THE HANGING OF
CONSTANCE HILLIER

Borgo Press Books by S. Fowler Wright

THE HANGING OF CONSTANCE HILLIER

AN INSPECTOR CLEVELAND CLASSIC CRIME NOVEL

by

S. FOWLER WRIGHT

WRITING AS "SYDNEY FOWLER"

THE BORGO PRESS

An Imprint of Wildside Press LLC

MMIX

CONTENTS

BOOK ONE: CONSTANCE HILLIER

BOOK TWO: THOMAS MOGSON

BOOK THREE: MARGARET HILLIER

BOOK ONE

CONSTANCE HILLIER

▲

CHAPTER I.

IT was not until the third day of the trial of Constance Hillier and Thomas Mogson for the murder of Lady Catherine Middleditch that the public interest reached its height, for it was that morning that it was confidently expected that Mr. Butforth, K.C., who had undertaken the thankless task of defending the female prisoner, would put his client into the box.

The first two days had been mainly occupied with the evidence for the prosecution, which had not been without its dramatic incidents, or its sharp encounters between counsel who were too skilful not to find opportunity for sudden rapier-like exchanges, even in a case which had seemed from the first almost too simple for any honour to be gained in its demonstration, or lost in its defence.

But they had been so occupied with redundant proof of the obvious, the unimportant, or the undisputed, that even the daily press, though serving a public avid for every detail of so sensational a crime, summarized or condensed the larger-part of the evidence for the Crown.

It may be convenient if, in glancing back upon the events of these two previous days, we give first attention to the opening statement of the Attorney-General, in which he outlined the case which the Crown had undertaken to prove. And we may do this the more readily, remembering Sir Ernest Coleman's reputation, not only for concise lucidity, but for a moderation in attitude and statement towards those whom it was his duty to prosecute which was something more than a forensic pose.

"It appears," he said, "from the evidence which will be brought before you, that on the 26th day of December, 19—, at about 7:30 P.M., Dr. Alex Bennett received an urgent telephone call from number 35, Castlemaine Gardens, the residence of Lady Catherine Middleditch, asking him to attend there immediately, as Lady Catherine had suddenly developed symptoms of an alarming character. Dr. Bennett will tell you—and it is not disputed—that he recognized the voice as that of Constance Hillier, one of the two prisoners who is now before us. He knew her as one of the two nieces of Lady Catherine who were in constant attendance upon her. He did not regard her as one who would be likely to telephone him with such urgency without serious cause, and he was somewhat puzzled by the fact that the symptoms, as she described them, were no more than such as might naturally follow the over-indulgence that is not unfamiliar to medical men at that season of the year. He was doubly puzzled owing to the fact that Lady Catherine Middleditch was, alike by her physical condition and by the habits of many years, extremely unlikely to have been engaged in any excesses of conviviality. Ladies and gentlemen, it is easy to be wise after the event. Dr. Bennett had just come in from the work of a tiring day. He appears subsequently to have blamed himself more than others would be likely to do. He thought it sufficient at the time to give certain instructions on the telephone, and to ask that he should be called again at a later hour if there should then appear reason to do so.

"About two hours later he received such a call from Miss Margaret Hillier, the prisoner's sister. He then went at once, arriving at Castlemaine Gardens within ten minutes of the call being received. By that time Lady Catherine Middleditch was dead.

"Dr. Bennett considered his position. He saw no cause to suspect foul play. The symptoms which had preceded decease, as they were told to him by those who had been in attendance, were not suggestive of any form of poisoning with which he was familiar. He was in regular professional attendance upon Lady Catherine, who had been an invalid for many ears. He hat actually visited her about three days previously, though he hat not then seen cause to anticipate any immediate danger. He knew that as a physician of repute— and his reputation is deservedly high—he could have given a certificate of death which would pass unquestioned. It might appear that, if there were any blame to be apportioned, that blame was his; but, in spite of that—perhaps for that very reason—he felt unable to do so.

He refused his certificate, and reported the death to the Coroner. The Coroner, very properly, ordered an autopsy.

"The posthumous examination was conducted by Sir Lionel Tipshift, Dr. Bennett being present; another doctor—Sir Roger Fairbanks, who as you are probably aware is regarded one of the greatest living authorities upon both vegetable and mineral poisons—was also present, at the request of the Earl of Weyford, Lady Catherine's cousin, and the head of her family, who was anxious that the suspicion which had been created by the refusal of the death-certificate should be dissipated beyond any shadow of doubt, in the interests of the family and, in particular, of that of Lady Catherine's nieces, because, as you will hear, they were the only ladies in attendance upon her.

"It is necessary—it is only fair to the case which the prosccution have set up—to direct your particular attention to the sequence of events, and to the way in which Sir Roger Fairbanks came on to the scene, because it was from his suggestion—from his suspicion—though he could, of course, have had no foresight of the direction in which it would lead, that the inquiries originated of which this trial is the result.

"It is common ground that the autopsy did not lead to the discovery of the presence of any poisonous drug, and while it disclosed certain functional abnormalities—putting the case in non-technical language—which were the immediate occasion of death, it failed to disclose any sufficient cause from which those symptoms could originate.

"Among those symptoms there was a marked congestion of the liver, and there was also a very slight but peculiar and unusual discoloration of that organ. Both Sir Lionel Tipshift and Dr. Bermett will tell you frankly that while they noticed and were puzzled by this discoloration, they were unable to regard it as of any certain significance, particularly in view of the negative result of their search for traces of any known poison either in the stomach or other organs, or in those parts of the body in which some deleterious substances are inclined to linger.

"But Sir Roger Fairbanks had observed this discoloration with a troubled mind, because he recollected a similar effect having been produced upon the livers of certain rats with which he had experimented a few months earlier with a new and rare drug which is, it appears, of a very volatile character, so that it would be difficult, if not impossible, to detect its presence even a few hours after death.

"You will appreciate Sir Roger's position. He was not there to suggest improbable causes of death, but to watch the interests of the surviving relatives. He said nothing at the time. But he was uneasy in mind, and he will tell you that his scientific curiosity was aroused. During the next few days he made further experiments, with the result that not only did he find that the post-mortem organs of rats to which this drug had been administered were in a condition similar to those which had appeared in the human subject, but he was able to observe that there was a close similarity peculiar and distressing symptoms which preceded death, as they had been described by those who had been in attendance upon Lady Catherine.

"Faced by this position, Sir Roger Fairbanks made a private report to the Earl of Weyford. He said that in his opinion Lady Catherine Middleditch had died from the effect of a certain drug—I may say conveniently at this stage that it is not considered in the public interest that it should be named, or its symptoms discussed, and I propose to avoid doing so as far as possible with the approval of the Court, and with the concurrence of my learned friends—though he was unable to suggest how or by whom it could have been administered or obtained. He said that this drug was practically unknown in any separate soluble form, excepting only that he had himself recommended its use in advising on a process for the manufacture of gramophone records of a new flexible kind. He explained that the holders of certain patents for the production of such articles, after laying themselves out for manufacturing them on a large scale, had met with an unexpected obstacle in the fact that the substance on which they were working became less pliable under certain atmospheric conditions, and Sir Roger was able to advise that this difficulty could be overcome if the records were dipped in a solution, of which this drug is the essential element.

"Sir Roger will tell you that it is not his habit to recommend the use of any substance for commercial purposes without exhaustive testing of its qualities or effects, such as its inflammability, or its action in contact or combination with other substances, or whether it can be dangerous to human life either by swallowing, or by its effects upon the skin its fumes, or in other ways; and it was in the course of such routine that he had acquired the knowledge which he was utilizing in this unexpected way.

"So far as he was aware, there was only one place in England and two in Germany where this drug was being distilled, and used for the purpose already mentioned, but, impossible as it might sound, he regarded it as a mathematical certainty that Lady Catherine Middleditch had died from its effects.

"He concluded by saying that while he was reporting privately to Lord Weyford in the first instance, if his lordship did not inform the police he should be obliged to consider whether his own duty as a citizen did not require him to do so.

"On receiving this report, the Earl of Weyford appears to have acted without hesitation. Within two or three hours of it being in his hands it was on its way to Scotland Yard.

"Obviously, such a report could not be ignored, and Chief-Inspector Cleveland, an officer of long experience and proved ability, was instructed to investigate the matter.

"Inspector Cleveland first interviewed the managing director of the Flexite Gramophone and Record Co., this being, as he was informed by Sir Roger Fairbanks, the only place where the drug was prepared which, as he confidently asserted, had been the cause of Lady Catherine's death. The managing director gave him all possible assistance and information. It appears that his firm do not purchase this drug, but distil it in their own laboratories. Their head chemist had been warned by Sir Roger of its particular properties and dangers, and had taken somewhat elaborate precautions in recording and controlling the quantities which were prepared. When ready for use, it is in the form of a finely granulated powder of a rather deep indigo colour. This powder is made up in small packets, each containing about three grains, and these packets are sealed and numbered, and issued separately—it will be understood that it is used in infinitesimal quantities—to the foreman of the department in which it is required to be used. Had he failed to use any appreciable quantity in the right way, it appeared to be impossible that the articles which he was treating could pass the tests to which they were subjected. Both the managing director and the head chemist assured Inspector Cleveland that the undetected leakage of a fatal dose was a practical impossibility.

"Inspector Cleveland appeared to he confronted with a very difficult task. He had to establish some connection between the works of the Flexite Co., which are in the neighbourhood of Uxbridge, though not in the same county, being over the Buckinghamshire border, and the bedroom of Lady Catherine Middleditch, perhaps twenty miles away.

"But the Inspector had learnt the value of patient, fearless, logical deduction. He felt that Sir Roger Fairbanks would not have expressed himself so confidently without good reason. He saw that the apparent difficulty really narrowed and simplified the inquiry on which he was engaged.

"After very careful investigation into the way in which the drug was prepared and guarded, he decided that there were five men who, with various degrees of difficulty, might. succeed in removing a quantity without detection, and of these five, after eliminating the head chemist himself, who undoubtedly had the superior opportunity both to manufacture and remove, he concentrated his inquiries upon Thomas Mogson, his chief assistant, and in the course of the following week he secured evidence that this man was known—was somewhat intimately known—to Miss Constance Hillier, and that for a period of about eleven months they had been in the habit of meeting at the Yellow Cat, which is a night-club in Thornhill Street, the proprietor of which has been convicted of various irregularities on two recent occasions.

"Considering the manner in which he had been directed to this inquiry, the Inspector may well have thought, when he had made this discovery, that he had established the fact that a crime had been committed, and the channel through which the poison had been obtained, to the satisfaction of any reasonable man. But the English law, when the liberty and perhaps the lives of its citizens are in question, is not satisfied with probabilities, however great. It asks, and rightly asks, for a weight of proof which will be of the measure of certainty; and, knowing this, the Inspector proceeded to obtain a search-warrant, and made an exhaustive investigation at 35, Castlemaine Gardens, where the tragedy had occurred.

"This search resulted in a discovery of a most directly incriminating nature. It is not denied by the defence—it is, indeed, not deniable—that one of the actual packets of this powder was found secreted among the personal effects of Constance Hillier, in its original wrapping, as it must have been received by her from Thomas Mogson.

"Confronted with this evidence—she was actually present at its discovery—and asked to explain how it had come into her possession, and for what purpose she had required it, she took refuge in an absolute denial. She said, and subsequently signed a formal statement which will be produced in evidence, that she had never seen it before, and could suggest no means by which it could have come among her possessions. The probability of that defence will be a matter for you to determine.

"Unfortunately for her, the police proceeded to the interrogation of Thomas Mogson before she could inform him of the denial which she had made.

"After being warned of the seriousness of his position, and informed of the finding of the packet in Constance Hillier's possession, he appears to have realized the uselessness of denial, and he also made a statement, at his own request, which will be brought before you. In that statement he admits supplying her with three packets of the fatal powder, this being the number which Inspector Cleveland had already traced as having disappeared from the Uxbridge offices, but denies that he did this with any guilty purpose. The credibility of that defence will also be a matter for your decision. The prosecution contends that he went to the elaborate trouble of purloining this rare and deadly drug, well knowing its properties, and the purpose for which it would be used.

"There remained the question of motive. The strongest motive is not proof of guilt, and its apparent absence is not vindication, but it is usually found, in cases such as this is alleged to be, that there is some powerful motive of hate, or greed, or jealousy, which has been sufficient to outweigh the bonds of kindred, and the natural instincts of mankind.

"In this case there appears to be evidence of abundant motive. It will be shown that the deceased woman had been a bedridden invalid for about fifteen years, during which she had required the constant attendance of her two nieces, whom she had ruled with a querulous tyranny. She was a wealthy woman, and they were entirely dependent upon her. She appears to have used this position to the utmost. It was her whim that she would not employ the services of professional nurses. Everything must be done by these two young women, one or other of whom must be in attendance upon her both by night and day. Their reward was to be wealth at her death. Their penalty was that the years of youth were passing in this unhappy servitude.

"Should they fail in any detail of the duties which her comfort required, they were under the constant threat that she would alter her will to their detriment.

"This appears to have taken place on at least three occasions, the last being only about three weeks before her fatal illness, and the procedure was always the same.

"Without saying anything to either of them directly, she would send for her lawyer, and require their presence in the room while she dictated the new provisions. On one occasion, she bequeathed the bulk of her fortune to various charities, and it was nine weeks before their assiduous humilities led to the revoking of these dispositions. On the last occasion, she signalized a more than usual resentment at some real or fancied delinquency of the younger sister by leaving the whole of her fortune to Constance Hillier.

"That was the position on the evening of December 26th. By the will of a capricious invalid, to whom she had already sacrificed fifteen of the best years of her life—a will that might be altered at any moment—Constance Hillier would become a free and wealthy woman, if Lady Catherine died. That evening Constance Hillier—and Constance Hillier only—was in attendance upon her. Constance Hillier had in her possession a subtle poison which had been procured for her, at her desire, at great trouble and risk. Of that poison Lady Catherine died.

"That she died by that means does not appear to be capable of any serious question when we remember that its symptoms were recognized by a doctor who was specially familiar with them, and who had no knowledge of such a poison being accessible to the female prisoner.

"It only remains to explain the method by which the drug was obtained from the Flexite Company's laboratories without suspicion being aroused. Its explanation exonerates that firm from any imputation of carelessness, and is of interest as showing something of Thomas Mogson's criminal ingenuities. It was done by means of a deliberately bad figure, a four being so written that the foreman, who received packet No. 24, read it as 27, and so copied it into his book, though he had himself signed for it as the correct number. He was thus made to be the actual perpetrator of the error, and he alone would have been shown to be in the wrong, had the difference been promptly noticed. But the device succeeded by its simplicity. When a few days had passed, and it had become evident that the error would not be remarked, Thomas Mogson was able to remove the three packets without any great probability of the detection of the trick, or that suspicion would fall upon him in the event of its discovery.

"Simple and successful as it may have been, it is not a device by which any man, quite apart from its moral aspects, would risk such a position as Thomas Mogson held, unless it were for some very powerful reason. It is the contention of the Crown that it was in pursuance of a very cruel and wicked compact between the two prisoners, who may have been already discussing such a conspiracy when the will was made, but who were roused by it to prompt and decisive action, so that they might benefit from its provisions to the full extent of the fortune of their unhappy victim."

Having completed his speech, without attempting a more elaborate peroration, the Attorney-General proceeded to call his evidence, the major part of which need not delay us, for it was no more than an elaboration of that which his own narrative has already supplied in clearer and conciser form.

It was not until the sister of the female prisoner, a slight, pathetic person, entered the box, that there was any atmosphere of emotional intensity, and her evidence amounted to little beyond admissions as to the routines of the household which had consumed her youth, and a confirmation of the fact that she and her sister had been in the room when the instructions were given for the last will, and that they had subsequently seen it signed. She also confirmed the fact that it had been her sister's turn to wait upon Lady Catherine during the earlier part of the day, and for her to have done so during its later hours, but there had been a voluntary exchange between them. Constance had wanted to have an entire day of freedom during the following week, and so it had been arranged that she should do the double duty on that on which the fatal illness occurred.

"On whose suggestion was that?" the Attorney-General asked in a quiet way.

The reply did not come quickly, and there was a breathless silence in the Court as the witness stood, looking straight before her, as though she had not heard the question.

It was noticed by some that the female prisoner, who had sat apathetically up to that moment, as though not being interested in the evidence that her sister was giving, raised her eyes, and looked at her in an anxious—or was it only a puzzled?—way.

Still quietly, but in a somewhat slower, more emphatic tone, the question came again. Did it recall something to the witness's mind, that she had perhaps forgotten? Something, perhaps, that for her sister's sake she was afraid to say? Even if your sister be a murderess, it may not be pleasant to say the word that will tighten the noose about her neck.

But this time the witness did not hesitate. She said firmly and clearly, though in a low voice:

"It was at my suggestion."

"You are quite sure of that?" She looked the Attorney-General full in the face, almost defiantly it seemed to some, as she answered:

"Quite."

"Very well."

The Attorney-General sat down.

"Any questions, Mr. Butforth?" asked the Judge.

Mr. Butforth had nothing to ask. The witness stepped down, having won some sympathy for herself, and perhaps done as much for her sister as was possible to her inexperience of such ordeals.

After that, there had been evidence from various members of the staff of the Yellow Cat. Here Mr. Butforth was able to do more for himself, if not enough to be likely to make any final difference to his client's welfare. The witnesses were not of the highest character. One of them, in particular, was less accustomed to the witness-box than the dock. The learned counsel soon had him rather badly rattled. A reminder that there were penalties for perjury, after he had been skilfully led to contradict one of his own assertions, reduced him to such confusion that he promptly did the same thing again. Mr. Butforth felt that he had earned the fee that endorsed his brief. When the time came he felt that the Judge would be obliged to direct the jury that they must disregard the evidence of that witness. Better still, should he omit to do so, there would be matter for an appeal for misdirection. It would fail, of course. But what would you have? No one can make bricks without straw.

The prosecution had established their main point, beyond serious denial. The two prisoners had been identified as having frequented the club together on numerous occasions, and it appeared that the man had been in the habit of incurring an expenditure which must have been a very heavy charge upon a limited income.

At the close of the second day, the case for the prosecution had been closed, and the morning of the third day saw the female prisoner enter the witness-box.

CHAPTER II.

CONSTANCE HILLIER entered the witness-box. As she left the dock a wardress followed her, and stood beside it. Not five yards was she to move away from, not for an hour was she to forget that on her shoulder rested the iron hand of the criminal law, in a grip that would only be loosed at the word of the four women and eight men whose eyes were upon her now, with varying glances of sympathy or repulsion, curiosity or speculation.

Those members of the public who had been fortunate enough, whether by chance or favour, to obtain tickets of admission to the crowded court, saw a sour-faced woman of thirty-three who looked older. The expression of her face was now of a terror hardly controlled, but even that emotion could not remove the permanent lines of ill-temper that marred her mouth. Yet the face might have been well enough in earlier youth, and the yellow hair was abundant still.

The Judge, looking at her with expressionless eyes, considered that her face could be made quite pathetic for the Sunday Press. Probably in a month's time some newspaper would be getting up a popular appeal for her, that she should not hang, and thousands would rush to sign. If they could see as he saw! He had tried three or four murderers a year for the last ten years, and he had not seen one yet who had not shown sufficient depravity in his face to be a warning to all but the foolish to avoid his company. If the public could see as he saw!

Meanwhile, Constance Hillier took the oath, holding the book to her lips in a hand that trembled visibly, and Mr. Butforth rose to examine her. His task was not an enviable one. She had to tell an unlikely tale, and her fellow-prisoner must follow her into the box, and tell one which was equally improbable. That would have been bad enough, even had their accounts agreed. There would have been the difficulty of persuading the jury of its plausibility, against the destructive criticism of the prosecuting counsel, and the toneless analysis of the summing-up. There would have been the earlier danger that one or both of them would break down under the ordeal of cross-examination. That would have been bad enough. But when the two prisoners were about to flatly contradict one another! And there had been no way out. The two statements taken by the police were, the one too definite, the other too detailed, to be explained away. And yet he had felt that if his client had refused to go into the witness-box, there was no hope at all. None. And he had discussed the matter with Basil Clackleton, who represented Mogson, and his learned friend had felt the same.

There was just one point he could make. Not a very savoury point. Not without a possibility that it would be turned against him by the prosecution, but—what alternative was there?

The fatal packet had been found in the lowest of a chest of drawers, which had been in the bedroom, and admitted to be in the exclusive use of Constance Hillier. Inspector Cleveland had given evidence that she had appeared to regard the scrutiny of the two higher drawers with comparative indifference, but that she had been visibly perturbed when she had been required to unlock the third, and that it had required a combination of patience and sternness to persuade her to do so. Naturally, he had made his search all the more thorough, until the packet had been exposed. That, at least, was capable of a different explanation from that which the prosecution had suggested.

With the inward feelings of one who steers over a cataract's edge, but with an outward aspect of assurance that was almost jaunty, Mr. Butforth rose to examine his witness.

Everyone familiar with legal proceedings, whether by personal observation or by the reading of Press reports, must have observed the constant difference of result obtained by counsel when examining their own or their opponents' witnesses. In the one case, the narrative will make steady progress, it will follow a direct course, it will usually be coherent and consistent. In the other, even with a witness of good character, who is endeavouring to assist the court, and who may be absolutely disinterested in the result, the progress made will be slow and tortuous, and liable to be productive of apparent inconsistencies in the evidence given; and this difference is emphasized by the fact that the rules of evidence do not allow counsel to put a leading question to his own witness, while one who is cross-examining is free to do so.

Doubtless, this difference arises in part from the fact that counsel has been previously supplied with a statement of the evidence which his witness is prepared to give, and his questions are therefore put more intelligently than can be those of one who is less fully in-

formed. But there is another reason, which is of an evident deliberation. The interrogations are often inconsequent and obscure, or confused in wording, so that the mind of the witness is perturbed or stu-
pefied by such questions as the classical example, *Have you ceased
beating your wife?*—to which either the "plain yes or no" which he
is bullied to give would be equally misleading.

Even allowing for the fact that the witness's own counsel has
the advantage of previous information as to the evidence which is to
be tendered, the difference remains too great to be explained without
admitting that English methods of cross-examination are based on
the assumption that an opposing witness is lying, and should be
trapped into admitting the truth, or that, if he be truthful, he should
be confused into some appearance of falsehood.

In the present case, it might be observed that the effect of the
slow clear questions, asked in a voice which was modulated to a
soothing friendliness, was to produce a narrative which gained in
confidence as it proceeded, and, while it was occupied with the circumstances and routines of the lives of the three occupants of 35,
Castlemaine Gardens, was of a convincing simplicity.

It was, indeed, difficult for the hearers to withhold some measure of sympathy from the prisoner, murderess though they could
scarcely doubt her to be, as she laid bare the lives which she and her
sister had lived under the domination of a capricious and exacting
woman, who appeared to have taken an evil pleasure in humiliating
them with the consciousness of their dependence upon her, and bait-
ing them with the fear that they might ultimately lose the reward for
which they had sacrificed their freedom and their self-respect.

But it was Mr. Butforth's difficulty, even in this, that he could
not expose the tyranny which Constance Hillier had endured for fifteen years without supplying the motive for the crime which was
alleged against her, and he was obliged to glide as lightly as possible
over those aspects, as he led the witness to the day of her aunt's
death, and to the subsequent discovery of the poison in her own possession. Even here, there was little to be asked or answered. She denied on oath that she had poisoned her aunt. She denied that she had
known or suspected that any poison had been administered. She admitted acquaintance with Thomas Mogson, but she had never had
any packets of poison from him, had never discussed poison with
him at any time or in any way, and knew nothing of how the packet
of the fatal drug had come to be in her own drawer. She was emphatic in this denial, repeating it with a weak vehemence, which was
unconvincing to those who heard it. Yet, perhaps, it was the best
thing she could do.

If there could ever have been a hope that she could have convinced the Court that she had acquired the poison for some innocent purpose, and that it had been introduced to her aunt's diet by some unlikely accident, her statement to the police must have already closed that avenue of defence against her. She admitted that she had been unwilling that the police should search the drawer in which the incriminating packet was hidden, but she said that that had been solely because of other private papers and books which it held, which she was ashamed that they should see.

Mr. Butforth sat down, having done what he could with a hopeless case, and the Judge looked at Sir Ernest Coleman with an interrogative lift of his eyebrows, as though he doubted whether he would think it necessary to cross-examine. But the Attorney-General rose.

"I have a few questions I should like to ask," he said easily. He turned his gaze on to the prisoner.

"How long have you known Thomas Mogson?"

"About—since—about eight months— No! About a year."

"Where did you meet him first?"

"At the Yellow Cat."

"Introduced by—?"

"I don't—I expect—I don't remember—"

"Well, never mind. When did you see him last? Now, be careful. When did you see him last?—before today."

"On the— When did I see him last? On the— It must have been Wednesday. The Wednesday before—"

"Before your aunt died?"

"Yes."

"Where? At the Yellow Cat?"

"Yes."

"You were engaged to be married?"

"Yes."

"When?"

"When...I couldn't say that. There wasn't anything arranged."

"When your aunt died?"

"There wasn't anything arranged."

"I see. Where did you part?"

"Part?"

"Yes. On the Wednesday night. Did you part in the Club, or in the street outside?"

"In the— I can't quite remember where. It used to be in the street."

"Never mind where it used to be. Where was it on Wednesday night?"

"We used to part in Oxford Street."

"Did you part there on that Wednesday night?"

"Yes. I took a taxi from there."

"Alone?"

"Yes."

"Very well. You say there wasn't any understanding as to when you could get married?"

"No."

"You could have hoped nothing from your aunt had you left her during her lifetime?"

"She—I don't know—she would have been very cross."

"And she might have lived for many years?"

The witness made no answer to that, looking as though the question had not penetrated her mind. She may have taken it to be less a question than a statement of obvious fact. The Attorney-General did not press it. He went on to ask:

"You had no means of your own at all?"

"I had—my aunt gave me—it was a pound most weeks. Some-times more."

"And sometimes less?"

"Yes, if she were cross."

"And you knew what Thomas Mogson's salary was?"

"It was £500."

"Is that what he told you?"

"Yes. I suppose so. It was what I knew it was."

"Well, it wasn't. Didn't you hear the evidence given yesterday by the secretary of the Flexite Company?"

"You can't listen all the time."

The Attorney-General looked his surprise at this answer. The Judge's eyes regarded the witness keenly, but he believed her with-out difficulty. A long experience of the criminal courts, first as ad-vocate, and then as judge, had familiarized him to the dull reaction of prisoners who sit through the weary hours while the slow process of evidence builds up a case which is already so familiar—perhaps so fearfully or so hatefully familiar—to them. And they must often have so little hope, so little doubt, of what the issue will be when the endless talk, the endless repetitions, will be over at last. He had once seen a murderer go to sleep in the dock.... To his experienced mind it was just a slight additional evidence of her guilt, where no addi-tion was needed. He was merciful, and of a scrupulous fairness, but he recognized this as a case in which the guilt was self-evident. He could have condemned both prisoners without hesitation after reading the depositions, and with a glance at what they were.

"Well," the Attorney-General went on, "you may take it from me that his salary was £8 a week. £416 a year. How often did you meet at the Yellow Cat?"

"About—I can't say exactly—about once a week."

"Not twice?"

"Not except—no."

"How much did it cost?"

"I don't know."

"You didn't pay?"

"No—not except—I paid the taxi home."

"Then you went home alone?"

"Yes."

"Always?"

"Yes, unless— Yes."

"Unless what?"

"Unless Mr. Mogson came part of the way."

"Why not all?"

"We—I didn't want aunt to see anything."

"See? But we have heard that she never left her room?"

"She had her bed by the window."

"You mean she used to watch what went on in the road?"

"Yes, when she wasn't asleep."

"Well, what do you think it cost?"

"I don't know."

"Two pounds? The Yellow Cat isn't a cheap place. Three?"

"No, not that. Not three."

"But it might be two?"

"Yes. I don't know."

"You say you didn't meet more than once a week?"

"No. We didn't."

"Then how many times had you met since November 29th?"

"Since—? November 29th? I don't know. Why?"

"Never mind why. Three times? Twice?"

"Since? Yes, I daresay."

But the Attorney-General was not satisfied with less than a definite reply.

After many questions and contradictions, it was elucidated with some certainty that it had been three times, neither more nor less, since the 29th November—that being the first day on which it would have been possible for him to supply her with the fatal drug. Beyond that, and probably without realizing the implication of her own admissions, the witness had given evidence that Thomas Mogson had never entered, and had not been in the vicinity of, 35, Castlemaine Gardens, to her knowledge, during the period mentioned. In the end, the Attorney-General had felt sufficient confidence in the strength of his position to risk the further question which is so often the downfall of the inexperienced advocate, and had survived it successfully. He had asked whether the witness could suggest any possibility by which at any time her fellow-prisoner could have obtained access to the drawer in which the poison was found, and had received a confused and reluctant negative.

"Then," he asked in slow impressive words, "if it has been shown that this packet could have come only through the hands of Thomas Mogson, with whom you associated, into the drawer which was in your own room, can you suggest any possibility by which it could have done so except by your own hand?"

There was a breathless silence in the waiting court as the witness gazed, as though fascinated, upon the face of her accuser, but no answer came.

"Very well," he said at length, "we will leave it there. It is a question to which there is no reply."

"If your cross-examination is concluded," the Judge interposed at this point, in the quiet voice of one who did not allow his mind to rise to the temperatures of those around him, "it will be a convenient point at which to adjourn."

Sir Ernest Coleman glanced at his brief. "No, my lord," he said, "I have a few further questions I should like to ask."

"In that case," the Judge answered patiently, "I still think it may be convenient to adjourn at this point." To his mind, the asking of further questions was as futile as the flogging of a dead horse, and as cruel as to prolong the slaughter of a living one. But he could not restrain the prosecution from the course of their selection. Perhaps after Sir Ernest had thought over the admissions he had obtained, he would be disposed to the same view.

CHAPTER III.

CONSTANCE HILLIER re-entered the witness-box. She had probably had some stimulant with her own refreshment, for her cheeks had a deeper flush than the morning had shown, and her replies soon became more voluble, if not more adroit, than they had been previously.

But the first question that she was required to answer was put in a quiet, almost conversational way, and was one of which the ultimate implication might not have been apparent even to one of greater mental agility than was hers.

"The furniture in your aunt's house was of a very solid quality, was it not?"

"Yes."

"Including that in your own room?"

"Yes."

"The chest was substantially made?"

"Yes."

"No one else had a key?"

"Not that I know of. How can you expect me to answer that?"

"This was the key, wasn't it?"

"Yes. It looks like it."

"It is it, isn't it?"

"I suppose so. Yes."

"You have never known of there being two keys?"

"No."

"It doesn't look like a key that would be easy to duplicate?"

"I don't know. It might."

"You don't really think that?"

Mr. Butforth rose to object. The prosecution should have called a locksmith, had they wished to introduce such a contention. It was a point on which the witness's opinion was of no more value than that of anyone else in the court. The Judge upheld the objection. The Attorney-General suggested that the jury might like to inspect the key.

The foreman—who had wanted to speak several times during the last two days, but lacked courage or promptness to do so—saw his chance, and said with some emphasis that they would. (Now he would be in the evening papers for certain. Would they say "The foreman of the jury, Mr. Edward Collins," or would they omit his name in the provoking way that the Press had?)

Mr. Butforth pointed out that the identity of the key had not been formally proved. The Attorney-General said that the witness had herself admitted it. There was a difference as to this. The Judge was not quick to interpose. He knew that the admission of any irregularity of procedure on his part would be a certain ground of appeal. It is by such errors that convictions may be quashed, and the guilty go free. He decided that the evidence should be admitted, but before he spoke, Mr. Butforth had given way. He had seen a look of annoyance on the foreman's face.

The key was handed round. Eight men and four women turned it over with suitable gravity, and an air of wisdom such as few of us possess. It was not a very large key, but of a rather intricate pattern. Not a lock which would be likely to yield to the casual selection of a key from another bunch. Probably not one which would be easy for any but an expert to pick.

"You always kept your drawers locked?"

"No, I didn't. Not always. Not all of them anyway."

"Perhaps the two top drawers would often be left unlocked?"

"I used to lock them more often than not."

"But the bottom one was always locked?"

"I'm not going to say that. We all of us forget sometimes."

"It would be locked unless you forgot?"

"Yes."

"And that was the drawer which you did not want the Inspector to search?"

"No, of course not. It was a private drawer. I don't suppose you'd want him to search yours."

There was a general smile at this unexpected retort. It was the first sign that the wretched woman had shown of a temper which was not normally far from the surface unless her looks did her some injustice.

Mr. Justice Troutbeck looked at her with some severity. "You mustn't answer in that way. You must remember the respect due to the court."

There was a sullen obstinacy in the witness's face as she replied without lifting her eyes, "Then he shouldn't ask such silly things."

There was a moment's silence, and then the Judge signalled to the Attorney-General to resume his examination. But the witness had gained more than she knew. Her opponent was too wary to pursue a line which might possibly wake some sympathy for her among the more susceptible members of the jury. He turned a page of his brief, and contented himself with one impressive deliberate question, such as that with which he had confounded her at the close of the morning sitting. "Then your evidence amounts to this, does it not, that the packet of the fatal poison was found in the place where you kept those things which you hid most carefully, even from the other members of the household? The place that you guarded most vigilantly from the access of those around you? The one place under your control that was kept hidden from every human eye?"

The wretched woman gave no direct answer. She looked on her tormentor for a time, as she had done before, as though in a fascinated silence. Then she said, with a weak reiteration of her useless defence: "I've told you that I didn't know it was there."

"That," counsel replied, "is for the jury to decide."

He sat down.

The Judge looked interrogatively at Mr. Butforth. But that gentleman shook his head. He had the right of re-examination, but what use could it be? No. Let his witness go back to the dock. Later on, he must try what a passionate speech could do to influence the less logical of the twelve on whom her fate depended. But he could do nothing now. Yet her ordeal was not over. The Judge had a few questions to ask for himself. They were not intended to trap her. Rather, they were meant to exhaust the last possibility of any genuine defence, to eliminate the last faint possibility that she was an innocent woman.

He had noticed, with some surprise, that while there had been evidence that Constance Hillier had been the only person in attendance on Lady Catherine on the fatal day, there had been no attempt from either side to ascertain whether, or to what extent, she might have been absent from the room during periods when the poison might, theoretically, have been administered by others or taken by Lady Catherine herself. But the fact was that both the prosecution and the defence had been in possession of information which, for different reasons, they had felt disinclined to elicit. It was no part of the business of the prosecution to show that she had been out of the room at all. It was of no assistance to the defence to disclose that she had been seen to retire to her own room—which was at the opposite end of a rather long passage—and had admitted that she had remained there for about half an hour while her aunt slept. There was a witness to this in a Mrs. Pearson, a woman who came in daily to do the rougher work of the house, and who had been occupied on the stairs and landing long enough to say that she must have been in her own room for at least twenty minutes. She had thus been in sight, more or less, of both rooms during most of the time that Constance Hillier had been absent from her aunt, and could testify, to that extent, that no one else had entered. Indeed, except Margaret Hillier, the house had had no other occupant.

The Judge elicited something of these facts, enough to see that he ploughed in a barren field. He leaned back, giving direction that the witness should return to the dock.

Mr. Butforth had a moment of debate in his own mind as to whether he had failed his client in not attempting to make some capital from that admitted absence. But he could not see what could result except a dearer demonstration of the impossibility of developing any plausible theory of defence. There was the connection with Thomas Mogson. There was the packet in the locked drawer. There was the poisoned woman. Worst of all, there was Thomas Mogson's evidence to come. It was a damning weight of circumstance against which neither he nor his client's solicitors had been able to construct any theory, even the most fantastic, which they could offer to the court. If only she had not denied so absolutely all knowledge of the hidden packet—! And even then—!

No, there was nothing more he could do.

He sat silent, with no more than his normal professional watchfulness, as Thomas Mogson entered the witness-box.

CHAPTER IV.

IF Thomas Mogson were an innocent man, he had cause to complain of the equipment with which Nature had armed him for the ordeal.

It was not merely that he was without any physical attractions, such as might have softened the hearts of at least one or two of the jury-women, though that disadvantage was sufficiently serious, for he was small and contemptible of body, his features were mean and meagre, his hair was thinning and dull, and his complexion that of a man who punctuates a sedentary life with unhealthy pleasures. But, beyond that, there was the impression of personality which is indefinable, and it was that of one who was at once furtive and insolent in his attitude to those around him. He had the look of one who would do even ordinary things in a base way.

He walked from dock to witness-box beside his attendant warder with quick short steps, and looked round the crowded court with an expression that was half-cringing, half-insolent, and which he probably mistook for an air of courageous innocence.

"Looks quite perky," a schoolmistress jury-woman, who had watched the proceedings with an aspect of alert competence, whispered to a stouter and somewhat older companion.

"He'll look more like himself when he sees the black cap," was the reply, with a grimness of tone that interpreted its otherwise somewhat cryptic meaning.

Meanwhile the witness, under the expert guidance of Mr. Basil Clackleton, was narrating in quick, jerky, confident sentences the various honours with which his industry and ability had been rewarded, and the records of a blameless life.

It was evident that he was a very competent chemist, and that the previous appointments which he had held had resulted in testimonials which had won him his position with the Flexite Co., against (he said) between seventy and eighty competitors.

28

Coming to the events that more immediately concerned the court, he admitted that for a year or more he had visited the Yellow Cat about once a week. He admitted also, with what he may have supposed to be an air of disarming frankness, that he had done so with the deliberate purpose of meeting such female acquaintances as are likely to be found in the vicious squalor of such resorts.

It was there, he said, that he had met Constance Hillier, and that the acquaintance had ripened at that time.

"And so," said Mr. Clackleton, "you took the packets, and gave them to Constance Hillier, not supposing that they would be used for any unlawful purpose?"

"Yes," he said, with one of his quick defiant glances round the court, as though daring contradiction. "That is just how it was. I hadn't the least idea.... "

"When and where did you hand them over to her?"

"In the taxi, after we left the Yellow Cat, on December 13th."

As he said this, there was a commotion in the dock. Constance Hillier had fainted.

The Judge adjourned the court for a short period while the fainting woman was carried below, and received the attention of the prison doctor. On its resumption, Thomas Mogson returned to the witness-box to continue his evidence, but Mr. Clackleton announced, to the general surprise of the court, and to the visible disconcerting of the witness himself, that he had no further questions to ask. Thomas Mogson had good cause for surprise, as there were several points in his defence which he knew to be set out in his counsel's brief, and which he had been given no opportunity of asserting. He was about to make an open protest, when he was silenced by the knowledge that the Attorney-General had risen, and that his cross-examination had commenced.

Mr. Clackleton sat with an inscrutable face, and the inward expectation of some amusement to come. In the brief interval of the adjournment, he had reviewed his client's evidence as it then stood, and had realized that the remaining points he had intended to reach must come out almost inevitably in cross-examination, and might be more convincingly elicited in that manner.

But knowing nothing of what was in his opponent's thoughts, the Attorney-General commenced, with an easy mind, the task of demolishing a defence, the main feature of which had sounded unconvincing enough, even as it had been already presented.

"It has been given in evidence," he began, "that your income was £416 a year. Is that right?"

"Yes."

"Have you any source of income, apart from that salary?"

"No."

"And you were engaged to be married?"

"There's nothing wrong in that."

"When?"

"There wasn't anything arranged."

"But you had been urgent for a date to be fixed?"

"I haven't said so."

"Do you deny it?"

"We might have talked about it."

"We have heard that your salary was to be increased from January 1st of this year. Was that correct?"

"Yes."

"How much?"

"By £52 a year."

"Not a very large amount on which to marry. But perhaps you had been saving carefully since the acquaintance began? How much did you spend each week at the Yellow Cat? Two pounds?"

"Yes. I daresay."

"Three?"

"It might be sometimes."

"More than that?"

"It might be sometimes."

"It was a good deal out of £8 a week, if you were really contemplating an early marriage with no other prospects than the increase of salary of which you have told us?"

"It didn't come out of that."

Thomas Mogson brought out this statement with a derisive chuckle. Whatever might be his feelings in the hours that followed, there was no doubt that he was now in actual enjoyment of the momentary confusing of his antagonist.

"Not out of that? But you have told the court that you had no other source of income?"

"That was what I said."

But here Mr. Justice Troutbeck, who had observed the witness's demeanour with no favourable judgement behind an impassive countenance, intervened with a note of sternness in his voice. "Mr. Mogson, you are doing yourself no good by that attitude. If you have an explanation to offer, it should be given promptly and clearly, with proper respect to the court."

Somewhat sobered by this rebuke, the witness replied: "I had it from the *Prize-Winners Weekly*."

"You mean," the examination continued, "you won a prize in a competition? How much was that?"

"I won £250 last February."

"And the expenses of your nights at the Yellow Cat were discharged from that source?"

"Yes, they were. I put it in a separate account to have a good time with it."

"And I suppose most of it was spent by the end of the year?"

"There was about a hundred left. Ellerson's have had that now." He added the last words with a note of bitterness in his voice. (Price and Ellerson were his solicitors.)

"Now tell me, Mr. Mogson, did you really propose that Miss Hillier should leave her aunt after all she had gone through for the past fifteen years and by so doing almost certainly abandon the prospect of succeeding to the wealth which she would otherwise expect to inherit, to marry you on an income of £468 a year?"

"No. I didn't know anything about it."

"About what?"

"About her aunt."

"What didn't you know?"

"I didn't know anything about the money—about the will—about her aunt. I scarcely knew she'd got one. I've heard all that here."

As Thomas Mogson made this reply, his attitude justified the vocabulary of the schoolmistress who had called it "perky." His tone, and an almost truculent aspect, might be compared to that of a chess-player who gives sudden disastrous check to an overboastful opponent. And however offensive the manner of his declaration might be, there was, perhaps for the first time in his evidence, a tone of sincerity, of confidence in his own assertion, that impressed his hearers.

Mr. Justice Troutbeck, still patiently open-minded, as he was keenly watchful of every phase of the drama of death over which he presided, had been observing the demeanour of the female prisoner throughout this examination. As it had followed its smooth current under the expert guidance of Mr. Clackleton, she had been in a state of agitation, which had been restrained with difficulty by the wardress at her side, and the urgent persuasions of her solicitor, from breaking out into audible protests, till it had culminated in the fainting-fit which had caused the adjournment of the court. Had she cherished to the last, he wondered, some wild and foolish hope that her lover would be chivalrous enough to take the blame on himself? That he would invent some ingenious explanation such as would free her from the guilt of murder? Or that he would repudiate his own admission, and join her in denial that they had trafficked together with the fatal drug? However that might be, it was with a curious difference of demeanour that she listened to the evidence which was now given. She appeared to accept it without protest, and without surprise.

Was it possible that it could be true? He watched the continuation of the examination with even closer attention. He heard Thomas Mogson assert confidently that Constance Hillier had always been reticent about her own affairs; that she hat not even told him dearly of the size of the household to which she belonged; that her aunt had been only mentioned, if at all, in the most casual way; that she had always refused to let him accompany her as far as her own door. He had, he said, gained an impression that she considered her relatives too "grand" for him to know, and it was owing to this reticence on her side that they hat continued, at her insistence, to meet only at the Yellow Cat.

The Judge was not alone in recognizing the quality of this evidence. Mr. Butforth saw very dearly that it was knocking away the last support from beneath his client's feet. (And yet what hope had there been before?)

The Attorney-General saw that he was doing no good to his own case, and this realization was increased by a side-glance from his learned friend, Mr. Clackleton. It almost seemed that he winked. The Attorney-General changed the course of the cross-examination abruptly, to inquire for what possible innocent purpose the witness could have supposed that Miss Hillier could have required the fatal drug. And as he pressed this point with sarcastic logic, the demeanour of the witness changed; his confidence failed; his answers were unconvincing, or died in a halting silence. He asserted that he had yielded blindly owing to his infatuation, and there were few who heard, who did not recognize it for the lie that it surely was. Yet there was a puzzled doubt in the Judge's mind, for the first time since the trial commenced. If it were true that she had concealed the circumstances in which she lived—? And he observed that this assertion was borne out to some extent by the woman's evidence that she had required Mogson to leave the taxi before it arrived at its destination. There was a lie somewhere—but where?

* * * * * * *

Mr. Butforth, discussing the case with a discreet circle at dinner that evening, said that it showed the injustice of trying two people together in such cases. No one knew how much or how little one or other of the pair was guilty. That they were equally so was an unlikely thing. But you try them together, and they find that their two necks are in one noose, and they can't loosen it from their own without tightening it on their companion in difficulty. So they just hang each other. And the more they struggle, the worse plight they're in. "It's like a pig," he said, coarsely enough, "when the butcher's roped its snout, and the more it pulls back the tighter it holds."

"And a good thing too," grunted Sir Richard Bulkington, in one of those brief intervals when his fork had failed to keep his mouth fully occupied. But whether he alluded to those who enter the august slaughter-house of the law, or to the victims of the pork-butcher which he so nearly resembled, is for the grammarians to decide.

CHAPTER V.

MR. BUTFORTH addressed the court. There was little doubt of his client's guilt in his own mind, but he had his duty to do, and his reputation to maintain If he called it making bricks without straw in conversation with the solicitors who had briefed him, he showed such ability in that method of manufacture that it seemed to many who heard, and to many more who read his speech, that he might have saved his client from her approaching doom.

He asked the jury to consider in the first place whether they were satisfied—fully and absolutely satisfied—that there had been murder at all. They had here the death of an elderly lady who had long been bedridden, and who was obviously in failing health. Such a death could not, in itself, be considered an unlikely thing. Her niece had been in attendance upon her when the fatal seizure occurred, as she had been—with a devotion and self-sacrifice, the fact of which was beyond dispute, whatever unworthy motives the prosecution might suggest—unfairly suggest, he urged, in the absence of any supporting evidence—in explanation of that devoted service.

She had been prompt to call for medical aid. It was at her own wish that she had been in attendance that afternoon. This had been brought out by the prosecution as though it were a point against her, but if it were carefully and impartially examined it would be seen that it had an opposite implication. It had been shown in evidence that Lady Catherine had a jug of milk constantly beside her, from which her attendant would fill the glass from which she sipped at frequent intervals. The milk was renewed in the morning, and again at night. Could not Constance Hillier have gone off duty at midday after slipping the fatal powder into the jug, or into the glass, and with a less probability that she would draw suspicion to herself than by remaining by the bedside for the whole period? Besides, she was under no necessity of arranging a special occasion. She had ample opportunity in the natural routine.

But when they considered this point further, they found that she had a natural and innocent motive for wishing to take her sister's duty on that day. She wished to have the additional time to enable her to do some shopping and to spend with her lover on the following Wednesday. But would her mind have been on such an adjustment, would there have been any purpose in taking on that extra duty, had she planned the murder of which she was now accused? Was it not inconsistent with the suggestion that she had resolved that her aunt should die? Was it not evident that she was anticipating that the routines of that quiet household would continue without change, and that her mind was occupied with nothing more than the securing of ample time in which she could meet her lover? If they were to decide this case on circumstantial evidence, was not this a circumstance which was convincingly in favour of the innocence of the accused?

This argument may have been too subtle to make much impression on the jury, but Mr. Justice Troutbeck did not dismiss it without a careful pondering. To his mind, it was the only point of interest in the whole speech. The rest was no more than the usual clap-trap, through which he must sit patient, alert, and inscrutable, always ready to decide the issue should there be a sudden challenging interruption from one of the opposing counsel.

But Mr. Butforth noticed that the attention of more than one of the jury wandered. Two of them had commenced a whispered conversation which he knew instinctively had nothing to do with the case. He changed abruptly to his next contention.

He had asked already had there been murder at all? It was not merely a question of whether they could eliminate the possibilities of suicide or misadventure—itself a quite probable explanation—but were they satisfied—satisfied as fully as they ought to be—of the cause of death? There had been no discovery in the body of poison of any kind A packet of a certain little-known substance had been found in one of Constance Hillier's drawers, and they were asked to assume that she had administered it to Lady Catherine with a guilty purpose, to assume that she knew it to have fatal properties, to assume that it was from that cause that Lady Catherine died!; and for the fact that it was poison at all they had the unsupported assertion of one man! A man, truly, of scientific attainments. An honest man, doubtless. But how sure scientists always are! How sure they always have been! And how sure are the scientists of today that the scientists of yesterday were most often wrong! How could we tell that the confident scientific pronouncements of today would not be the admitted fallacies of tomorrow? Was it not common knowledge that people had been condemned to death forty or fifty years ago, both in this country and France, for arsenic poisoning, on "scientific" evidence which is now recognized to have been no proof at all? (Here the Judge interposed, though he may have been deliberately slow to do so, to point out that there had been no evidence to justify counsel in such allusions.)

"I beg your pardon, my lord," Mr. Butforth answered, with a respectful cheerfulness, having made his point already. 'I will say no more than to emphasize, as I am entitled to do, that the whole of this prosecution is based on the unsupported assertion of one man, an assertion that there has been poisoning, where it is admitted that no poison can be found, where it is not asserted that any previous case of such poisoning has occurred. No edifice can be stronger than its own foundation. Would anyone hang a dog on such evidence? Would an insurance office issue a policy, would a bank grant an overdraft, guaranteed only by a single assertion of such a nature? Are we to accept a lower standard of proof when the life of a fellow-creature is the awful responsibility, the dreadful stake?"

Mr. Butforth, having made this protest with an appropriate passion, dropped his voice suddenly to a conversational key as he continued. "You will doubtless be asked by my learned friend, Sir Ernest Coleman, to consider the extreme improbability of such a co-incidence as that Sir Roger Fairbanks should have first diagnosed the poison, and directed the police to trace it, and that it should then have been found in the room, if not in the actual possession of the accused. But human life, whether by the operation of capricious chance, or through an overruling destiny, is full of such coincidences. Of course, it is improbable. All coincidences are. That is why we remark them. Which of us cannot point to more than one in our own experience which we should tell with hesitation, even to our most trusted friends, because of its amazing improbability? If an English man or an English woman may be condemned on such evidence, or on such an argument, however skilfully worded, which of us is secure?

"But," he went on, "there is one principle of English law, one of our most ancient and cherished privileges, which still endures, though it may be sometimes forgotten in recent years. It is not required of my client that she shall prove her innocence. It is for the prosecution to prove her guilt." Mr. Butforth proceeded to analyse the evidence in detail, arguing that it amounted, at the most, to no more than a case of suspicion, capable of other explanation, which the defence was under no legal necessity to invent or supply. And this evidence, such as it was, depended for its vital link upon the assertions of Thomas Mogson, the truth of which his client had denied explicitly, and on oath. And—as he was sure that the learned Judge would direct them—such evidence was inadmissible from one of the accused as against the other, unless supported by independent testimony.

"You are called here," he concluded, looking at the jury with an intensity which strove to establish an individual contact with every member, "by the requirement of our English law, to say whether the prosecution have proved their case. The law requires proof. It places the life of a fellow citizen in your hands. It does not require more than that—that you shall condemn, if the case be proved. It does not ask you to guess. If you say among yourselves that my client is probably guilty, and condemn her upon that supposition, you are doing something that the law does not ask you to do, and the guilt, I will not say of murder itself, but of the taking of a human life, must be on your own heads. It is not a responsibility that can be shared among you. It is one that is awful and individual. If you allow yourself to be overborne by argument, or tired out by delay, while there is a doubt in your own mind—and how can you avoid a doubt, when deciding on a case which is built on surmise and theory, and buttressed only by conflicting ant mutually destructive evidence?—the terrible responsibility is yours, both by human law, and at that tribunal before which we must all stand at the last—and, perhaps, the awful remorse, if you should decide this case without mercy, and the truth should ultimately be revealed."

It would be of some psychological interest if it were possible to observe the effect of such a speech upon a jury who should be required to render their verdict immediately on its conclusion, ant to contrast or compare it with the verdicts which follow at an interval of from twenty-four to forty-eight hours.

In the present instance, its effect must have been largely neutralized by the succeeding speeches for Thomas Mogson, the reply for the prosecution, and the final summing-up of the learned Judge.

The procedure being as it is, it is at least possible that some persons who have been hanged—whether innocent or not—would be walking about today, had their counsel discarded forensic eloquence for the more enduring effect of a colder logic.

The speech which Mr. Basil Clackleton delivered in defence of Thomas Mogson was not designed to seal the doom of the female prisoner: rather, he was careful to point out that it was entirely consistent with a double innocence, yet it could not be urged without the implication that Constance Hillier had lied when she said that she had no knowledge of the fatal packet. His defence of his own

37

client was to urge that he had procured the poison innocently. Its actual, if not its logical effect, was to make the question at issue rather one of whether both the prisoners were guilty, or whether Constance Hillier alone deserved the poisoner's doom. Obviously, he could not accept her assertion that she had never asked for or received the fatal packets, and she probably did no good for herself when she broke out in audible interruption, reiterating foolishly that she had never seen them at all.

After that, the Attorney-General replied for the Crown in a speech the tone of which may be described as a deadly moderation. Declaiming nothing, he used the weapon of ironic understatement. He urged the jury to give full weight to the arguments which they had heard, with an implication that to weigh them carefully would be all that was needed to prove their hollowness. To the suggestion that it was a mere coincidence that the police had found this most rare poison, for which they had been directed to look by one who could not have known it to be there, in Constance Hillier's drawer, after it had already been diagnosed as the cause of death, he gave no more than a passing smile. "Well," he said, "if you can believe *that*...." He left the conclusion of the sentence to their imaginations.

The jury felt, perhaps for the first time, that they were being addressed as intelligent equals, which was as it should be. They got on very well with the Attorney-General.

The summing-up brought a note of quiet, almost of serenity. to the proceedings. Mr. Justice Troutbeck had the name of a very shrewd and yet merciful Judge. He was one who would habitually admit the possibility of a prisoner's innocence till the last word was said. In this case, he was so scrupulous that no point which had been made either by prosecution or defence should be disregarded that he left two or three of the jury who had resolved to let him make their minds up for them, rather bewildered as to where they were.

"Blowin' hot and cold, I call it," was the irritated comment of the manager of a travel agency, as they filed into the jury-room.

"There was an ever-present air of ambiguity," a shop-walker replied, in the good English which was equally at the service of a peer's widow or a publican's wife.

"I wouldn't quite say that," the foreman interposed in a voice that was firm yet conciliatory. "He depends on us to have enough sense to read between the lines. He doesn't mean them to get off on appeal, because it wasn't all set out from their side."

The foreman was convinced of the guilt of both, and in a great hurry to get away. He had a shrewd idea that they would end in a unanimous verdict of guilty, and that it depended mainly on himself whether they took ten hours or ten minutes to come to that conclusion. He addressed a broad-chested, rather rubicund man, with a large and fleshy nose, and an overbearing manner. "What do you say, Mr. Linkater?" He knew very well what Mr. Linkater thought. Mr. Linkater had cursed the swine every night for keeping him away from the wholesale egg and butter business from which his income came.

"What do I say? I say I hope we'll have ended this damned rot, and got out in an hour, of course. Half a dozen sensible men could have ended it all on the first day. Wanted the old girl's oof, and she wouldn't peg out. That's as clear as day. You could bet all Billingsgate to a rotten egg. You can understand how they felt. But they shouldn't have yanked her off as they did, all the same. You can't do that in this country. I say, let the vermin swing."

The foreman was not sure that this tone was the best to win over the more hesitant or fastidious of their colleagues. He said diplomatically: "It isn't for us to say that. Not exactly. We only say whether they are guilty or not. It's the Judge's part to pass the sentence that he thinks right. And, of course, the Home Secretary makes his own inquiries, and he always gives a reprieve, if there's any doubt. And, of course, there's the Appeal Court to go to, if we make a mistake."

The last sentence contained a truth of a very misleading kind. The Criminal Appeal Court deals with questions of law, rather than fact, and a very casual reading of its proceedings might have shown the frequency with which its judges decide that they "cannot" interfere with a jury's verdict. But there has probably never been a murder trial in recent years, where the jury have had difficulty in reaching a unanimous decision, where the argument has not been used to wear down the resistance of those who are unwilling to assent to a conviction.

On this occasion it visibly impressed more than one of those for whose benefit it had been spoken. When they had entered the room, of the eight men, there had been four whose minds were made up for a double conviction, two who were inclined to give Mogson the benefit of the doubt, and two who were uncertain in mind, and disposed to follow whatever might be the general feeling. Of the four women, two would have been disposed to welcome a verdict of not guilty with relief, one—the schoolmistress—was inclined to a reluctant verdict of guilty against both the prisoners, and one would cheerfully have hanged anyone, either man or woman, who had been shown to enter the Yellow Cat.

39

There may be no grosser defect in English criminal judicial procedure than the custom which imprisons juries in murder trials until the verdict is rendered. It has outlived the social conditions from which it grew, and can only continue as long as its victims accept it meekly. That juries are found to submit to its insolent implications is a matter which concerns themselves only. Its effect upon the administration of justice is more serious, because it falls upon those who have no power to protest against it. In the majority of cases in which a jury is absent for many hours, it is an almost inevitable deduction that there is a difference of opinion among them. It would require a more than childlike simplicity to believe that these differences are always harmonized by debate. They must end, whether after two hours or twenty, when the more obstinate section—which may not be an actual majority—have overcome the resistance of their opponents. There may be times when a coin spins. There are advantages in the jury system, and strong arguments for its retention, but it ceases to be a bulwark of liberty, or a probable instrument of justice, when it is used to bully those whom it calls together, by such methods, towards a unanimous verdict.

So we may reflect; but in the case with which we are dealing it is improbable that the result would have been different under conditions more favourable for a just decision.

In fact, there was an interval of forty minutes before the Court was able to reassemble, and the jury filed back into the box. It is actually probable that they would have taken longer in arriving at a unanimous verdict had they been under no coercion to do so. But there could have been no difference at last.

There were few who had been present during the four days that the trial lasted who did not confidently anticipate the verdict of guilty against both prisoners that the jury gave. Fewer still who doubted that it was a just decision. But of those few who had anticipated a different ending—though not, perhaps, from any consciousness of innocence—Thomas Mogson was certainly one. He had entered the dock with an air of rather nervous confidence, and looked at the jury almost as a man smiles at his friends, as they stood awaiting the formality of the question, the answer to which might mean liberty or death to those who heard it.

Even the significance of their downcast or averted eyes did not appear to disturb him, his demeanour contrasting with that of the wretched woman who stood beside him, though as far distant as its space allowed. As for her, she stood as one dazed, gazing at the Judge's face with the frightened, fascinated look of a cornered animal that can neither fight nor fly. "She'd scratch his face if she could," was a female comment from the back of the court.

Thomas Mogson listened to the fatal query. "Do you find the prisoner, Constance Hillier, guilty or not guilty?

"Guilty."

"And that is the verdict of you all?"

"Yes. Unanimous."

That didn't disturb him at all. He had rather expected that. That explained why they'd all looked so damned solemn as they had come in.

"You find the prisoner, Thomas Mogson, guilty or not guilty?"

"Guilty."

Thomas Mogson did not hear the further query. With an exclamation of "Oh, my God!" he collapsed in the dock.

It was half an hour before he was physically able to take his allotted part in the final tableau.

Homo sapiens is always inclined to take himself over-seriously. When he has decided to take the life of one of his fellows, he expects his victim to continue to treat him with respect and even politeness.

Thomas Mogson, and his physically and mentally bewildered companion in the guilt which the jury had laid upon them, must stand up respectfully while the Judge told them of the fate to which they would be consigned. They must also go through the obsolete formality of being asked whether they knew of any reason why they should be allowed to live.

Constance Hillier had nothing to say. It may be doubted whether the question penetrated her mind. Thomas Mogson had regained something of his former front of assurance. "Only that I'm quite innocent, my lord," he answered firmly. The Judge took no notice of that. It was a question on which Thomas Mogson's assertion had ceased to have any legal value.

He addressed the prisoners together. "You have been found guilty," he told them, "after a full and careful trial, of conspiring together in the perpetration of a cruel and cunning murder, designed in such a way, and by such a method, that I can well believe that you shared the anticipation that it was beyond discovery. But it is an old proverb that *Murder will out.* By what we may regard as an almost miraculous chance, or, if we will, as a direct interposition of Providence, the one man was called in—and that not by the police, but by the relatives of one of yourselves, with no thought of the consequences which would follow—the one man who could point a finger in the direction of the evidence which would prove your guilt. It is not a case where it would be right to hold out to either of you any expectation of mercy," and his voice shook with emotion for the first time as he said these words, "I can only recommend you, in the short period of earthly life that remains, to do what may yet be possible to prepare your souls for God." He then passed sentences of death in the usual form, ending with that quaint derisive formula "and may the Lord have mercy on your soul."

Firmly rejecting the basic principle of Christianity in favour of the Mosaic law, it yet ventures to express the hope that the Creator may be more complaisant or less particular in the standard of His requirements. Or perhaps it is only that He may be considered more competent to deal with a difficult case.

CHAPTER VI.

MRS. PARKER considered her position. She did not pause for this purpose in the cleaning of the gas cooker in her little kitchen at No. 4a, Holland Mews, a routine proceeding requiring the service of hand and eye, but leaving her mind at liberty for a more urgent function.

It was a bare hour from the time when Mr. McErrol, the urgent emissary of the *Sunday Pail*, was due to call upon her to receive her decision, and she was still in doubt as to whether she should accept his offer.

Mrs. Parker was a small, active, hard-featured woman of thirty-five. Fifteen years earlier she had been a fresh-coloured attractive girl, alluring enough to the inexperienced eyes of Hendrik Parker, a blond young giant, parented by a Swedish housemaid and an English butler, and carrying on the blameless trade of a master-carpenter in a side-street in Soho.

Married within six weeks of their first acquaintance, they had lived together in apparent concord for over six years, during which period they had added three vigorous children to the population of London, and then the morning had come when Hendrik had packed up his clothes, and announced, with his habitual economy of words, that he was going back to his mother's.

Ivy Parker (*née* Smith) did not pause in her occupation of washing her reluctant offspring, as she observed this departure in an angry and incredulous silence. When three days had passed, she visited her mother-in-law, with whom she had a few words, and a week later the enigma was occupying the attention of a stipendiary magistrate.

The magistrate recognized that the case had some unusual features. Mrs. Parker had nothing to say against her husband, except that she wanted him back, as a wife should. Mr. Parker had nothing to say against his wife, except that he wouldn't go. He appeared to be a sober man, of good character, which, considering his occupation, was not surprising. The plumber may go back—at your expense—to fetch the tools, the forgetting of which is one of the routines of his trade, the iron-monger may improve a dull day by charging a hammer to the account of every customer who may be likely to overlook the error, but the carpenter will come with a full bag. His thick pencil will figure his estimate on the wall with a laborious accuracy. He will diffidently suggest a sum which seems absurdly inadequate, and in a tone which invites you to reduce it further.

Finding that persuasion was of no avail, the magistrate inquired as to the extent of the defendant's earnings. It appeared that they amounted to from three to four pounds a week. Sometimes more. He said that he should make an order that thirty-five shillings weekly should be contributed to the support of the deserted wife and children. Hendrik Parker looked his surprise. He was not quick of speech, but he justified the moral status of his occupation by finding words to suggest that two pounds would be a more adequate figure.

Leaving the court, he stopped his abandoned consort to tell her to let him know if she needed more. Mrs. Parker, in spite of the bitter anger in her heart, had a regretful realization that she might have done better for herself had she preferred a more informal method of settlement, but she only said that she wasn't one to take more than the law had given, and if it weren't for the kids....

Since then the two pounds had come regularly, and Hendrik had stayed away.

There were two customary methods by which the deserted wife could augment her income. She could advertise that she was prepared to act as "housekeeper" to a "widower," which is the accepted euphemism for intimating that she would be willing to consider uniting her fortunes with that of a man who had been similarly separated. This is the logical, almost inevitable issue of a law which encourages judicial separation without divorce. But she did not like it for several reasons. She had a sure two pounds a week, the receipt of which would sooner or later be placed in jeopardy by such an arrangement. She had to consider that, having three children on her own hands, her advertisement would be unlikely to attract replies from men who had less than two of their own. That meant five—and probably more to come. There is a proverb about those who go further, and fare worse. No, she did not like the idea.

The alternative was to leave her children during the day, so long as any of them would be too young for school, in the care of a neighbour who specialized in such custodies, and go out to work.

She resolved to try this expedient, and was fortunate in securing such a position almost immediately in the service of Lady Catherine Middleditch.

Having once gained this position, she had kept it without difficulty. She was an excellent worker, cleaning a room with the ruthless efficiency with which she had controlled the routines of her own household, and the furniture, being unable to imitate her husband in walking out, submitted without audible protest.

She also gained a reputation for honesty, refusing even to make the shopping profits common to her kind, if either of the Misses Hillier should entrust her with some commission in the emergencies to which every household is liable. If she knew of a backstreet butcher who would retail Canterbury lamb to his more numerous customers, of the same quality that was supplied to Lady Catherine at three pence per pound higher by the obsequious Purveyor of Meat on whom she bestowed her custom, she gave her employers the full benefit of her commercial knowledge. But Ivy Parker had a basket, as daily women very commonly do. There was nothing wrong in that. It was needed at times to bring a clean apron, or remove a soiled one. It supplied a change of shoes in wet weather. It had also opened very willingly from the first to accept any stale provisions or cast-off garments that the generosity of her employers might offer to its capacious interior.

There were three healthy young appetites to be remembered at 4a, Holland Mews. If you have been told that you can take a jar of dripping home that would otherwise have been thrown away, you may require to be told the same thing every week for months—if you are a very scrupulous woman—before you will venture to do so without permission, but even so, as the months—and the years—pass, there will come a time when it is a recognized perquisite which will be taken without concealment, or verbal license asked or given. Vested interests grow.

Lady Catherine Middleditch kept a tight grip on the household finances. She had never been too ill for that. But there had been a limit to the possibilities of even her supervision while she had been confined to her own bed.

When Mrs. Parker cleaned her employer's room on Thursday mornings, she was subjected to many questions. If her answers were indiscreet, there might be trouble for Miss Hillier or Miss Margaret to follow. There came a time when things happened which Miss Hillier would have been very sorry for her aunt to know.

It had been quite a natural thing to say to Mrs. Parker, as she helped her to tie down the gooseberry jam which they had been making yesterday, "I shouldn't say anything to the mistress, if I were you, Ivy, about what happened yesterday. It will only upset her for nothing."

And if Mrs. Parker had already intended to ask if she could have what was left of the pork—which wouldn't be wanted again now that the butcher had delivered such a large joint—was she bound to keep silent because Miss Hillier had just asked a favour from her? It would have been most unfair.

And if Miss Hillier hesitated for a moment, even then, before she said, "Very well, Ivy, I don't suppose we should use it again"—there must have been nearly two pounds left of that pork—did it show anything except what a mean woman Constance Hillier really was? Even Miss Margaret would give her aunt's provisions with a freer hand than that.

So the years had worn out the brown bag, and it had been succeeded by one of even more generous receptivity, and the time came when it was left entirely to Mrs. Parker's discretion to fill it with such things as were more needed by her own children than by Lady Catherine's household, and these tacitly permitted levies became an increasingly substantial part of an honest woman's remuneration.

It is necessary to understand these circumstances if we are to do neither more nor less than a scrupulous justice to Mrs. Parker's actions in the tragic events which had so suddenly disturbed the Middleditch family.

Her position, which, a week before, had appeared impregnable, had become extremely precarious, and she realized with dismay that she was threatened with a financial disaster of the first magnitude. All things are comparative. She was not the first to realize that it is more difficult to revert to a lower scale of expenditure when it has been exceeded than it was to endure it previously. The children were at their most expensive age. The eldest was too young to earn. Even the youngest required clothes, and her appetite was a marvel to see. Mrs. Parker considered that she might quite easily obtain another position at the weekly remuneration that she was now getting (or even two shillings more) but she would be very unlikely to get one which would enable her to continue a household budget in which meat was an infrequent debit, and tea and sugar and matches a half-forgotten dream

She observed a good deal, and she overheard what she could. She asked Miss Margaret, and got no more than a doubtful assurance that she hoped it might not be necessary to part with her. Evidently nothing would be decided till the result of the trial was known.

It may be true that rats are prompt and businesslike in their desertion of a sinking vessel, but even a rat will not leave a floating plank for one of inferior quality as long as it *does* float, and may continue to do so. When the reporters came to Mrs. Parker's—as, of course, they did—she sent them empty away.

That was before the case had come on for trial. Mrs. Parker had not liked Miss Hillier, but she had not thought her to be one who would murder her aunt. (Probably the discovery of a poisoner is always more or less of a surprise to other members of the household.) But when she spread out the evening paper on her kitchen table, and read the verdict, she realized that her opinion had ceased to have any practical value. She had to think what Miss Margaret would do now, and she had a conviction that, whatever it might be, it would mean the closing of No. 35.

It was while this gloomy reflection filled her mind that Mr. McErrol's taxi stopped at the door.

That was two hours ago. She had admitted, in reply to his pressing and ingenious questions, that there were things which could be told of the "goings-on" at 35, Castlemaine Gardens, during the last eight or nine years, and she had received an offer of the substantial sum of one hundred pounds if she would tell them in such a way that they could be published on Sunday as "Mrs. Parker's Narrative." He had swept aside her scruples as being superfluous now that Constance Hillier had been convicted of murder. He understood the reticence which had kept her silent till then. It did her honour. But it would be absurd to continue it longer. The public wanted the truth, and they had a right to have it.

Mrs. Parker was impressed by this eloquence, but it did not vanquish her hesitation, which sprang from a different doubt. Was she sure that the comfortable position which she had held for nearly nine years was really lost? Was she sure that Miss Margaret might not make it more worth while to hold her tongue? She must have time to decide.

Mr. McErrol replied that he could call again in two hours. That was the most he could give. The value of such news is a very transient thing. Also, it depends on being first. Other papers might be foraging in other fields, and reaping more or less of the same crop. How could he tell? Anyway, it was getting late on Thursday now, and they went to press on Saturday afternoon. He made it dear that she must take her chance now or it would be lost for ever.

CHAPTER VII.

WHEN Mr. McErrol made his final call, about ten minutes before the appointed time, Mrs. Parker was still in a state of indecision. She did not like the thing that she was asked to do. She felt frightened. She was not reassured by a new proposal that she should tell her tale anonymously, and that its source should not be exposed, if that could be avoided. She was not a fool. Miss Margaret would guess in about thirty seconds. When she guessed—well, if Mr. McErrol knew her as well as she did. Yet she saw that if she missed this opportunity, and were told tomorrow that her services were no longer needed, she would be in the proverbial position of those who hesitate between two stools.

Mr. McErrol played his last card. He brought out a packet of one-pound notes. They were new notes, clean and uncreased, in little packets of tens. Ten packets in all.

Mrs. Parker's eyes glistened with cupidity as she gazed upon them. Yet she had the nerve to say, "If that's all as you offer, Mr. Mackerel.... It's worth twice that if it's worth your print in the *Sunday Pail*. You don't know what I can tell."

Mr. McErrol saw victory in his grasp. He employed the shock tactics which have the approval of some of the highest exponents of the military art.

"You pick them up, Mrs. Parker, and come along with me now, and give us a good tale, and there'll be another hundred for you to bring back."

He rose with the words, and Mrs. Parker said weakly, "I couldn't do that; not unless Bessie Furguson could come in. There's the three children in bed."

"Where's Mrs. Furguson?"

"It isn't Mrs., it's Miss. She's at No. 3."

"Well, come along, and we'll find out." Miss Furguson was in. She would oblige Mrs. Parker for the usual consideration.

Mrs. Parker had a last moment of indecision. Dare she leave the notes in the house? She decided to put them into her bag, and she clutched it with both hands as Mr. McErrol shepherded her impatiently to the waiting taxi.

"*Daily Pail* offices. Button Lane, off Fleet Street. Stop at the first entrance you come to."

Mrs. Parker sat clutching her bag, an excited, bewildered, and rather miserable woman.

CHAPTER VIII.

THE law of England, like that of most "civilized" countries preferring the risk of punishing the innocent to that of the guilty escaping, refuses bail before trial to persons who are accused of murder, thereby furnishing one evidence among many that the idea that an Englishman is accounted innocent till he be condemned by a jury of his peers is subject to very important qualifications.

It followed that from the moment when Inspector Cleveland had called at 35, Castlemaine Gardens, and departed in Constance Hillier's company, she had been seen there no more, and even her sister had not been allowed to visit her at the gaol in any real privacy. The only subsequent intercourse had been in two very painful and somewhat hysterical interviews, during which she had vehemently protested her innocence, which was hardly surprising in view of the probability that the conversation was liable to be reported by an overhearing wardress.

Apart from these interviews, and the uncertainty of her sister's fate, Margaret Hillier had had sufficient troubles to face during the seven weeks that intervened between the arrest and trial. Inspector Cleveland's inquiries had been conducted with a discreet secrecy until the moment when he had appeared at the door of No. 35 with two assistants, and a warrant to search the house. When he left, he "invited" Constance Hillier to accompany him to the police-station, and it was a journey from which she did not return. Margaret had found herself left solitary in the house of death. The first night she slept alone, its solitary occupant, with such thoughts as we may imagine, if we care to do so.

The next morning her aunt's solicitor, Mr. Risdon, had called upon her. It was then but sixteen days since Lady Catherine had died.

Mrs. Parker had opened the door, and showed him into the drawing-room, where Margaret entered a few moments later.

Mr. Risdon was a clean-shaven man of middle height and middle-age, and a manner suitable to the time of life that his appearance indicated, His peculiarity was that this condition appeared to be essential to himself, rather than to a transitory period of life, It was difficult to imagine that he had ever been young. He showed no sign of age. Would he become short of breath if he should sprint to the street corner in his, perhaps, fiftieth year? It would be a foolish question to ask. He was not a man who would sprint. Probably he never had sprinted. His walk was neither brisk nor slow. His appearance neither weak nor robust. You would know him at once as a man who would drink wine—and would drink sparingly. It was difficult to imagine that he would be disconcerted by any circumstance, or stirred to anger, or roused to haste; or that he would be slack or hurried of speech.

He showed no awkwardness in meeting the sister of the woman who had been arrested on the previous day, nor did he fail to say what the circumstances required. He expressed his regret that he had been away on business in Germany during the previous fortnight, so that this had been his first opportunity of calling since he had heard the distressing news of Lady Catherine's death. But he had cabled to his partner to render any assistance that should be needed, and he understood that some money had been advanced to deal with the current payments of the household.

"Yes," Margaret Hillier assented. "We had no money at all." She was very pale, and showed evidence of restrained emotion, but it was under the control of a firm will. Five years younger than Constance, she retained more of the freshness of youth. Normally, she was lighter of step, more alert of movement. Laughter might be strange to her lips, but her face was free from the moral slackness or ill-temper that her sister's showed. She added, "I am needing some more now."

Mr. Risdon did not offer to supply it. He said, "I did not expect that there would have been any immediate stringency. I was aware that Lady Catherine kept a sum of fifty pounds in cash in reserve against any unexpected emergency."

Margaret made no direct answer to that. She said, "I have less than two pounds." After a moment's silence, she asked: "What are you going to do about Constance?"

The eyes that met those of the lawyer were cold, the voice was toneless. Mr. Risdon, sensitive to atmosphere, though he would show no reaction, was conscious of a latent hostility, but there was nothing that he could observe or resent. He answered, "I have arranged to see her at...."—He was about to say "Pentonville", but changed it to, "...three o'clock this afternoon." He added, "There has been a formal remand this morning."

"I suppose you will have no difficulty in defending her from such an accusation?"

"I hope that it may be disposed of without difficulty, but it is too soon to express a final opinion. It seems to have some unusual features. I shall know more when I have seen Miss Hillier."

No one listening could have judged whether either the man or the woman spoke with sincerity, or whether the slow words were merely those which they felt to be most suitable to the circumstances in which they met.

Margaret answered: "Constance wouldn't have done thing like that. I don't suppose there's been any poisoning at all. I should have thought with a family like ours...."

"I'm afraid that doesn't make much difference. Not when matters have developed to this point. Sometimes, perhaps, at an earlier stage."

"Can't you get them to drop it?"

"Not, I'm afraid, without a hearing in the magistrate's court. Of course, he may refuse to send it for trial. But that rarely happens in a case that the police bring. No, I'm afraid we shall have to see it through."

"I suppose there'll be no difficulty about the money, now you are back?"

"I have no doubt that adequate arrangements will be made for your sister's defence, I have already asked your uncle to see me to discuss the position."

"I meant here."

There was a long moment of silence before he answered. "I scarcely think, under all the circumstances, that it will be advisable for this house to be kept on. It is only held on an annual tenancy, which is terminated by Lady Catherine's death. In fact, I am arranging for an inventory to be taken tomorrow, with a view to an early sale."

"I shouldn't allow that."

"I'm afraid, Miss Margaret, it hardly rests with you to decide."

"You mean it's for Constance to say?"

"You will remember that I am the executor under Lady Catherine's last will."

"You always were."

"Yes. Your aunt placed a confidence in our firm which has continued from three generations. A confidence, if I may say so, which has never been abused."

52

"I suppose as executor you will consider the wishes of those to whom the money is left?"

"I shall consult Miss Hillier's wishes, and act in her interests to the best of my ability, subject, of course, to the unfortunate complication which has arisen."

"And why not mine?"

"You are not, unfortunately, a beneficiary under the last will."

"But I think I am. There is a document that you have not seen."

"Then I should like to see it."

Margaret left the room, and returned with a sheet of letter paper which she handed to Mr. Risdon. He read this:

35, Castlemaine Gardens, W.6
April 18th, 19—.

We agree that whatever will may be made by Aunt Catherine, we will share everything equally when she dies.

CONSTANCE HILLIER
MARGARET HILLIER

Witness to this: IVY PARKER

The lawyer considered this remarkable document. "I'm, afraid," he said, "this has no legal validity."

"You needn't say that to Constance. Not that she'd want to go back on it, if you did."

"The question may not arise." He had the thought that he would have matters of greater urgency to discuss with Constance Hillier that afternoon. He added, "But it is obviously not a document of any legal value. It shows no consideration. It's not even stamped."

"You mean it's no good because it's not stamped?"

"Not exactly. There would be a penalty to be paid. There are other reasons."

He folded it up slowly and was putting it into his pocket as one who does not observe his own actions, when Margaret interposed, "I should like that back, please."

He hesitated, and then returned it. He had considered that it could do Miss Hillier no harm in her sister's hands, and its production might do her no good. It made it too evident that one or both of them had looked forward to Lady Catherine's death with an anticipatory mind. Perhaps the less he knew of it the better.

"I shan't give way about that," Margaret was saying, in her calm way. "If necessary, I shall dispute the will."

"I don't think that you could do that."

"I thought anyone could dispute a will."

"Yes-s. Not exactly. We'll hope the question may not arise."

Mr. Risdon could see other possibilities that might complicate the financial consequences of Lady Catherine's will. But he must not assume his client's guilt. Still less must he assume her conviction.

He rose, saying that Miss Margaret would hear from him further. She must rely on him as a friend.

She made no answer to that.

CHAPTER IX.

THE next morning the Earl of Weyford called upon Mr. Risdon at his office in Bedford Square. The Earl was small and old. He leaned on a heavy stick. As he removed his hat, he showed a bald head, the colour of a Langshan's egg. It had a fringe of hair that was straight and white and well-trimmed. A white moustache stood out from his upper lip, falling over, smooth as a waterfall on its outer surface and somewhat lengthened on either side of his mouth. He had a manner which was alternately abrupt and hesitant. He had a reputation for petulance and indecision, but the actions of a long life had shown that when his mind was made up it was usually in the right way.

"Terrible business, Risdon, terrible business," he began, before he was seated, as he extended a vein-blue hand. "I suppose if I'd left it alone...."

Mr. Risdon, who thought the same, only remarked that you can never tell. "But what's the truth, Risdon, what's the truth? That's what I'm here to know."

"I suppose that's for the court to decide. It's too early to say much. I saw Miss Hillier yesterday afternoon. She denies everything. I can't get beyond that yet. I'm seeing Butforth at his chambers tonight. He'll be the right man for this, if he'll take it on. I suppose I shall be doing right to give him the brief?"

The Earl saw the implication of the question, without waiting for a more explicit approach. "You want your instructions from me, Risdon? Isn't there plenty in the estate?"

"Yes. Lady Catherine didn't spend much. There'll be about £10,000 more than what came to her. But there are one or two points that...I thought I'd talk it over with Butforth tonight, before I start proving the will. Still, I don't see...."

But the Earl did. He pulled out a cheque-book with a rather shaking hand. He wrote a cheque for £500.

"You mustn't spare anything, Risdon. But make that do, if you can. You know I'm not a rich man. I shall look to you to get it back in the end."

Mr. Risdon blotted the cheque. He touched a bell on his desk. A clerk came in and was told to write a receipt. Mr. Risdon pulled a drawer at his right hand a few inches open, and slipped the cheque in. He said, "I've decided to have a sale at No. 35 as soon as possible. It's no use the expenses going on as they are, I don't want to advance them, anyway; and I can't realize the investments till the will's proved. Of course, we usually arrange for an advance at the bank till we can get probate, but as things are, I scarcely know what they'd say."

"You mean, if you sell the furniture?"

"Yes. It ought to bring in a good deal. There are some old pieces that look valuable. I meant to send Gray & Wisden's clerk up this morning to take an inventory, but as you were coming in...." Mr. Risdon did not mention a conversation of the previous morning.

The Earl hesitated. He did not like the responsibility of a sudden decision being thrown on his shoulders in that way. It is so easy to say "Yes" or "No," and think of something half an hour after that makes you wish that you hadn't. But it did seem the most sensible thing to do. Even if this ghastly affair didn't prove as bad as it looked, he didn't suppose that Constance would want to keep that house on.

"Yes," he said, "I expect it's the best way." He got up to go.

He went to lunch at his club, telling his chauffeur to call for him again in an hour, and went on after that to see Margaret Hillier. He didn't like going at all. He had not got on well with Catherine, and the house was strange to him. Consequently, the two nieces who had lived with her were strange also. But he had promised Violet that he would go. You couldn't leave the girl alone in the house like that. So she had said, and, of course, she was right. Violet was a grandchild who lived with him, her parents being in India.

So he drove to Castlemaine Gardens, hoping that Margaret wouldn't be of an hysterical kind. He never could stand scenes. But he need not have worried about that. Margaret said the correct things. Beyond that she was quiet and inscrutable. She received her cousin's messages politely, but, surprisingly, she refused the invitation which they contained. She said she was best where she was till the trouble was over. Mrs. Parker came in during the day. She did not mind sleeping alone. Not in the least. What was there to mind? She couldn't stand talk. No, she would rather be by herself for a time. Only, Mr. Risdon had said something about selling the furniture. Couldn't anything be done to stop him? She had had to tell Mrs. Parker already not to open the door without knowing who was there. Things were bad enough without that.

Faced by a woman who knew her own mind, and obviously meant to have her own way, the Earl capitulated easily on a point on which he had been doubtful before. He said he would tell Risdon to let things remain as they were. And money? Yes, she must have some to carry on with. He would tell Risdon that. He felt that she had trouble enough, and that she should be kept free of avoidable worries.

She felt she had done well, and was unguardedly cheerful as she said good-bye at the door.

As he drove away, he wondered whether she were more troubled that her sister was charged with a capital crime, or relieved that her aunt was dead. Perhaps it was natural enough. Anyway, she had a good nerve. And it was bad luck for her the will being as it was, however it might turn out in the end. He wondered how Violet and she would have got on if he had brought her home....

Meanwhile Margaret was looking at the little store of money locked in her own drawer. There were a few pounds that she had saved from what her aunt had given her. There was the fifty pounds that had been found when she died, in the little bag that was always beside her. It had been Constance's idea that they should say nothing about that, to which she had agreed easily enough. Beside that, there was three and nine-pence in a cardboard box. That was all that was left of the money that had come from Risdon & Clarke's. She went down and told Mrs. Parker to tell the grocer that she would have some money from her lawyer before the end of the week, and his account must wait till then.

Mr. Risdon had a note from the Earl of Weyford next morning. He read it, and did not look pleased. He was not greatly surprised that Margaret had decided to remain in the empty house. "Doesn't mean to give up possession, if she can help it," he commented, half-aloud. He rang for a typist, and dictated a letter sending her ten pounds. He felt he had no option, in view of what the Earl had written. He would have liked to make it even less than that.

CHAPTER X.

IT was on the afternoon of the day following Constance Hillier's conviction that the Earl of Weyford called again at Mr. Risdon's office. The anxiety of the last two months—an anxiety of prestige rather than of any personal sympathy for a woman whom he scarcely knew—appeared to have shaken a constitution already weakened by advancing years and some definite infirmities, and he leaned more heavily on the stick he carried, and his hand was less steady as he extended it to the lawyer, casually introducing, as he did so, his granddaughter, Miss Violet Scovell, who had entered beside him.

"This dreadful business, Risdon, this dreadful business," he began, "I don't know what can be done, but I felt that I must talk it over. I can't sleep or eat. Three hundred years, Risdon, three hundred years, and now for it to come to this!"

It is a fact that the Weyford earldom is of that unbroken antiquity, but it may, at a first thought, appear improbable that any family should have held a recorded position of such duration without some even more sinister incidents than that a relative—not in the direct line—should be convicted of a capital crime. But it is not without parallel. The records of historic families which maintain their position over the centuries are of two opposite kinds. They may show emphatic assertions of character, aggressive and turbulent, in which event they will be punctuated with imprisonments, conspiracies, divorces, illegitimacies, and a variety of picturesque criminalities, alternating with demonstrations of intellect, or heroic or patriotic deeds, of more admirable descriptions. Or otherwise they may show a continuing record of the more negative virtues, of cautions, abstinences, and evasions, by which the family fortune has been steered without disaster through the shoals of circumstance for succeeding centuries. Of such families it is only marvellous that so long a succession of heirs have held positions of prestige and wealth without leaving more than the faintest impressions of their existence upon the minds of their contemporaries, or the history of their race.

The family of the Earl of Weyford had been of this latter kind. The barony conferred by King James I upon Sir Robert Scovell, for services of which there is no record remaining, even survived the embarrassments of the Civil War without apparent difficulty, the son of the first baron acting with such politic discretion throughout that it has proved difficult for the historians of his county to decide to which party his allegiance was given; and the advance of the family rank and fortunes which took place after the accession of William and Mary is of a very uncertain significance.

Sprung from this prudent stock, the feelings of the present earl may invite our sympathy, as his family connections were thus exposed, and his grandniece convicted of sordid crime, and condemned to ignoble death. But it would do him injustice to suppose that his mind had failed to react in other and more generous ways. Having little mental occupation of urgency and being debarred by physical infirmity from taking the relief of bodily exercise, his mind had concentrated itself upon the incidents and background of this crime—if such it were—during the past two months, until prolonged and agitated reflection had done much to supply the deficiency of a somewhat sluggish imagination, and he had entered even into some measure of understanding sympathy with the restricted lives of those two young hag-ridden women, which did much to explain, if little to condone, the final catastrophe. But he had a mind that placed a very high value upon the observance of his country's laws, as well as those which he believed to be divinely given, whether through the pages of the New Testament, or the Mosaic code. Whatever might be the moral aspects of murder, the central impregnable fact was that it was forbidden by English law. It was by reverence for established order, by careful, even timid observance of the rules of the game, that his ancestors had held their extensive Berkshire acreage. If he regarded a socialist as superior to a murderer, it was only because the laws of his country displayed a greater tolerance, but even the laws of a Labour Government deserved respectful obedience when once they had found their way to the Statute Book.

It followed that his anxiety that his niece should be defended to the best advantage had sprung from two sources. He had desired to save the family name from the disgrace of such a conviction, and he had felt the duty of extending his support to one of his own blood while her innocence remained a legal, and perhaps an actual possibility. But had he been, or should he become, convinced of her guilt his course of action might be of a less certain complexion.

Yet even now, the final word of the law might not have been pronounced. There was the right of appeal. He had said no more than the literal truth when he remarked to Mr. Risdon at their previous interview that he was not a rich man. Though the threat of national starvation was but twelve years old, the government of the day had no use for agriculture, except for the draining of impoverished estates by means of Death Duties when their owners died. His own precarious and mortgaged income could only continue to hold his ancestral estate together till his death should bring destructive crisis upon it. But if Mr. Risdon told him that Butforth regarded the evidence as inconclusive, or that there were just grounds of appeal, he was still ready to find or guarantee such funds as the legal appetite might require.

To his first explosive protest, Mr. Risdon had returned no more than a conventional answer, but he addressed his mind to a carefully worded explanation in reply to the query that followed.

"What I want to know, Risdon, what I want to know is: did she do it or not? That scoundrel Mogson, did he lie all along? We must appeal, Risdon, if the verdict's wrong. It's only the jury, after all. You couldn't tell what the Judge thought. What does Butforth say about that?"

He had an instinctive feeling that the judge's opinion was of a superior order to that of any dozen of unofficial jurymen, and a conviction—which may have been sound enough—that he was more likely to be right than they.

"The summing-up," Mr. Risdon answered, "was very fair. There would hardly be two opinions about that. Butforth says that may be our greatest difficulty. I had it over with him last night, but we'd discussed the question of appeal before then. You see, the way the case was going, it was almost certain that we should have to face an adverse verdict. Mogson will appeal, of course. Price told me that they should brief Clackleton this morning, and get it lodged at once. I wouldn't like to say that he told the truth, or how far. If he wasn't in it up to the neck, he's a very unlucky man. But that's the only ground of appeal—that it was against the weight of evidence. A jury's got the final word on a question of fact, and you can't go beyond that. The Court of Appeal itself has to take a back seat. But if there are only three witnesses, and they all say that they saw a man turn to the right, the jury can't bring in a verdict that he turned the opposite way. But if it's a question of whom they believed, or how far, then it isn't easy to get the Appeal Court to interfere."

"You mean you think that Mogson may get off, but Constance won't?"

"No. I didn't mean that. I don't think he's got a chance. But they're bound to try it, for what it's worth. Our position's more difficult. Butforth asked me to put it to you, and let him know what you think. We've got no real ground of appeal—legal ground, I mean. I'm not saying whether she did it, or not. As to that, I know no more than anyone else, and I don't know that my opinion's more valuable."

"It's a dreadful thing—" Miss Scovell spoke for the first time— "to think how she must feel if she really didn't do it at all."

"Well, as to that, I don't know that she'd feel any worse than if she did. But if you put it that way, Miss Scovell, I'll say what I mightn't have done otherwise. Speaking between these walls, there's no doubt that they're both guilty enough. The only real doubt is who suggested it first, which we're never likely to know, unless they confess. But anyway, it must have been Constance Hillier who did the actual thing. There's no getting over that."

"I suppose not. But I thought—grandfather thought—suppose it was just possible that Mogson had been in the house with her, and she didn't like to say? Or could he have got in without being seen? I don't say there's much chance of that. But she might have had him in without Aunt Catherine knowing."

Mr. Risdon turned his eyes to Miss Scovell, and really observed her for the first time. Not, perhaps, a very beautiful girl. Not one who would draw the glances of all those among whom she moved. But one who might hold those that were once fixed upon her. One who would be likely to keep her friends. And she had an arresting voice—low, and musical, and very clear. And very intelligent eyes. Mr. Risdon was led to remember that though the earls of Weyford had done little in the direct line, there had been some notable women of their blood who had married into other families. There are several such instances in the records of the English peerage. Under our system of inheritance, a family retains its males, and exports its women, and if it be one of those—as such there are—which breed women better than men, it may be responsible for the reputations of others, while it gains none of its own.

Mr. Risdon had little liking for women, and he was being interrupted in the course of what he had to say, which he always disliked, but he answered without visible sign of annoyance.

"I don't think we need consider seriously the possibility of Mogson getting into the house without her knowledge, and I can see that you have come to the same conclusion. But the possibility that she might have wished to conceal the fact that she used to have him inside is on a different plane There was a time when I thought it was most likely that it was there that the truth lay. Of course, it wouldn't show that she was innocent, if she did. But it would just raise a doubt. Legally, it's of no value now, whether it were true or not. She chose her line of defence, which was just a denial of everything, and it's too late to change. But if I got—if I could get even now any reliable evidence that Thomas Mogson had been in that house, there'd be something that we could put before the Home Office, and that might just possibly—I wouldn't say more than that—just possibly mean a reprieve.

"But I don't want to raise any hope on that ground, because I've altered my mind. I don't think that Mogson ever entered that house at all. It's the one point on which they both said the same thing, and it was about the only one of which they both spoke as though they were telling the truth. I'm told that the Judge said afterwards that he'd been impressed in the same way. Of course, that's all in Mogson's favour, not ours—as far as it goes. Clackleton'll try to use that on appeal for all it's worth, and a bit more. But, anyway, so it is.

"But that isn't the point I was going to put to you," Mr. Risdon turned more directly toward the Earl of Weyford again as he said this. "The point is that it just happens that the Courts are sitting in such a way that if an appeal's entered, it's likely to come on for hearing a few days *after* the date for which the executions are likely to be fixed. That's always liable to happen, though it doesn't often. But it will this time. That's practically inevitable.

"Now Mogson's going to appeal, which means that the date of his execution will be postponed. We can do the same if we like. We haven't any real ground, and there isn't a chance that we shall succeed. Butforth's firm on that. Not the least.

"But the point he wants me to put to you's this. He says it's psychological rather than logical, and it's a poor chance, but it's a bit better than none.

"If we both appeal, there are four possible results. We might get both the convictions quashed. That's not worth considering. It wouldn't happen. Or we might get them both confirmed, in which case we should be back where we are now, with just a shade of difference against us, because it's said to be just a little more difficult to get the Home Office to consider a reprieve after an appeal's failed. Butforth says they mayn't put it into words, but they act as though they have the feeling that you can ask for mercy or for some more law, but you can't expect both. I don't say there's much in that, but anyway, we'd be no better off than we are now.

"Then, theoretically, we might get Mogson's conviction confirmed, and get off ourselves. But there's really no chance of that. If you think it out, you'll see that it isn't sense—not on any evidence we've got now, or are ever likely to. And so we come to the last possibility—and this is one that we can't dismiss so easily—that Mogson might get off, and we be left in the cart—and if that happened we'd be a lot worse off than we are now.

"In a sense, that's the position that may arise, whether we appeal or don't. We can't help it. But Butforth's point's this. No one likes hanging a woman. Many people are against it, whatever she may have done. There's hardly been a case in recent years where there hasn't been a reprieve except one, and then there were two people who hanged each other in a quite illogical and very natural way. Either of them might have got off, standing alone, but it wouldn't have done to reprieve both, and you couldn't say a word for either that didn't make it worse for the other.

"Now this case is a good deal of the same kind, and there'll come a time when the Home Secretary will have this case on his desk, and be considering whether it's one on which he can 'advise' a reprieve. Now is it better that he should have to consider the two at once—or possibly have ours before him while Mogson's appeal's pending? You see, Mogson's appeal will only defer the date of his own execution, not ours, and he'll have to make up his mind one way or other, while Mogson's appeal is still on the file."

"You think under those—in that event—he might advise a reprieve?"

"No, I don't. It's Butforth's idea, not mine; but I don't think he does either. It's a slim chance, but it seems to us it's the only one. It might mean postponing our execution, and when it's once been postponed there may be a better chance that we get through in the end. But if you ask me, I don't think it will, and if it does I don't think we shall get off in the end. But we'll think out some excuse to appeal if you feel it's the better way."

The Earl of Weyford had listened to this somewhat long and lucid explanation in exemplary silence, though he could not entirely conceal the nervous tension which he endured. His hands worked restlessly on the knob of the stick on which they rested as he sat. He mate half-articulate exclamations at times which he controlled with a visible effort. Why did Risdon talk of it in the possessive case? Even of "our" execution? As though we were actual partners in guilt and penalty! He was not content to recognize it for the polite and customary formula which it really was. Why, again, did Risdon show so little interest in Violet's theory, which they had talked over together till it had assumed approximation to fact? Was she guilty or not? That was what mattered; had always mattered to him. Still more important—though he might not have recognized this for truth—could they, even yet, demonstrate her innocence to the world? But to Risdon it was a game of chess! It was sickening to an honest man, who had kept his name unstained through the difficulties and worries of over seventy years, as his ancestors had done before him. In these impatient, but perhaps natural emotions, he did some injustice to men who were giving their best advice and efforts to the saving of Constance Hillier's life if any such possibility remained, and in the case of Mr. Risdon, to one who was doing it in the midst of private worries of a very urgent kind. He rose to go, saying abruptly, "Very well, Risdon, very well. You must do what Butforth thinks best. I suppose what it really means is that it's got to go on. But I shall see what I can do in other ways. I must see what I can do before then."

He had a vague idea that he would see the Home Secretary—perhaps the King—there must be ways. As his mind abandoned the last hope that it might yet be possible to establish Constance Hillier's innocence, and the shadow of the gallows was at his feet, his mind moved to the resolution that this last indignity must be averted at any cost.

He went out in a rather stumbling way, with Violet's firm young hand under his arm. At that conference, the last faint hope of saving Constance Hillier's life had been thrown away. But they could not know that.

"I still think," Violet said, as they reseated themselves in the waiting car, "that someone ought to find out whether Mogson really ever went to the house.

This was on Friday. On the following morning she was walking to St. Margaret's Church (it may be remembered that the third Sunday in February was a fine day, though rather cool) when she passed a row of placards announcing the leading features of the Sunday newspapers. Most of them were concerned with the East Islington by-election, which was decided a few days later, or with the Chelsea-Blackburn Rovers cup-tie of the following day, and she passed them with unobservant eyes—do we not all train our civilized eyes to be as unobservant as sedulously, and with as urgent cause, as we should need to train them to observation under more natural conditions of life?—when she waked abruptly from a wandering thought as she came opposite those of the *Sunday Pail,* which announced on three conspicuous placards:

THE TRUTH ABOUT CONSTANCE HILLIER

WHAT HAPPENED AT CASTLEMAINE GARDENS?

AMAZING REVELATIONS
DID CONSTANCE HILLIER HAVE A CHILD?

CHAPTER XI.

THE article which appeared in the *Sunday Pail* was widely different from the wording and substance of the statement which Ivy Parker had signed for that enterprising periodical at about midnight on Thursday, to be sent home thereafter in another taxi, tightly clutching a bag which by then contained two hundred of the precious pounds, and very agitated in mind as to whether she would have courage to face Miss Margaret tomorrow morning, with the guilt of betrayal in her heart, and only supported by the fact that it could not become public before the end of the week. She endeavoured to harden her resolution with thoughts of the week's wages which would be lost if she did not continue her service until Saturday afternoon, and of them cabbage-pickles on the top shelf at the back which Lady Catherine couldn't eat now, poor soul, and which yet could never be transferred to the pantry at 4a, Holland Mews should she lack the courage for which she prayed.

In the first place, the editor had decided that it would be best to avoid disclosure of the source of the information which they had obtained, which involved the redaction of the whole narrative, and the elimination of Ivy Parker's very numerous first-person-singulars, and of her more exclamatory passages.

Next, Mr. McErrol, to whom the editor had entrusted the completion of the good work he had begun, had to eliminate all avoidable references to Margaret Hillier, and to tone down those that remained. Margaret Hillier still lived, and even the sister of a murderess may evoke the law of libel if there be sufficient provocation, and one who is the grandniece of a peer may have money or friends to enable her to do so. It is from the friendless and the unfortunate, from those who are broken in health or fortune or reputation, that such papers as the *Sunday Pail* can most safely select their victims.

But Lady Catherine Middleditch was dead. The law of England is explicit that you *cannot* libel the dead. Possibly the original idea may have been that no one would be so base as to find pleasure in such a deed. Possibly no one does. But profit is a different thing.

Mr. McErrol knew that there was little need for care as to what might be written about Lady Catherine, except he must remember always that she had had important connections. The editor's policy was well-known throughout the office. You must never risk offending anyone influential, unless for a big scoop, or to please someone more influential still. But with a murderess in the familiar—well, even an earl couldn't be over touchy about what was written concerning any deceased relative!

But as to what was said about Constance Hillier, it might be true or false, but, if it would make good reading, there was no need to trouble at all. You can't libel a convicted murderess. Not to matter, that is. And if there should be any unavoidable allusions to Margaret or others, they must be as oblique as possible. The conditional mood provides grammatical constructions of appropriate kinds.

These were points on which the editor could rely upon Mr. McErrol's caution, and go home to an easy bed. Everyone on the staff knew the unfortunate experience of McErrol's first adventure in journalism. He had begun by omitting the magic word "alleged" in alluding to an unconvicted burglar, and then had been so severely admonished, and so strictly enjoined to use the talisman on all doubtful occasions, that he had made his paper a laughing-stock on the following day by describing a charge of drunkenness which had been brought against an alleged taxi-driver by an alleged policeman, and of the gallant conduct of an alleged fireman in rescuing an alleged cat from the roof of a burning building.... It had been nearly two years before he got his next job.

Violet Scovell bought the paper, and then, after a first glance at the front sheet, resolutely closed it, and turned back home, to find a place where she could read unobserved, catching one swiftly-obliterated look of consciousness on the face of the footman who opened the door as he saw the paper beneath her arm, and concluding correctly that it had been already spread out on the table of the servants' hall.

Margaret Hillier did not see it till the afternoon. She had not left the house (or at least not by the front door) since she had read the news of her sister's conviction on Thursday night. On Sunday morning, when she found that Mrs. Parker did not turn up as usual, she thought little of it at first. She did not think that Ivy would desert her, while it was to her profit to stay. But as the hours passed, she grew suspicious, and recalled some singularity of manner of the previous evening. She had a look round the kitchen. Yes, they were all

67

gone, the little personal things that any woman would have lying round after so many years of service. Not even an apron left. Not even the old overshoes which had outlived their usefulness. Mrs. Parker had gone.

Margaret always got her own breakfast. Now she cooked her solitary dinner. After that, she wrote a letter, and went out to post it. On the way to the pillar-box which is beyond Castlemaine Gardens, at the further end of Little Compton Street, she passed the newspaper shop on the left-hand side, and saw the placards bearing her sister's name. Margaret Hillier did not lack courage. She walked in at once to purchase the paper. But it was sold out. She had to search Kensington to the borders of Hammersmith before she could find a copy that was unsold, and that one bore evident traces of having been in the hands of a previous reader. Unlike Miss Scovell, and doubtless under a more acute temptation, she could not resist a number of hurried glances as she walked, which, though she would not be observed to read it, devoured so much, that she had little left to learn when at last, white with an almost uncontrollable fury, she could sit down in the darkening privacy of her own room in the lonely house, and read the page-long narrative without further need to control her feelings. From the first glance at the paper, she had had no doubt of the source from which the article was derived, and if Mrs. Parker could have seen her face she would have congratulated herself upon the prudence which had kept her away.

CHAPTER XII.

MARGARET HILLIER paced up and down the room between the intervals at which she read and re-read those maddening "revelations" in uncontrollable agitation. It was not only the glaring headlines and the column on the front page, which was continued on a full sheet inside; there were the photographs, which had another page to themselves. Constance in the centre, with Lady Catherine and herself on either side. They were caricatures rather than portraits, and that of Constance Hillier (which had appeared previously) had been touched up to a more sinister expression of mouth and eyes. And at the side of that there was a picture of "35, Castlemaine Gardens—where the crime took place"; and below that, all across the page, the picture of an ugly shadowed Victorian house, "the Nursing Home at Hillingham where Constance Hillier is said to have stayed."

So they had even traced her to there! Damn that woman! *Damn! Damn! Damn!* What should she say to Bill Langford now? How explain this new scandal, and maintain his sympathy, his belief in her? And he would be looking now for the signal-light she would put in the window when the darkness came. But she could not put it yet. She could not see him yet. She must have time to think. And, for a time, that was just what she could not do. If she had that woman here now! She felt as though No. 35 might have been the scene of another and more violent homicide.

Yet she cooled after a time, as she must, and faced the position with a brain that was not often abdicated from its control. She could not deny everything. She had the sense to see that. It was too circumstantial, too detailed. And Bill would recognize the condition of the wall! It was strange how the event had repeated itself to a point. So alike—and yet so different! No, she couldn't deny it all. Even he mightn't believe that. And yet it was five years old! And the child had died. Who could have thought that it would be resurrected now? But after all (she was much cooler now) was there so much that she need deny? She went over that article again very carefully to judge what it would imply to a reader who knew nothing of what had really happened. There were the anecdotes about her aunt, about her cruelty and caprices. Malicious anecdotes of the particularly poisonous kind that are partly true. But they made good reading, and what else mattered to the *Sunday Pail*? She didn't mind overmuch about them, though they represented her sister and herself as having been held in a mean and abject servitude.

Apart from that, she was relieved and somewhat puzzled by the skilful way in which she had been kept in the background. No, it was not really so bad, now that she read it in a quieter way. It was a case for the truth—the minimum truth of course—and that should carry her through well enough. When she had written to Mr. Risdon to say that she would call on him tomorrow she had had nothing on her mind, except to find out, once for all, where she stood about the money, and decide how she should go on now that Mrs. Parker had bolted. She wanted to get away from this hateful, nightmared house, and she didn't mean to let him in, to do just what he liked. She saw that there would be an additional subject of conversation now.

She went upstairs, and lit the lamp in the window. Five minutes after she would put on her thick coat, and go down the garden, sure that Bill would be waiting at the gap in the wall where the old pear-tree fell. It was not wise for him to wait about, as his mother kept too close a watch on the length of his garden absences. That was why she had arranged that bedroom signal, so that no time should be lost waiting for her to appear. She would have liked to bring him into the kitchen, and talk there in comfort. But there was his mother to be remembered again. And her own character. To Bill Langford she was a shy and very modest girl. That was the right character to maintain. More than ever now. It had better be no more than a few words tonight...and a few tears. He might not have seen the paper at all. If not, she would tell him herself. It would be much the best way, and, sooner or later, he would be sure to hear.

CHAPTER XIII.

VIOLET SCOVELL came to Mr. Risdon's office alone the next afternoon. She explained: "Grandfather meant to come when I telephoned this morning, but he's been worse since then. Dr. Cross says it's a slight stroke, and we must keep him quiet at all costs, but it isn't easy to do.

"He says he wants these newspaper tales stopped, whatever it costs, and I only got him to stay in bed by promising to come and see you, and get something done.

"He says you're to issue a writ in his name, if that's possible, and if not you're to offer to buy them off. He'll pay anything up to £1,000, if they'll publish something to say that it isn't true.

"You know, some of it couldn't be. I mean, no one could know for a fact. There are things that Aunt Catherine is supposed to have said in her own room, that no one but Constance or Margaret could have heard, even if it were true. And even if some of it is, it seems a dreadful thing to publish it now, when she's in prison, and can't say anything to defend herself."

Mr. Risdon was already familiar with the offending article. It was lying on the desk before him. In his private mind, he didn't see that anything could be done, and he didn't think it was worth while to make a fuss. He was not naturally a man of sentimental excesses, and that morning he had a pressing preoccupation in the letter he had quietly slipped under his blotting-pad as Miss Scovell entered the room. But the Earl of Weyford was not a client whose wishes could be ignored, and he addressed his mind to the problem which had been put before it. He expressed suitable regrets for the indisposition of the Earl, and added, "I can fully sympathize with your grandfather's feelings in the matter, and you can assure him that everything will be done to prevent further publication, and to secure a contradiction, if possible. I should have been glad to obtain Cons— Miss Constance Hillier's account of the matter, but I have

71

heard this morning that she has been removed to the prison infirmary, and is too ill to be seen at present."

"I think grandfather will be easier in mind if I can tell him just what you are proposing to do."

"Yes? I wonder.... Perhaps I had better leave it to your discretion as to how much you say, when you see the condition he's in. You see, it's not much that I can.... Beyond, of course, protest, and perhaps bluff. But I don't think that would be much good here. The *Sunday Pail* keeps a tame barrister on the premises to advise them about these things. But, in the first place, if you wish me to be definite, I can't issue a writ in the name of the Earl of Weyford. He's got no cause of action at all. I can't issue it in the name of Lady Catherine, because she's dead. If I could issue it for Miss Margaret, I might make them sit up, but they've been too cunning for that. There's not a word about her that you can take hold of from end to end.

"It's Constance Hillier that's attacked, and even if it's all false, as it may be for all I know, well, you see the hole we're in." (Surely that was definite enough? There are some things that should be understood without speech.)

"You mean she couldn't issue a writ while she's in prison?"

No, he didn't mean that. Not exactly. He knew that the right to engage in litigation is the one that the law is most loath to withhold from those on whom its penalties fall. The gaol-doors may open to a prisoner's lawyer when his own wife is refused admittance. His friend's letters may be returned, but if his enemy issues a writ the Governor will allow it entrance without demur. The law is polite to its own customers, even though on other issues it may be exerting itself to gaol or hang them.

No, it wasn't that, but—couldn't she see? He said: "I don't want you to go back and tell your grandfather that people can't engage in litigation when they're in gaol, because that's not quite exact, and as to whether we could issue a writ for libel on Miss Hillier's behalf in the existing circumstances—well, frankly, it's a point on which I should like to take counsel's opinion before advising, if it were seriously proposed. But, as a practical issue, what damages could there be, while the present conviction stands? And besides that—well, you've got to face the position. An action for libel stops of itself if the plaintiff—dies."

"You mean that if anyone does one wrong thing, you can say they've done anything else you like?"

"No, that's going too far. It isn't safe to call a man a bigamist because he's forged a cheque, though it's the kind of risk that a certain class of paper takes often enough, and gets away with it nine times out of ten. But when anyone's been convicted of murder, the papers reckon he's fair game. It mayn't be good law, but, as a practical question, there isn't much can be done."

"Then you'll have to pay them to stop?"

"I'm afraid that would be equally hopeless—if not worse. If I made such an offer in writing they might publish the letter, for all I know. They'd probably kick me out of the office if I called to offer them half a million. They'd say they were vindicating the dignity of the Press."

"The *dignity*...but...."

"Yes, I know how it looks to you, and you're right enough in a way. If the man who delivers my morning milk said he'd overheard a scandalous report about the people opposite, I shouldn't encourage him to talk, and I shouldn't think any more of him if he said he was only telling it to those who would give him a penny for the tale. But it seems different to most people when it's done on a large scale. They say the public has a right to know. I've no doubt everyone on the staff is additionally proud of the paper because it's been the one to get hold of these tales. But if we offered them money to print anything or to leave it out—well, we'd most likely get kicked."

"But grandfather says he knows for a fact that Mr. Bryson paid *Jack Sprat* £500 not to print something that they were going to about him."

"Yes, I daresay he did. But that's a different matter entirely. Everybody knows that some of the weekly prize-competition and financial papers lay themselves out for that kind of thing. Of course, there are others that are as straight as the best dailies, and their standard's about as high as you can ask, if you allow people's private affairs to be discussed in the Press at all. But if it had been one of those—one of the wrong sort, I mean—they'd probably have called on your grandfather first and asked him to buy the article. That's the usual routine, either that before they start, or a suggestion of an advertisement afterwards if they'll print another article to say they've made a mistake. If they go on attacking anyone, you can be fairly sure that it's someone who won't be blackmailed, and who won't trouble to prosecute."

"But you say the *Sunday Pail* isn't that kind?"

"No. It's one of the more 'popular' of the Sunday papers. Of course, the higher-class ones wouldn't have printed such an article. But it's quite a reputable paper of its own kind."

"Do you know who the editor is?"

"Yes, Birchall—Rodney Birchall."

"I think I'd better see him before I go home."

"Well—if he'll see you. You'll have to find out about that. And it's a chance whether he'll be there."

Mr. Risdon did not think that it was a very wise thing to attempt. But he had the caution of his profession. Suppose he attempted unsuccessfully to dissuade, and then some good *did* come out of it? He contented himself with an offer to telephone to inquire whether the editor were available.

"No. He might say 'no' on the phone. I'd rather call."

Miss Scovell went, and Mr. Risdon lifted his blotting-pad, and his attention reverted to the letter which had engaged it before she came.

CHAPTER XIV.

MR. RODNEY BIRCHALL is a man of unusual rotundity. It is commonly believed in the offices of the *Sunday Pail* (and may be true) that when some years ago there was a temporary breakdown of the lift on which he relied to elevate him to his fourth-floor office, he had commandeered the porter's very limited accommodation at the stair-foot rather than attempt to climb the height on his own legs.

However that may have been, he now sat wedged some what tightly into a very ample chair before a broad and vacant desk, his heavy-lidded eyes fixed upon the card which he turned over in his swollen fingers, while the boy stood waiting for his decision.

"Show her up," he said at length, and when the boy had gone he sat motionless before the empty desk until Miss Scovell appeared.

There was nothing unusual in that absence of occupation Mr. Birchall had made it a rule of life never to do anything that he could throw upon the shoulders of others, and never to be hurried under any circumstances. It is not a recipe for success which can be recommended promiscuously. It is evident that it is not one which could be universally practised. But in his case its results had done much to justify it. The proprietors of the *Sunday Pail* knew that its operations were watched by a leisured mind, and that a cool judgement controlled them. The staff knew that they worked under a patient silent watchfulness which expressed itself without comment by advance or dismissal. They knew him also as a man of great and varied abilities in the profession to which they belonged. There were few subjects on which he could not have dictated a leading article without preparation, should the occasion require it—or probably half a dozen at once, each adapted to the minds of the different readers of the papers to which they would be supplied. He allowed little latitude either to the news or literary editor as to choice of subjects or the space which they should receive. Nothing could be regarded as settled till his green pencil had initialled it, and marked the space and position which could be allocated to its expansion. And the circulation figures which Miss Weston laid on his desk every Thursday morning, together with a synopsis of the contents of the issue to which they referred, became of an increasingly satisfactory character.

As Miss Scovell entered, he told the boy to place a chair for her, and said good morning in a genial voice, though he did not rise, or offer his hand, and when she was seated he remained silent, leaving it to her to introduce the subject on which she called.

Violet Scovell was not a girl of aggressive personality. She was naturally disposed to stand aside and watch the drama of life rather than to intrude herself into the contest, and this disposition had been cultivated by a youth which was without the insistent urgencies of less sheltered lives. It was of the atmosphere of her family also, which was more concerned to be than to do, and even in its activities would be less so to do the right thing than to avoid the wrong. But she had a very stubborn, though not a confident courage, a courage of the kind that will not be easily subdued by its own fears. And, beyond that, she had a personality which was no less charming to those to whom she disclosed it because it was only the intimacy of friendship or the stress of emotion which overcame its diffidence from the general gaze.

Now she said, with a quiet directness, seeing that she was expected to open the conversation: "I came to see you about the article you have published about my cousin."

Mr. Birchall's heavy eyelids lifted, and his glance was on her for a second, and then withdrawn.

"Your—? Was there anything in it which was incorrect?"

"I could not say that. There were things in it which went beyond what anyone could have known. It seemed a very cruel thing to do."

"Which went beyond—? Suppose we say also that might have gone much further, and still been no more than the truth?"

"I cannot say as to that, but my grandfather—the Earl of Weyford—has been made too ill to come out himself, and I have come to ask you to do what you can to put it right."

"Miss Scovell," he answered in a more serious tone than he had used previously, "if you have any facts to give us which would modify anything already published, I can promise you that they shall be fully and fairly stated. You cannot ask more than that."

"No," she said, with an acuteness which he was quick to recognize, though he gave no sign, "but I can ask something different, I do not see why such matters should be discussed in public at all."

"But I may. I am afraid I can only repeat, Miss Scovell, that if you can give us any facts of which we are ignorant, they shall be fairly treated." He looked at her again as he added suddenly: "Do you, in fact, know anything about these matters at all?"

"No, I never heard any suggestion of them. Except I know that Constance was ill about five years ago, and was away for some months."

Mr. Birchall recognized, though he did not remark, the disarming candour of that admission. He recognized also that, whatever her cousin might have been or done, she was of a different quality. His chair creaked as his heavy body moved somewhat in her direction, and she felt for the first time that he was not merely rebuffing her, but speaking with an almost friendly sincerity.

"Miss Scovell," he said, "I can quite understand how you feel, and the fact that I cannot admit that we have done anything beyond our duty to the public we serve does not prevent me sympathizing with any distress which it may occasion.

"It is unfortunately impossible to distribute news according to the requirements of the modern world without at times causing annoyance or pain to individuals, but the great power that is in our hands is always at the service of—if I may say so without appearing to boast—of truth and charity. If you can bring me any fresh evidence which would justify a doubt as to Constance Hillier's guilt, or any extenuating fact of whatever kind, you will find that all the influence of our circulation is at your free disposal to assist her cause."

Violet Scovell was a good judge of men. She recognized a core of sincerity in the rather journalistic style of this declaration. She paid it the compliment of a like sincerity when she asked in rather halting words if it would not be better to maintain the standard it indicated rather than to descend to the level of the article that had brought her there.

"Miss Scovell," he answered again, in the same serious and somewhat sententious manner, "you make a mistake which is natural to one without journalistic experience, and (I suppose) without business training. Should we disregard the requirements of our readers, should we seek to supply only what we think may be best for them, we should have no readers at all, and our influence would be gone. You cannot carry on any business on such principles. Would you deal with a grocer who sent you only the brand of bacon which he considered most suitable for your wellbeing, assuring you of his superior qualifications for knowing what you require? Should you allow your baker to dictate to you whether you should eat brown bread or white?"

There was a profound and confusing truth in this argument—the truth that power is gained by service, the truth of, "if any would be first among you let him be the servant of all," and beneath it was a fallacy that she could not reach. But she recognized the generosity of the offer which had been made. Surely, with such a medium to use, something could be done to save her cousin from the terrible fate, the full ignominy of the sentence that had been passed upon her? Anyway, it would be something for thought, and perhaps hope.

She had a well-founded instinctive feeling, also, that she had made a friend of the ungainly bulk of flesh that was now listening to her quiet words of thanks as though unconscious of what she said, while he touched the bell which would bring the boy to show her out.

"Miss Scovell," his voice called her back as she was at the door, "has there been any insanity in your cousin's family?"

"No," she said, "I don't think so." Her mind stirred to a dim recollection of an Uncle Lawrence, concerning whom there had been whispers, vague and dark in her childhood. "At least, not anything special."

"Well, that's the best line to take. There's nothing in it, of course. There's been insanity in most families, more or less, if you know where to look. But it helps the Home Office with the public, if it feels inclined to give a reprieve in a case like this. Tell your lawyers to work it up. Mentally unhinged by the life her aunt led her. Aunt a bit queer herself. Insanity supported by the stupidity she showed in denying everything even when half the truth had come out. It's the only chance. It ought to have been worked up from the first. Two good alienists in the box. It wouldn't have altered the verdict, but it would have started things on the right line. Let me know if you've got anything to go on now."

Miss Scovell was rather puzzled She was sufficiently sane herself to see the absurdity of the suggestion that if her cousin had become insane it would have been unobserved by those about her, and resulted in a cunningly contrived conspiracy to poison her aunt. Insanity, as she understood it, was a disease of the brain; and those who joined in such a conspiracy showed their brains to be in working order, whatever might be thought of their characters. Neither was she familiar with the cynical underlying assumption that experts can always be hired, either by prosecution or defence, to give the evidence which the case requires.

Yet it is a sound argument enough, if we define sanity as the normality of the human race. To the idealist it may appear to have a hollow sound. It is significant that it has gained in importance as the authority of religion has lessened. The old belief that the mind rules the body is to be exchanged for its opposite, and the body now rules the mind. We are to abandon the idea that faith can remove mountains, for the belief that a grain of dust can remove faith. Christ does his best, no doubt, but Antichrist trumps the trick—and trick seems to be about the right word.

As to sanity and normality being synonymous, do not our lawcourts already accept this construction when the wealthy die? Jones could not make a valid will. Since he retired, and had only to please himself, he had become an eccentric man. He is said to have worn a dinner-jacket in the morning, and a lounge suit for his evening meal. Shall we allow a man to dispose of his own property if he be shown to have eaten eggs and bacon at 8:00 P.M.? If a man would be accounted sane by his fellows, let him keep step with the crowd.

Very well. Most of us don't poison our aunts. Therefore it is an eccentric thing to do. Eccentric people are mad.

Nothing—at least, nothing decisive—came of the interview. The Earl of Weyford did not think that Constance Hillier was insane, and family instances of insanity were remote and few. The fact was that the Scovell brains had never been overworked, and had shown no tendency to collapse. As to eccentricity of any kind—well, suicide would have seemed less repugnant, providing, of course, that suicides were sufficiently numerous to avoid any suggestion of oddity in the act.

But it gave a subject for talk, and the attitude of the *Sunday Pail*, as Violet reported it, did something to mollify the anger with which the Earl of Weyford had regarded this fresh exposure of the indiscretions of his female relatives.

He got somewhat better as the days passed, though he was not allowed to leave his room.

Mr. Butforth, reading the article in the *Sunday Pail*, congratulated himself on the advice he had given. A faint chance, but the only one. It was what happened so often. When the verdict was given, and people were free to talk, the true character of the murderer would be revealed. There had never been any chance for a reprieve. It was too repulsive, too sordid, a crime. People don't like poisoners. Poisoners of their own families least of all. And it wasn't as though there were any possibility of her innocence, however faint. No. He had seized the only chance. And he didn't think much of that.

The dislike of hanging a woman—the fact that the man's fate would be still in suspense when the decision must be made—there was no other card they could play. And to his mind it was no more (nor less) than the game of chess to which the Earl of Weyford had compared it in his worried thoughts. He had no more doubt of Constance Hillier's guilt than had the Attorney-General, or the Judge or jury who had heard the best defence that he could set up. He had done his best in a hopeless case.

CHAPTER XV.

THE same afternoon that Violet Scovell called at the offices of the *Sunday Pail*, Margaret Hillier ascended the stairs that led to those of Risdon and Clarke with her usual lightness of step, but with a hard set face that only conventionally relaxed as she shook the lawyer's hand, for there was no more than a conventional cordiality between them.

"I thought," she began abruptly, "I'd better see you to find out what's going to happen now."

There was ambiguity in this statement, which was not lessened by the wording of the note which Mr. Risdon had had from her that morning, which simply stated that Mrs. Parker had left her, and that she proposed to call upon him on the next afternoon to know what was going to be done about everything.

"I can assure you that everything will be done that is reasonably possible."

"About Constance? Yes, of course. I suppose you'll get her off somehow. Uncle's influence ought to be good enough for that. What I want to know is what's going to be done about the house and the will. And about that wretched article in the *Sunday Pail*. I suppose Ivy Parker's at the bottom of that, and that's why she hasn't dared to turn up since. I hadn't seen that when I wrote yesterday. You can see that things can't go on as they are. There's heaps of money, and I've been kept a lot shorter since Aunt Catherine died than I was before—that is, for the house. I have to write, or come begging here for every pound, as though it wasn't our own money that's being doled out. So I thought I'd better come and get it straight out between us."

The last sentence was uttered in a rather more conciliatory tone than had been those that preceded it. She may have been conscious that she had not commenced the interview in the most diplomatic manner, but the fact was that she expected little from Mr. Risdon's goodwill. He was a man to whom she was instinctively antipathetic, and after the strain of her many weeks in the solitude of that tragic house she was determined to force the issue, and reliant mainly upon her great-uncle's influence to overcome whatever difficulty might confront her. Of one thing, she had told herself as she walked from the bus to Mr. Risdon's office, she was resolved at whatever cost. She was not going on longer like this.

Mr, Risdon, cool, watchful, and unresponsive, had a thought that we may be disposed to share. Did she care so little for her sister's fate that she could think only of money at such a time? Yet, he reflected, sisters may be uncongenial to one another. Even a sister may not seem very attractive in the guise of the poisoner of a mutual aunt. Besides, the fact was not new. And Margaret Hillier was not one to show her feelings to all she met. And she had had several days for thought in that lonely house since that of her sister's conviction. Remembering that, he noticed that she was looking weary and heavy-eyed, though the alert decision of her manner might remain. Doubtless, she had suffered, though she might not be one to disclose the wound.

It is to be remarked, beyond that, that there may be more hypocrisy in the profession of grief than in almost any other relation of human life. Mr. Risdon was not Constance Hillier's brother, it is true. But he was her lawyer. He had seen much more of her during recent weeks than her own sister had been allowed to do. It would not have occurred to him to lose any sleep because she lay ill in the prison infirmary, with the shadow of the condemned cell waiting for her to enter as soon as the prison doctor had given her strength to walk there on a wardress's arm. He was not expected to show such grief, but had it been a convention that he should do so....

Now he said, "I am sorry, Miss Margaret, that you should adopt that tone. It obliges me to put the position more plainly than I should otherwise have felt it necessary to do. The property of which you allude is your sister's, not yours. Until recent times, it would have been forfeited to the Crown under the conditions which have now arisen. The time has passed when such claims were enforced against those of the natural heirs. But if your aunt's last will be allowed to stand as I am disposed to think that it may) then the final disposition of the property will depend upon the will which your sister makes."

"The will that...." A sudden look of terror came into her eyes. There was a thought in her mind that her lips were slow to speak. "You mean that...you are not trying to get a reprieve?"

"No. You must not suppose that. Everything possible will be done. But I should be wrong to hold out any confident hope. I shall advise your sister to make a will for the disposition of whatever property may be hers."

"She hasn't made one yet?"

"No. Since the verdict, she has been too ill to be seen, even by her legal advisers."

Margaret thought of the document which she had already shown. It gave half. As her sister's heir, she might have more than that. It might all be left to her. Again, if there were no will, she might get more than half. She was not sure. There were no very close relatives. She wished her knowledge of the laws of inheritance were more exact. It was a question that she did not like to ask. She paid passing tribute to what she felt might be expected of her, and may have spoken no more than the truth, when she said, "I shouldn't have raised this question at all now, if you hadn't doled out the money in the way you do."

"You must try to appreciate the special difficulties of the position in which I am placed."

"I don't see it at all. Mr...someone I've talked it over with didn't either. He's a solicitor, too."

"If you have consulted someone else professionally, Miss Margaret, I'm afraid I shall have to ask you to communicate through him in future."

She did not look pleased at that suggestion. Her face showed confusion. He wondered whether it were an invention entirely. Then she said, "I couldn't do that. He's not really a solicitor. He's a solicitor's clerk." She added quickly, as though to lead the conversation away from this topic: "I suppose you'll remind Constance of the agreement between us." (Half, she thought, was at least better than nothing. If Constance could make a will, she might leave everything to a Dogs' Home. No one could tell what Constance would do under such conditions as these.) "I've told you before, Miss Margaret, that that document has no legal value."

"I don't know about that, but I know Constance ought to be reminded of it, if she's making another will."

"*Another* will?"

"Oh, I don't mean that. I mean another from aunt's."

"Very well," he said, though coldly enough, "I will undertake to remind her of that document." And then, in a suddenly altered tone, "Have you always been on good terms with your sister?"

"Oh, yes. We hit it off well enough. Yes, generally. Except sometimes. Constance won't go back on that."

He thought the words to be more confident than the tone though there was not much hesitation in that. She added, "But what I came to know is how I'm going on for the time. For this week, and next."

As the words left her mouth she was conscious of an implication that went beyond her thought. "I mean, from week to week." Would he have understood her to mean, "This week and next, till Constance—dies?" She had only meant from week to week, till something gets settled for good.

He answered with another question, giving no sign that he had noticed the ambiguity of her speech. "You still want to keep on the house?"

She was silent to that. How she hated those sombre rooms, and every memory that they held! But she did not mean to walk out for him to walk in as executor. Not if she could hold her ground.

"I don't want to give it up till things are more arranged than they are now. After that, we can decide what's best to be done."

That sounded reasonable. For the moment, at least, he felt that he must agree, though there were reasons for this which he did not mention. He agreed also that she must get someone to replace Mrs. Parker. She could not be alone there. He would advance her five pounds a week. No, not six. Five would have to do. To that she agreed, having no choice. But the mention of Mrs. Parker brought up the other object of her visit.

"I should like to prosecute that woman," she said, with a rather venomous intonation, with which it is not difficult to sympathize, "she deserves han—" The sentence stopped abruptly, and the lawyer replied without appearing to notice the unfinished word.

"I don't think anything can be gained by that, even if there should be any legal ground. The mischief's done now, and after that it's no use going against people who've got nothing to lose.... Is there anything in the article that you can point out to me as being specifically false? I don't mean in the way things are put, or the comment made; I want, if possible, a definite fact. Preferably one that could be *proved* to be false. I'm writing to the *Sunday Pail* to-night, and I want all the help you can give me."

He passed her a copy of the article as he spoke, and watched her expression as she glanced down the offensive columns.

"It's so difficult," she said at last, "after all these years. Of course, it's all lies. Papers oughtn't to be allowed to print things like that."

His thought, answering her words, was, "Of course, it's mostly true." He said, without heat, as one who diagnoses rather than feels, "Yes, it was a dastardly thing to do at such a moment as this. I appreciate your difficulty in regard to events at that distance, but any—discrepancy—might be helpful. There is the question of the wall. They say that it was broken down at the foot of the garden. It is on such points that discredit of such a tale can be suggested most easily. Suppose, for instance, that the condition of the wall should show that it had not been broken down during recent years. Better still, suppose that there should be no garden, or no wall, at all. There is the possibility of a hedge."

Miss Hillier did not seem stimulated by this suggestion. She said, "The wall's broken down, right enough. Of course, Mrs. Parker knows. You won't catch her out over little points like that. I wish we could."

"And I suppose it's true that these young men—they don't give any names—used to visit you and your sister—and you them?"

"They used to come in sometimes. There's no harm in that. It's the way it's put."

"Yes, I know. Did you visit also at their house?"

"Not much. Aunt Catherine didn't know. She wouldn't have let us have any friends. That shows what a wicked lie some of it is. There couldn't have been any rows. We had to keep too quiet. Why, till there was the trouble about Constance, Mrs. Watson didn't know anything about it at all."

"Watson was their name?"

"Yes."

"And they used to see you without their parents' knowledge at No. 35?"

"Yes. They came in sometimes, but the rest's make-up, mostly. How could Mrs. Parker know when she'd gone home?"

"Yes. I appreciate that. But she might say that she'd known enough to be told the rest. There's the tale about the kimonos, for instance. Could she have seen that?"

"It didn't happen like that, anyway."

"A basis of fact embroidered by a journalist's imagination, and a woman's tongue? But the central fact cannot, I suppose, be seriously challenged? Your sister did go to the Nursing Home at Hillingham?"

"Yes. You couldn't deny that."

"In her own name?"

"Yes. Aunt Catherine paid the bills."

"Then she knew all about it?"

"No. She only knew that Constance was ill, and the doctor said she must go away."

"And it's true that she had a child, and the child died?"

"Yes. It only lived for a week."

"And your aunt never knew?"

"No."

Mr. Risdon considered the position for a moment of expressionless silence. "I'm afraid we can't do much," he said. "Not beyond protest and warning. "

He shook hands in a cool way, and closed the door on his visitor, as he reflected in a coldly impartial mind that Margaret Hillier must have shown some loyalty to her sister, at least of a passive kind...Or had there been her own secrets to be kept also? Had the two sisters in that sombre household been mutually in each other's power, and both in that of the woman who had betrayed them at last?

Margaret walked away with the visions of those five-year-old episodes filling her mind. The slow monotonous days of living in that quiet house, in attendance upon the capricious, bullying, exacting invalid. The friendless existence which, whether it sprang from circumstance, or their own characters, or the almost penniless condition in which their aunt had kept them at that time, offered them no relief of outside companionship or amusement. The conditions of servitude which had never even allowed them out together. Always, night and day, one of them must be in her aunt's room, or ready to answer an instant summons. Even in the acquaintances which they had formed with the youths in the next house, the four had seldom been together. It had been Constance and Eric, or herself and Jonas. She saw these episodes of their lives now, looking back, in their full ugliness. There had been no real friendship, no love, no comradeship in those intimacies. It was not only that, looking back, she saw the unlovely lewdness of these accidental acquaintances: she knew that, at the back of her mind, she had known it then. There was no time when she would not have discarded Jonas in half an hour at the opportunity of a more congenial companionship, and yet, what she had allowed to happen...well, it was known to no one but herself and him, let others guess as they might. When Constance had been upstairs in their aunt's room, and Ivy Parker had gone home, and even Eric could not have been looking through the back-sitting-room blind (as she had known him to do) because it was the night when he was always kept late at the bank, what might have happened between Jonas and herself could be known to none but themselves. Of course, Constance had known, more or less, at the time. There had been rivalry between them of an ugly kind, ignorant questionings and discussions, even bitter boastings and counter-claims of their own dishonour. She remembered how Constance, ignorant, bewildered, white with fear, had first told her of the doubt that possessed her mind. She had been ill—visibly—probably more from terror than any direct physical cause, for weeks before that. So ill that it had become evident at last to the tyrant who ruled their lives. And Lady Catherine had unconsciously played into their hands by saying that no doctor should come to her. She was well enough to walk to see Dr. Haines, in the next street. She would have no running-up of bills with the expensive physician in whose attendance she herself indulged.

So to Dr. Haines Constance had gone, and, of course, the truth had come out. And there had been angry interviews and discussions, and Mrs. Watson had been told, and then the father, and there had been repulsive scenes of unmannerly denial, reproaches, accusations, evasions, tears.

Constance must be sent away. There had been general agreement about that. The manager at the bank was a man of strict principles, and Eric Watson was already out of favour. There had been a suspicion of drunkenness, and a stern warning. If he should hear of this...If Constance went, Mr. Watson would pay. So it had been offered at last, but that could not be contrived, unless Lady Catherine should know. And to keep it from her had been the one object before all. So in the end it had been she who had paid, having been successfully misled as to the nature of her niece's illness. There had been no doubt of the reality of that. She had been ill still when she returned to tell her sister of an experience which had been unrelieved by any atmosphere either of hope or love; and of the memory of the dead face of a week-old child. She had brought back also the counsel of a "sister" at the nursing-home, who had made a mockery of her disaster, telling her how she could live viciously without the risk of the unwanted life. Things might have got back to their old footing had not Eric's father arranged that his son should be transferred to another bank, and the whole family moved away.

So the years had passed, and gradual pressure had increased the shillings that their aunt had doled them, till their services had been rewarded each with a weekly pound (more or less, as her whim was) and they had sought, always separately as they must, such pleasures as their opportunities allowed, and their natures craved.

And now there were other occupants of the next-door house, and masculine youth again, of another pattern from that of the earlier time, and the solitary remaining occupant of the house had won sympathy—and perhaps love?—from Bill Langford, sister of a murderess though the jury's verdict had branded her to be.

CHAPTER XVI.

MR. RISDON considered his position. He considered it without excitement, in the patient careful way in which he had faced it for the last fifteen years. It had been steadily improving, year by year, during the whole of the period, but it was very difficult—now. If Lady Catherine had lived for another seven years, as he had hoped that she might—or even five—he might have reached the time when he could have faced the future, we must not say with a quiet, for he was quiet now, but with an easy and confident mind. As it was, nothing but a miracle, a confession, or a gamble, could save him from the pit which had opened before his feet.

Dismissing the first of these possibilities, he considered the alternatives which remained.

He might confess his position to the Earl of Weyford, and abide the issue. He might go to him, and say, "When Thomas Clarke died, and I succeeded to the entire control of the business (my father having died in the previous year) I found a neat record of a deficiency of about £15,000 in the securities which you had left in our charge, as your ancestors had done for more than a century past. I cannot say whether it had had anything to do with his death. I suppose that Thomas Clarke committed suicide because he thought that the position could not be hidden much longer. So, at first, I thought also. But Lady Catherine's affairs coming into my hands at that time, owing to her husband's death, enabled me to realize sufficient of her securities to adjust the deficiency in your own, without any suspicion being aroused.

"From that time I have been replacing the money at the rate of from £500 to £800 yearly. In that way, to that extent, I have shown that I am an honest man. But, in the meantime, to conceal the position which I inherited, to retain my practice, and the prestige of an old firm, I have lied and misappropriated, and—on two occasions—forged"—but it might not be necessary to mention that—"and I am still about £4,700 short, which it is now imperative to restore to

Lady Catherine's estate, and that I cannot do unless I take it from yours, from which the defalcations were originally made."

That was a possible course to take. It was the "right" course by the standards which most people would apply, as it had been at the first, when he had discovered the deficiency. But, as he had decided against it then, so he decided against it now. It was not that he thought the Earl of Weyford would take criminal or even civil proceedings against him. He was not of that disposition. It was more probable that he would offer a voluntary adjustment between his own estate and that of Lady Catherine—difficult if not disastrous, though it must be, for the Earl's finances had been increasingly embarrassed by the agricultural depression and taxation of the post-War years. But Mr. Risdon, a cool-headed, exact man, knew that things could never be the same again if it were once told. While it was private to his own mind, it was in itself, as it were, a smaller thing. It did not affect his status in his own eyes, or in the eyes of those among whom he moved. He could not suppose that the Earl would be entirely silent over such a loss, even if that were possible. The fact would become larger, more important, with each one to whom it should be communicated. To give it publicity would be like the nurture of an evil weed—a weed which would be poisonous to himself, destroying his practice, and with it his power to make the restitution at which he still aimed. And he remembered, to support a resolution already made, that the Earl was ill. It would be a selfish cruelty to disturb him with such a tale. It might cause his death. There would be no gain in that. There were two executors of the Earl's will. It would make ruin sure.

He had another thought, cold enough, but not ungenerous in itself. He did not wish to see the Earl embarrassed, and his descendants further impoverished, so that money might be transferred to Lady Catherine's nieces. So he must rely on himself.

It was fortunate that he was under no suspicion. There was one thing—one little unavoidable thing—which had evidently puzzled his bankers, and caused a letter which had given him anxious hours of thought before he had answered in the matter-of-course and somewhat offhand tone which he should have seen from the first was the right one to adopt. And he had gone into the bank, had made a reason to do so, on the following day, with the cool courageous judgement which he had shown throughout. And he was sure that there was no suspicion at all.

He owed that to himself. For fifteen years they had known him as a man exact and punctilious in all matters of account, one who kept the money of his clients separated with a scrupulous care. He was a single man, without vices or extravagances, one who did not speculate or involve himself in commercial investments, of good practice, and repute.

He had twice been obliged to arrange charges on Lady Catherine's securities without her knowledge, witnessing the signatures which he had forged, and those deeds were still in the strong-room of the bank. But those signatures had never been doubted—could never be doubted now. He had been so cautious that on each occasion he had actually visited his client—as could be proved—on the dates on which the documents purported to have been signed. But the destination of the money which had been raised by these means would be less simple to explain. No, those deeds must be withdrawn, and destroyed.

Having decided not to seek the path of confession, he took the only other which opened before him. For fifteen years he had studied the fluctuations of the stock markets, never venturing himself into those perilous depths, but learning all that he might, to fit himself for such an emergency as this. It had always been in his mind, as the last resort, if time should fail, as it did now. He had little cause to sympathize with the woman whose criminality had driven him to the desperation of this resort.

Having reached his decision, he rang for a stenographer, and dictated a letter to Messrs. Thornton & Briscoe, stating that he had received instructions from a client, who wished to remain anonymous, to undertake some rather extensive operations, and suggesting an appointment for the following day.

CHAPTER XVII.

MR. WHITAKER was polite and conciliatory. He took the Home Secretary patiently, as he had taken his predecessors. He even treated them with an outward deference, which was insufficient to hide the gulf by which they were parted.

Mr. Whitaker was a professional; Mr. Armfield an amateur. Mr. Whitaker's position was impregnable: Mr. Armfield's depended upon the caprice of a popular vote, and a Premier's favour. Every five years, more or less, he would have to beg and flatter and lie for a renewal of support which he might not get. Beyond that, nothing was more evident than that Mr. Armfield did not possess his present authority owing to any special ability in grading penalties and con-donations of crime. Yet for the moment (in the absence of any out-break of popular clamour, such as might make it a question for the Cabinet to consider) he had the final word.

Mr. Armfield understood the position equally well. He expected deference. He expected guidance also. Mr. Whitaker knew. Mr. Whitaker could point the safe path which every politician desires to take. But in this instance Mr. Armfield was ill at ease. He did not like hanging a woman. An absurd atavistic instinct disturbed his mind. The importance of the tribe depends upon its number, which women supply. He did not observe that since children have ceased to matter, having, indeed, become rather a nuisance than otherwise, this feminine immunity is as absurd as it would be to continue to give the first places to women (or children) in the boats of a sinking ship. "I don't like the idea of hanging her, Whitaker, while the man may get of. I think we ought to have a short reprieve at the least, till we see how his appeal goes."

Mr. Butforth, had he heard this remark, might have compli-mented himself on the shrewdness of the advice he had given. Its weakness lay in the fact that if you lack strength to reach your desti-nation you may just as well stay at home. It's no use going halfway. Mr. Armfield's hesitations would do no good to Constance Hillier.

She was only concerned as to the side of the fence on which he would come down.

"I don't think we need worry about that," Mr. Whitaker answered. "He won't."

"Won't what?"

"Won't get off."

"You think there's no doubt about him?"

"There's no reasonable doubt of his guilt. But I didn't mean only that. There's no ground for the appeal. There was plenty of evidence on which the jury could come to the decision they did, and when that's the case, the Appeal Court can't interfere. And the summing-up was particularly fair."

"But suppose he does?"

"Well, if he can make the Appeal Court believe that he didn't do it, it won't help her. Rather the other way. I don't see how we can hang him and reprieve her, and I don't see how you could reprieve her first and then hang her because his appeal failed."

"You think it would mean reprieving both in the end?"

"Yes, I expect it would. And if you reprieve them, you may as well abolish capital punishment. That's how it would be understood. You can't have murder much worse than when a woman plots to poison her aunt."

"You think there's no ground for a reprieve?"

"No. I can't say I do. They don't seem to be even troubling to get up a petition. Not that we ever take any notice of them. It's a curious thing that it's often the worst murderers that can get the most signatures to those documents, and a case that really does call for some sympathy gets no notice at all. They just get pulped, and the paper's made over again, and may be used for something more worth while.

"I've been advising on these cases for about eighteen years—one or two every month, and sometimes more—and I've made it a rule to apply two tests to every one as it comes in. If there's the slightest doubt of the jury having gone wrong, I always suggest a reprieve. I've been responsible for letting two or three scoundrels live on that count, and heard since that they talk of the crime themselves, and perhaps boast of it, now they know they're safe from the rope. The other test is to look for any circumstance that calls for a measure of human sympathy. Any taint of insanity, or nervous disease, any provocation, or evidence that it wasn't premeditated; and, of course, you have to consider previous character and record. If there's nothing favourable to be found—well, I reckon that we oughtn't to interfere with the law."

"And in this case—taking the woman alone—when you look at it in that way?"

"Well, it's just ploughing a barren held. There's no doubt of her guilt. There's nothing to be said except that she denies it herself. Most murderers—all poisoners—do. They're not even trying an appeal. They know they're in an utterly hopeless position, whether the man can get clear or not. They've practically thrown up the sponge."

Mr. Armfield paced restlessly across the room. "I suppose you're right," he said irritably, "but I don't like these cases where there's no real proof. No one saw her do it. Why shouldn't she be telling the truth? Why shouldn't someone have put it into her drawer?—to throw suspicion upon her, or just to save themselves?"

"Of course, that's been considered. In fact, it was examined thoroughly before the prosecution was authorized. It's a possible thing, however unlikely—in her own drawer, you know, her locked drawer! But when you examine it, it doesn't really depend on that. That's no more than additional evidence that bears down a scale that's already full. You've got Mogson's admission to get over. He says he gave her the poison, whether innocently or not. Why should he admit that, if it's not true? It isn't sense. And she doesn't merely deny having put it into her drawer, she denies that she had it from him at all. If she had it for an innocent purpose, why not say what it was? And, if so, how did it get into the old woman's stomach? The more you examine the defence, the more hopeless it becomes. Even without his admission, you might call it a well-proved case. The poison got somehow from Uxbridge into the woman's body, and these two persons were the two, and the only two, who could bridge the gap, and—as you'd expect—they were the two who had something to gain by her death. Think of the will."

"Very well. I've no doubt you're right. If the public don't make any fuss, I suppose I mustn't interfere."

"There's no likelihood of that. She's not an attractive woman, and it's not an attractive crime."

Mr. Armfield went on to the House. He hated the idea of the execution of women. But he had done what he could. Constance Hillier must hang.

CHAPTER XVIII.

CONSTANCE HILLIER was well enough to be moved to the condemned cell. The prison doctor had been skilful and kind. The nurses had been kind and tactful. We hang people in England as kindly as possible. Every prison official is instructed to that effect. But, most important of all, they must have them well enough to be hanged on the appointed day. Now it was Friday afternoon, and, for the first time since she had been sentenced, she had been pronounced well enough to receive visitors. She was to meet her sister, and, after that, she was to be allowed an interview with her lawyer. Then she would be conducted to the condemned cell. And when she was there she was to receive an official visitor who would tell her—tactfully, of course—that there was no hope of a reprieve, and that she must prepare her mind for being hanged on Tuesday at 8:00 A.M.

But her sister must not see her alone. There is a reason for this. We may be sure that there will be a reason for anything which has an appearance of brutality.

She had been condemned to death by the law. Any duly appointed person might kill her at the appointed hour without committing any legal or moral offence. Any person in England—except herself. It might seem to a logical mind that if she had been judged unfit to live, and if she be required to admit the justice of this verdict, no hand could take her life so innocently or so decently as her own, and that every facility and encouragement should be provided to enable her to carry out the law, as a good citizen should. But the English law does not agree. Its dignity requires that there should be a deliberate killing by another hand.

So Margaret must see her sister in the presence of a wardress who could watch that nothing passed between the two, no knife, or little packet of some fatal drug, which might make impossible the ceremonial performance for which a limited number of tickets had been issued for Tuesday next. Constance Hillier was judged unfit to live longer than 8:00 A.M. on that day, and it appeared to be considered equally important that she should remain alive till that hour when a man would be paid to kill her. Was he to risk losing his fee?

So the sisters met in an interview which was very awkward, very futile, very painful in every way, even to the wardress who was required to observe it. But it was not outwardly very emotional.

Constance had not been normally a demonstrative woman. Like the rest of us, she must have had hopes and fears and passions, anticipations and dreads, but she had been accustomed to conceal her emotions with a shut mouth, which was often a sullen one.

Now she made no allusion to her approaching death, and it was not a subject which Margaret was likely to begin. It might have been doubted whether her mind was on her conviction at all, had she not asked in a sudden energy, at the first, "Has he told the truth? I keep asking them, and they won't say. They won't say a word!" It was not easy to judge whether she hoped or dreaded what such telling of "the truth" might mean.

Margaret could tell her nothing. The secrets of prisons are well kept.

Then she asked after household matters, and were her clothes safe? And Mrs. Parker? She had left? Why? Margaret evaded that.

And so the house was being kept on? There ought to be plenty of money now.

Margaret said that Mr. Risdon would give very little. He was coming to see her, so she had heard. Coming that afternoon, to arrange about money matters. Margaret mentioned that she had shown him their agreement. Constance didn't mind him knowing that, did she? Constance made no answer. Margaret was not sure that she heard. She had gone very white. She spoke with a sudden bitter energy. "That hateful house! We'd better get away out of this!"

The watchful wardress saw that mind and body were giving way. Perhaps she was not as well as they had thought. Her arm went round her (kindly, of course) so that she did not fall.

Margaret found herself hurried away.

There may be cases when such interviews take place with the same frankness, with the same abandon, as though they were unobserved, but this did not appear to be one.

Margaret walked out with a cold, set face, but the taxi-driver noticed that her hand shook as she laid it on the opened door. She was still shaking as she got out, and her foot slipped on the step. She would have walked in without paying him had he not followed her up the steps.

"They won't really do that," she was saying over in her own mind. "They don't hang women. They wouldn't really do that." It had seemed real to her, for the first time, as she entered the cold gloom of those sombre walls—walls as emblematic of human cruelty as of human crime. Suppose (she could not get the thought from her mind) it had been she? Suppose it had been she? Back in her familiar surroundings, with the new servant fussing about her, and the tea-tray at her side, her mind reverted to the interview which was to follow her own, and which might make her a rich woman, or turn her out naked to a friendless world.

What would Constance do? It had never been easy to foretell. They had had moments of intimacy, of confidence, as sisters must, but there had been little closeness of love, even in childish years. Yet she did not seriously doubt that Constance would do what was right in this. Only, there was one little thing about which she was not sure. If Constance knew *that*. But she did not think that she did.

Meanwhile Mr. Risdon had had a somewhat difficult time with a client who did not appear able (or was it willing?) to see any urgent reason why a will should be made, nor any great concern as to what its provisions should be. She said at last that she would like her cousin Violet to have it. In the end, it was more by Mr. Risdon's decision than hers that her property was left equally between Margaret and Violet, with himself as executor. She did not show either affection or ill-will toward her sister. She did not seem to care.

The will was simple and short. Mr. Risdon drew it up at once, and it was signed and witnessed before he left.

CHAPTER XIX.

THE Saturday edition of the *Pictorial Post* announced that Constance Hillier had been giving no trouble to the prison authorities. She had been ill at first, following her conviction, and had been admitted to the prison infirmary, but had since recovered, She was eating well, and had actually gained about three pounds in weight. The accuracy of such statements is usually as dubious as the sources from which they come, but it is quite likely that such an increase had occurred as the result of the judicious feeding and inactivity of the prison life. Cannibals have demonstrated that it is possible to fatten those who are aware that every added pound will bring them nearer to their appointed doom. It would be fallacious to conclude that people enjoy being carefully prepared for slaughter, whether in a Congo village or an English gaol.

The care of the prison authorities had not been limited to getting the body of Constance Hillier in fit condition for a punctual hanging. Her soul had also had their attention. They offered her the advice and assistance of a gentleman who had made a special study of the means by which criminals may avoid any unpleasant post-mortem consequences of their misdoings. It appeared from the information that he offered for her consideration, that the Deity would be favourably impressed by her confession; that is, that she would inform her questioner accurately as to her past actions; but he did not explain why He (already aware of these circumstances) should regard it as meritorious for her to impart the knowledge to the Rev. J. T. Stimkins. The justice of the Deity also differed from that of England in that it was somewhat placated by contrition, although this approach to pardon was complicated by some theological pitfalls which could only be avoided by an expert guide, such as he recommended himself to be. Beyond this, she would have the further advantage, on arriving at the Throne of Ultimate Judgement, of being able to report that she had been hanged by her fellow-men. She would have "expiated her sin!"

But Constance Hillier declined to confess. She made a fierce hysterical inquiry as to what efforts he was making to avert her doom, and when he replied by advising her to resign herself thereto, and fix her thoughts on her eternal welfare, she made an absurd appeal, "if he believed in God, that he would help her to get out of here."

He retired from this outburst to reflect for a time upon the unreasonable nature of women, and returned, as he conceived it to be his duty to do, to be met with a sudden violence of language from a woman whose self-control had broken down with the realization of the nearness of her physical destruction, and who told him that she was "sick of his hateful lies."

She could not know that these words would have the kindly effect of giving Mr. Armfield a good night's sleep. For his restless indecision had caused him to instruct his secretary to telephone the gaol on Monday afternoon, with a hesitant idea at the back of his mind that if it should be reported to him that she were still seriously ill, he might even yet find a reason for the reprieve which he would have preferred.

It is improbable that this impulse would, in any case, have become sufficiently vertebrate to have any decisive consequence, but the report which he received was of a nature to remove the hesitations that had vexed his mind. The wretched woman, blasphemous and stubborn in criminality, must go to her destined doom.

For the prison doctor had assured the Governor, and the Governor was able to assure the Home Secretary, that Constance Hillier was fit to hang. The doctor was accustomed to dealing with these final hours, and if bromides failed, he had many stronger drugs which could be administered in food or drink sufficient to control the more violent and exhausting paroxysms of terror or despair, and give such deadening sleep when the last night came as would insure that she would wake with strength to walk the short distance to the waiting rope.

There was a period when you might see a cow slaughtered any day as you walked along the public street. That was stopped, which was better for us, though not for the cow. At a later date we ceased the public slaughter of our fellowmen. Recently, we have stopped the hoisting of a black flag, and when Constance Hillier was hanged it was nearly 9:15 A.M. before the notice of the execution was posted on the gaol-doors. We improve every year.

BOOK TWO

THOMAS MOGSON

▲

CHAPTER XX.

IT was 8:17 A.M. when Margaret waked from a troubled sleep, and pulled the watch from beneath her pillow to see the time. She had a queer feeling of relief when she realized that she had slept through the fatal minutes while her sister had swung at the rope's end.

You must not blame her overmuch for that. She had been awake for most of the night debating feverishly whether Constance would be reprieved, or her troubles end when the morning came. She had thought (or tried to think) that she would be allowed to live. It is so seldom that a woman hangs in these merciful days. Now she looked at the watch that had been her aunt's (it was a rather valuable one, small and old, and quaintly enamelled, one of many things which were now in her possession or use, thanks to her resolute action in keeping Mr. Risdon out of the house, and his hesitation to assert his authority as executor of a will that he had not proved), and she almost hoped that there had been no reprieve, and that it was over now.

It was early spring, and the rare London sunshine patterned her bedroom wall as she lay. The sky without was the pale blue that is the best that London knows. Sparrows twittered joyously from the roof. Life was good, and she had felt younger during the last few weeks, in spite of the dreariness of the empty house, and the anxieties that had vexed her mind. She might have looked worried and worn, but there had been a new hope underneath, giving her fortitude to endure, and pushing upward, though it might be as invisible to those around her as a daffodil under the frozen ground. Now she made haste to dress, that she might be down before the woman came in. She had told her not to come till 8:30 today: she could not have endured having her about at the time. She wished to descend unseen to pick up the newspaper that would have been pushed through the letter-slit in the front door.

She did this, and was back in her room before she heard the sound of movements below, but, of course, there could be no report of what had happened in the morning's paper. Only—yes, here it was: *It was understood on inquiry last night that the Home Office has declined to interfere with the sentence on Constance Hillier. The execution will therefore take place as already announced, at 8:00 A.M. today.*

Well, it was over now. She must try to forget and look forward to the freer life of the coming days. She would have been glad to know whether she were rich or poor (we can hardly blame her for that either). Doubtless, Mr. Risdon would inform her now.

She was anxious about that, but not overmuch. She did not think that Constance would really leave all the money elsewhere— and there was the chance that the will could be upset if she did. One or other of the wills, anyway. But she wouldn't do that. To whom should. he leave it? Not to Mogson, even if he weren't where he was.

Margaret had a good reason for thinking that. Whatever relations might once have existed between them, she had very good reason for thinking that there had been no love since the arrests were made.

Besides, there was the agreement. Constance had not been a very affectionate or generous sister, but, as a rule, she would keep a bargain which had been clearly made. And if there were no will, Margaret felt that she would come off well enough, though she wasn't exactly sure whether she would get the lot.

Anyway, she expected that it would be better than if Constance had been in gaol, controlling the money from there, as she supposed she would.

She wanted to know. That was surely natural enough. But it wouldn't do to inquire to day. Nor to show herself outside. It wouldn't look well. It would be best not to inquire at all, but to wait till Mr. Risdon should communicate, as no doubt he would.

She dressed slowly, her mind busy with many thoughts, and then looked at the watch again, and finished in some haste, for she had a healthy appetite, and she had ordered breakfast for nine o'clock.

CHAPTER XXI.

MR. RISDON proved the two wills at once, and obtained probate without difficulty. The ultimate disposition of the property was one to which no serious objection could be made. The effect of the two wills was that the Treasury could collect double Death Duties, an illustration (which does not concern us now) of how radically inequitable such levies are.

Margaret and Violet met at Mr. Risdon's office, by his invitation, to hear the dispositions which Constance Hillier had made for their benefit. Margaret came in deep mourning, which she had ordered with some hesitation. The wearing of black garments when a relative dies is a rather ugly convention, which few have the courage to resist. It is no evidence of grief that we go out to buy new clothes. Its sole advantage is that it announces a fact without verbal advertisement. Margaret was not sure whether the decease of one who is hanged be a fact which should be advertised at all. It is a point on which books of etiquette may not be helpful. But she did not wish to appear callous—particularly not to Bill Langford. Probably she chose the wiser alternative.

The two cousins shook hands with some outward cordiality. Margaret rather liked Violet. Violet was sorry for Margaret, and anxious to do anything in her power to express, her sympathy. She was surprised by the provisions of the will, and somewhat disconcerted. She did not really want the money. She had a small private income, which was more than sufficient for her personal expenses. But she knew, vaguely, that her grandfather's estate was not free from embarrassments. She had heard him regret that it could only come into her father's hands in a reduced and encumbered form. That might be very soon now. The Earl of Weyford had not rallied as his physicians had hoped. He was critically ill. When he died, it was understood that her father would resign his commission in Burma, and that he and her mother would come home. She saw, in a quiet practical mind, that the money might have its use—if it could be taken honourably. How much would there be?

She might have asked that, but Margaret was first. She had heard the provisions of the will with an impassive face, as she had resolved to do. It might have been worse. She had got the half that had been agreed between Constance and her. She asked at once: "How much will there be?"

As to that, Mr. Risdon was somewhat vague (how provokingly cautious lawyers are!). It would depend upon the realization of securities, for which the moment was not very favourable. Then there was the lease of 35, Castlemaine Gardens. That might be worth anything from £3,000 to £5,000. And there were the contents of the house. Also, there was nearly £2,000 in the bank in Lady Catherine's name, which could be drawn on now that probate had been obtained.

On the other hand, the Death Duties would be a heavy charge. He thought they might each expect to receive ultimately from £12,000 to £15,000. He would not like to be more definite than that. They would have to consider the sale of the household effects now. He supposed that Miss Hillier would not wish for any further delay?

Violet said she did not want to disturb— But Margaret interposed. She had thought that over also, and her mind was made up. It had not been an easy resolution to face. There was a reason why she did not want to leave No. 35. But her judgement told her that it was the wiser thing to do. Wiser in *every* way. And she was of a resolute disposition to follow where her judgement led. She said: "I don't want to stay there an hour longer than I need, nor ever to see the place again."

There was no doubting the sincerity of those words.

Violet said: "I had a letter from Father yesterday. He said, if Aunt Catherine's things are being sold, there are a few that he would like Grandfather to buy, rather than that they should go into strangers' hands. Of course"—she turned to Margaret—"you have the first claim, if they should be things that you wish to keep, but he would like to feel that they are in the family still."

Mr. Risdon interposed. "I should advise that an inventory be taken in the first instance, and either of you could then withdraw such things as you may wish to keep, at a valuation which will be put on them by the auctioneers, who will be acting in the interests of both. I can arrange for a clerk to come up tomorrow, if that will suit you, Miss Hillier."

"It can't be too soon for me."

Violet said: "Shall I come round and bring Father's letter, and we can look at the things he mentions, and decide what to do?"

"Yes. When you like...the morning would be the best time."

But the mornings were not convenient to Violet. She sat with her grandfather at that time of day, relieving the nurse. The appointment was fixed for five-thirty on Thursday next.

CHAPTER XXII.

THE next day was that of Thomas Mogson's appeal. These events are rarely of any practical value, except to the legal gentlemen concerned. The convicted individual has (we may suppose) a rather anxious morning, though it is possible that someone may be sufficiently humane to inform him beforehand that they invariably fail. The Criminal Appeal Court is not exactly a sham, but its limited powers are mainly exercised in quashing convictions of guilty persons which have been faultily obtained, and the counsel employed by the Crown to prosecute in murder cases are usually too expert for their manœuvres to be frustrated in that way.

Mr. Clackleton spoke on his client's behalf for three or four hours, as he was expected to do, going over the evidence in great detail, and arguing, with some ingenious subtleties, that it supplied no reasonable ground on which the jury could be justified in presuming his guilt.

During the course of this pleading Thomas Mogson, who had elected to be present, and whose first appearance indicated something of the mental stress which he had undergone while awaiting the new ordeal of this appeal, gradually brightened, and looked round the court with an almost insolent cheekiness, as though to say: "Now answer that if you can!" He even looked, as the morning advanced, with a recovered perkiness, at the faces of the three carmine-clad judges, whose immobile faces gave no sign of their thoughts as they sat patiently waiting the conclusion of arguments the strength or weakness of which they could have weighed equally well had they been presented in a dozen sentences.

But the jaunty confidence of his gaze turned to a cringing fear, rather horrible to behold, when the learned judge who sat on the right hand of that high tribunal turned his head, as a vulture may do that had long sat motionless on his perch, and the cold intelligent eyes were fixed speculatively upon him, as one who surveys an unusual specimen of a familiar species.

It was a few minutes after the usual hour of the luncheon adjournment when Mr. Clackleton sat down. It would have been the part of the Attorney-General to reply on the reassembling of the court, which Thomas Mogson might have found a less pleasant experience. But he was spared that ordeal. The scarlet figures came to life. They leaned together, whispering. The Lord Chief Justice spoke. They did not feel that it would be necessary to call upon the Attorney-General. The decision of the Court was that Thomas Mogson had had a fair trial. The summing-up of the learned judge had been able and impartial. There had been ample evidence on which the jury could arrive at their decision. There was no ground for interfering with the verdict. The appeal was dismissed. Mr. Justice Ackling and Mr. Justice Sampson briefly concurred.

The end came so suddenly, so quietly, that Thomas Mogson had hardly realized his doom before the warder was guiding him down the stairs, with a firm hand on his arm. But he was still not without hope. There was the chance of a petition which his lawyer had undertaken to prepare if the appeal should fail. The law had taken one life. It might be content with that.

And, if that failed, there was a further hope still, in the rear of a cunning mind. A hope that he could tell to none, even to his own lawyers. At the very worst, at the last moment, *suppose he should confess*. "Ah!" he thought to himself, and straightened from a dejected attitude, as he sat in the closed car that was taking him back to gaol, *"what about that?"* It was a question more easily asked than answered.

But Mr. Clackleton was annoyed. Not by the result of the appeal. He would have been a most surprised man had it succeeded. But he thought his arguments might have been treated rather more seriously.

Still, it would have meant that they would all have to come back into court after lunch for no practical purpose, and—well, we can all see that.

CHAPTER XXIII.

IT was a dull March day of low unbroken cloud, and the dusk was closing before its time, when Miss Scovell's car stopped at the door of No. 35.

"I've told Peters to come back in an hour," she said, as Margaret met her in the hall, and led the way into the rather sombre sitting-room on the ground floor. It was a room that had been little used, and not altered at all, since its owner had gone upstairs for the last time nearly sixteen years earlier, and the heavy dullness of its substantial comfort had not been relieved by the substitution of a gas-fire for the cheerful glow of a Victorian grate.

To Margaret it was too familiar to arouse reaction. Mr. Risdon had regarded it only as the storehouse of certain pieces of furniture which would realize well under the auctioneers' hammer—and of others which would be hardly worth carting it away. But to Violet it was heavy with the shadows of the dreary history of the house, and of the sordid wickedness of its final crime. She could easily understand that Margaret should wish to leave it behind for ever.

Mrs. Wrigley, who had followed the abdication of Ivy Parker, brought in tea. Margaret, avoiding a too-abrupt approach to the business which had brought them together, made an allusion to her which resulted in explanation of the free supply of daily women which are obtainable from the purlieus of Kensington, in contrast to the difficulty in securing those who are willing to sleep in. Violet showed a sufficient interest in this natural-history fact, of which she had been previously ignorant. She inquired politely as to Margaret's future plans. Margaret was thinking of somewhere quiet. Perhaps Cornwall. Or would it be too hot in the coming months? Violet thought not. She realized, with a generous sympathy, how confined had been the life of that gloomy house. Even Cornwall had the unfamiliarity of a foreign land. But her time was short. She pulled out her father's letter. As she did this the door-bell rang. There was the sound of Mrs. Wrigley's shuffling feet in the passage. Voices followed. The door of the room opened, without the formality of knocking. "Mr. Langford to see you, Miss." Mr. William Langford entered the room.

He was, in appearance, a boy of about twenty, though, in fact, he was three years older. He entered quickly, with an athletic lightness of movement, which did not indicate his profession that of a solicitor's clerk. It did indicate some familiarity with his surroundings.

"I thought I'd better look in before...," he began, and then observed Violet, and stopped.

Margaret said: "Our neighbour, Mr. Langford.... Miss Scovell, my cousin.... Mr. Langford's mother lives next door."

Bill Langford appeared to hesitate for a second as to the etiquette of the introduction, and then held out his hand. He had a frankness of manner, which was of his own nature, and a shyness behind it which came from the solitariness of his childhood.

Violet shook hands with a self-possession which gave no clue to her mind. She thought: "What a good-looking boy!"

Margaret saw their eyes meet, and was not pleased. All this was in ten seconds of time.

Bill said: "I just looked in to say...to see if there's anything I could do."

Violet thought that he had called with a more definite purpose, which was not to be mentioned now. She would have withdrawn had the circumstances allowed it.

Margaret said: "It's very kind of you, and of Mrs. Langford. You might tell her that I'll come in later."

The remark (Violet thought again) surprised and disconcerted him, but he replied readily and conventionally enough. It was easy to judge that Mrs. Langford was not in the forefront of this acquaintance. But there was no harm in that. Why should Margaret think that the position required a lie? Violet was reminded of the ugly hints and accusations of the *Sunday Pail*. It was true that they had been aimed mainly at the woman who now lay in a shameful grave, but the suggestion of unseemly license was connected with those who had come in from the same next-door house. Yes, she could understand how Margaret felt. She was sorry for her again.

The incident was forgotten as they discussed the contents of her father's letter together. They went over the house. They turned over Aunt Catherine's old-fashioned jewellery. Was it of any real value now? They were not expert enough to know. There was a quaint brooch which Violet would like to have, unless Margaret wanted it. No, she did not care for it at all. But not, Violet said, if it were of great value, in which case, let it be sold. The valuation had not been completed. That was to be done tomorrow. The time passed quickly. When Mrs. Wrigley interrupted them to say that the young feller with the car had come back, it was evident that they would not finish that evening. Violet said that she could not stay longer. Her grandfather had been worse since yesterday. He had asked her not to be long away. She would come tomorrow at the same time.

When she had gone, Margaret's thoughts reverted to what she had said to Bill. She had had no intention of going in to see Mrs. Langford, nor any wish to do so. Probably Bill understood that. But he might not, and, in any case, he might expect that she would do what she said. He might even have felt that it was wise or necessary to inform his mother of the coming visit. She had her character with him to maintain. Yes. She had better go. In any case, it might do more good than harm. She went upstairs to put on her hat.

CHAPTER XXIV.

MRS. LANGFORD was not in her first youth. An earlier generation would have retired her to the ranks of the middle-aged, or ridiculed her for a pretence of that which was no longer hers. She had, in fact, been a widow for nearly eighteen years. She had been twenty-four when her husband died, and had formed an early resolution that she would consider no second marriage till her son should have ceased to be dependent upon her. She had not faltered in this resolve as the years passed, but she had added a second, to which she had held with an equal firmness—she would not resign her youth till she had taken some further toll of its possibilities. It was a thought that she did not hint even to her dearest friend. A thought—above all, Bill must not guess—that if he should marry young, as she hoped he might, she would still be—not old.

Meanwhile, she was known only as one who was too devoted to her only child, and to her tennis-court triumphs, to have any thoughts beyond these two absorbing interests. It was always difficult to be sentimental with Edith Langford. The twenty years had been punctuated with some offers of marriage that had been laughed away.

Now her son had been caught (that was the word in her mind) or was in danger of being caught by a woman ten years his senior (if not more) of whom she knew only that she was the grandniece of an Earl, probably of some inherited means, and the sister of a poisoner. She had observed her also (from her window) as having an alert and upright carriage, a brisk walk, and, she thought, a rather hard face.

Perhaps it had been a mistake that she had not encouraged Bill to mix with girls more freely...but he had been of a reticent disposition, and rather shy...and her first concern had always been that he should not be brought up in an unmanly way, being an only child.

So she thought, as she sat alone waiting for Miss Hillier's promised call. Why was the woman coming? What had she to say to her?

She had the instinctive hostility that a mother most often feels to the woman who would take her son, and to augment this there was some reasonable prejudice against her greater age and the sinister shadow that had fallen upon the household of which she was the survivor.

Against this was the hope, held through the slow-passing years, that Bill would marry at an early age, and a resolution that when such a question arose it should be faced reasonably, as being his choice, not hers. How much of human folly she had witnessed in the obstruction which other mothers had placed (so often to no effect) in the way of their own children under such circumstances!

No. She would be fair. Above all, she would be fair. She would judge the woman for herself. She did not doubt that she would be— was fond of Bill. That (she supposed) would not be difficult, and any woman would be grateful for a boy's sympathy under such conditions. To a lonely woman so placed, sympathy would open the door very easily to a warmer feeling. She had read the article in the *Sunday Pail*, but she wouldn't allow herself to be influenced by a thing like that. It was not playing the game at such a time, when no reply could be made. It was—yes, damnable was the word.

This was the thought in her mind as she rose and crossed the room to meet her expected visitor.

"It was nice of you to call before you left," she said in a tone that was only slightly less cordial than the words. "Bill told me you would be coming in. I'm sorry that he's had to go out."

Margaret did not doubt, nor resent, that his mother had made some excuse to have him out of the house. But she did resent that the woman opposite to her—who must be forty—looked no older than herself—perhaps even younger beneath the shaded electric bulbs and before the flickering light of the fire. Well, who could wonder, remembering the dreary servitude of the last fifteen years? But it was over now.

"I felt I must call," she said, "to thank you for all that you and Bill have done for me during this—dreadful time, before I go away."

Mrs. Langford was not aware that she had done anything except to tacitly discourage, while outwardly ignoring, Bill's acquaintance with their next-door neighbour. She knew that Bill had tried to confide in her on more than one occasion, and that she had deliberately evaded the conversation. She had the belief, on which Mr. Risdon had subconsciously acted in a very different connection, that a fact increased in importance when it is spoken aloud. If he should learn his mistake, as she had hoped he would, he could forget so much more easily if there had been no mention of it between them.

But she could not tell how much Bill might have used her name, or what she might be supposed to have done. Miss Hillier's words might be sincere, but she could not be sure.

She said: "I am glad if Bill has been able to help you. I would have called myself, but felt that—as a stranger to you—I could not tell how you would feel." As she said it, she wondered if it were not a breach of courtesy to make even so indirect an allusion to the trouble in her visitor's family. There is no recognized code of etiquette for those who meet women whose sisters have just been hanged. She added quickly: "The house must have been very lonely since your aunt died. I should think you will be glad of a change. Are you going far?"

"Cornwall, I expect. At first, anyway. I thought at first that I should stay for the sale. But I've arranged now to keep back the things I want, and Miss Scovell's picked what she doesn't want sold, and I think I can get away. If I don't like Cornwall...."

The attractions of Cornwall were sufficient to occupy five minutes' conversation. A glass of wine was offered, and declined. Miss Hillier must get back. She had much to do. Mrs. Langford hoped that she would look in again before she left. They parted with friendly words, and the knowledge in both their hearts that they were at deadly war. That is a woman's way, and sometimes, though less often, a man's also.

Margaret went back thinking: "I wonder what she'll say to him when he comes in."

Had she listened she would have heard nothing against herself. Bill's mother was not a fool. But when he mentioned Miss Scovell, he learnt that she had heard of her before. A nice girl. He was encouraged to talk of her.

CHAPTER XXV.

MARGARET HILLIER, enjoying the pleasures of a leisured life at the Trevelyn Hotel, Trethegar, breakfasted in her private sitting-room on the morning of Friday, March 27th. She was sensible enough to see that it is no use to have money that you don't spend, and her present outlay would scarcely equal the interest which would be produced by the fortune she had inherited. Besides, Bill had told her that he would come into some money on his twenty-fourth birthday, which was only a month ahead. He had not said how much, and she had not asked, but he had implied that it was a substantial sum.

She had only been at Trethegar for a few days, but already she looked younger, she had gained weight, the vigour of her youth asserted itself with a new emphasis in his atmosphere of sunlight and ocean winds. She felt the impulse of a new spring. It was not merely the spring of a new season but of her own life also. A late spring, but of rapid growth, as such springs are. She had always been alert of movement, her body, even when physically tired or depressed, being driven by a fierce and restless will. It had never been thoroughly subdued, even by the repressions of fifteen years. Now she took long inland walks, she rested on the hot sands, she ordered what food she would without thought of cost. She had come clear of the nightmare of fifteen years, and though the path that had brought her here was not of a kind on which it is good to look back, yet it had no power to disturb her now. She had no intention of looking back. It was a closed book. A drama, the last scene of which would be acted on Tuesday next. On Tuesday at 9:00 A.M. So she had just learnt from the *Cornwall Echo*, which was beside her plate:

> We are officially informed that the petition of Tho-
> mas Mogson has been considered, but that the Home
> Secretary sees no reason to interfere with the due
> course of the law. This decision was communicated

to the condemned man yesterday afternoon through the usual channels. It is understood that he received it with resignation, and appears to have abandoned hope of a reprieve. Since his conviction he has given no trouble to the prison officials, passing most of his time in reading, and paying much attention to the ministrations of the prison chaplain. The execution will take place as already arranged at 9:00 A.M. on Tuesday next, the 31st inst.

Margaret had read this with a satisfaction which had offset a little stir of uneasiness which she had felt as she had read Bill's letter, which was also beside her.

She had no doubt that Thomas Mogson deserved his fate. She felt that if he were hanged it would close the whole episode with a completeness which she could not feel if he were held in gaol. She wanted it over—over for ever when she went back in the confidence of recovered youth, to arrange her marriage—for June. That was how she planned it to be. That would not be too soon, nor too long. She had no wish to wait. She knew that there must be needless risk in delay. She knew that she would get no help from his mother. But she was confident that she could manage Bill.

Thinking this, her mind reverted to the letter that she had just received. It informed her that the cat had come back, as she had feared it would. Bill had caught it, and Mrs. Pettifer had had it again. If it didn't stay this time, Miss Scovell had been kind enough to offer to send it to some friends who, she knew, wanted a cat, and who lived too far away for it to find its way back.

There was no other allusion to Violet in the letter, not even to say how he had met her. But that was easy to guess. Margaret had asked him to look after several things for her during her absence. She had given him a key to the back-door and, at his own suggestion (a tribute to the legal atmosphere in which his days were spent), a formal written authority to enter the house in her absence. She had also written a friendly note to his mother, mentioning that she had given away her cat to Mrs. Pettifer at the paper-shop in Little Compton Street, and would it be asking too much for Bill to look round the garden to see that it had not returned? She could not endure the thought that it might mew vainly at the closed door.

She saw that it was natural that Violet should have come back for the things that she had wished to have, though she might have sent, or Grey & Wisden would have arranged delivery. Of course, they, or Mr. Risdon, would give her access. In Margaret's absence,

Violet would be the natural one to consult should any matter arise which required the decision of those who were primarily interested.

No doubt, it had all happened quite naturally. Anyway, it was not sufficient to disturb her mind. She had confidence in Bill. She had letters which he would regard as committing himself in honour to her, though the general verdict might be less certain to do so. He was not one to break faith. Also, she had some confidence in herself.

She might have been further annoyed had she known that there had been something beyond a casual meeting. Violet had overestimated the size of her car, or underestimated that of the articles which she had come to remove. She had promised that the clerk who had been sent by Grey and Wisden should return with the keys before their office closed. Bill had first come on the scene as a volunteer to help in the carrying of articles which Peters, a small and rather stout man, regarded with a reluctant aloofness, and at the sight of which the clerk had developed a professional interest in an ancient bureau. His suggestion that he could let her in on a second visit had been well received. It would be a convenience to her. The hesitation of the auctioneer's clerk, who remembered that his firm was now in possession of the house, and responsible for its contents, gave way before the production of Miss Hillier's authority, which was thus used to a purpose that neither she nor Bill had foreseen. Miss Scovell understood that she could obtain access to the house, and remove the remainder of her possessions, any time that Bill was at home, which a phone call would ascertain....

There was another circumstance of which Margaret was not aware, which might have disturbed her satisfaction in the ham-and-eggs which she had consumed, and the toast and marmalade, with really excellent Cornish butter, with which her meal was concluding. Thomas Mogson had no intention of being hanged on the 31st. He had given much thought to this subject, while he had appeared to be absorbed in a long and careful study of the Hebrew prophets. You can hardly blame him for that. The result had been to leave him in some doubt as to his final end. But he felt no special anxiety about the 31st. He thought he could arrange better than that.

At the same time, he saw that a reprieve would be the safer way. It was a respite of a more assured permanence. He would wait the event.

When the prison Governor received final instructions that the execution was to go through, he went himself, with the chaplain and another official, to inform the convict that he must prepare to meet his doom. That was his custom. It was likely to be a singularly unpleasant episode, even when the convict was no more than that lousy dog, Mogson (he was a man of regrettable language when his feelings were stirred), and he would not require of his subordinates what he would not do himself.

In this instance he was puzzled by the manner in which the news was received, and it was a point on which he was an exceptionally experienced man. "Looked almost as though he enjoyed the joke," he remarked, unbending to his subordinates as he left the cell, and speaking with some natural exaggeration in the relief of having got through a distasteful job better than he had expected. "Wonder whether the fool still thinks he'll wriggle through."

That was precisely what the fool did think. Half an hour later Thomas Mogson told his attendant warder that he desired to write. They brought him foolscap paper of good quality, and a choice of nibs. They informed the Governor, who was not greatly interested, nor surprised. It was a frequent sequel to such communications as he had just made. Sometimes they wrote defences or justifications or denials in a last-minute effort to gain the sympathy of those who had still power to remit their doom Sometimes they confessed, either with a similar object (why hang a contrite man?), or under that curious urge which possesses so many criminals to "unburden" their minds. It did not matter much, either way. It would be his duty to read the document, and forward it to the proper quarter, from which its contents would not be disclosed, even to the relatives of the executed man. Why vex them with the knowledge that he has confessed a guilt which, in most cases, they will continue to deny among their friends, and perhaps even in their own thoughts? How decide as to the truth or falsity of documents which are not sworn, and which sometimes impute responsibility or guilt to others? What use is there in further words? The law is ringing down the curtain on a dishonoured life, to which we can do no better service than to forget.

Thomas Mogson wrote quickly. He was making a statement which, whether true or false, or (as was most probable) of a hybrid kind, had been the subject of much quiet thought during the leisured hours that the law prescribes for those whom it will hang on its own day. He knew just what he meant to say.

It was the next morning when the Governor read it. He had finished breakfast, and found it waiting him on his office desk. It was actually about the same time that Margaret was congratulating herself on the paragraph in the *Cornwall Echo*, for the sun rises somewhat earlier in London than in the West. After the first indifferent glance, he made a sudden exclamation of astonishment, or perhaps of horror. He read on to the end. He read a second time. "Simpson," he said, "I'm afraid there's a ghastly business here. Get me through to the Home Office. I want to speak to Whitaker."

But when he got through to Whitaker, he found his news received in a cooler way than he had expected. "Yes, you can send it on, for what it's worth. We shall investigate it, of course. Probably three parts lies."

All that day, and on Sunday, the Governor waited in expectation of instructions to delay the execution that did not come. On Monday morning he got through to the Home Office again, and was informed that the matter was occupying the attention of Mr. Armfield, but that no decision had yet been reached. He even went so far as to cause some delay in the preparations of the hangsman (who arrived at midday on Monday), and told him that he had better not be in a hurry to book his usual room for the night, as his services might not be required.

Thomas Mogson may be supposed to have waited in a keener anxiety, but he was supported by an even greater confidence. He could quite believe that the instructions would not arrive till the last moment. He supposed vaguely that there was a routine to be observed. Probably the Home Secretary would be away for the weekend. Monday afternoon would be the most likely time, say about four o'clock.

But four o'clock came, and five, and six, and there was no news. And instead of the news that he was expecting he was offered the ministrations of the prison chaplain!

"They won't hang me, I tell you! *They can't! They can't!*" he cried in a voice that was almost like a wild beast's snarl. "They can't, now I've told the truth. I'm about the only witness they've got. The only one they can hope to have."

The Governor looked at it in the same way, but the hours passed, and there was no reprieve. To Thomas Mogson there came a dreadful fear. *Suppose the Home Secretary were away for a long weekend.* Suppose he should walk into his office at 9:30 on Tuesday morning (he did not suppose that so important a man would arrive earlier than that) and read his confession *too late*. But it could not, must not, be! He could not sleep, he could not eat through the night. There was no comfort in the opiates which are provided for such as he, so that they will wake heavily from a drugged sleep, and be urged with a hand on each pinioned arm a terrified, bewildered, half-unconscious way to the fatal drop. He was in a frenzy of terror when the morning came, and the minutes passed at such a frightful speed. He heard eight o'clock strike, and there was still no news. Now it was eight-fifteen—eight-thirty—eight-forty-five. Would he be a live man when the clock struck nine? Yes, he heard it strike. Thank God, thank God. At that moment he was conscious of something that was almost a genuine prayer. Had they meant to hang him, he would not have been in his cell when the clock struck!

But the truth was that the Governor was responsible for the delay. He had tried to ring up the Home Secretary at his private address at 8:45 A.M. to make certain that there had been no mistake, and there had been some delay on the line. He had said that the final steps were to await his instructions, and it had been 8:54 when he got through. There was a conversation which lasted three minutes. Then he said, "Yes. Tell Phipps he's to go ahead."

It was 9:02 when the executioner and his assistants entered the cell to pinion a fighting, struggling, protesting man. He kicked Phipps in the stomach once before they got his legs under control. It was no more than a random kick, given blindly, without malice, as he struggled to delay his captors, for the reprieve that was sure to come, but it did win him some extra seconds, for Phipps doubled up on the floor.

At 9:09 the drop fell. Thomas Mogson's confession had gained him about seven minutes of conscious life.

CHAPTER XXVI.

IT was Saturday afternoon, and Thomas Mogson was still unhanged, when Violet rang up to say that she would come in about half an hour if Mr. Langford were sure that it would be quite convenient to him.

Bill was quite clear about that. Indeed, his time was so free that when the question arose of how some fragile articles should be packed in the car, he was able to accompany her back to help to hold them in positions of safety. And, observing him to be so unoccupied, and after he had been so kind, Violet could hardly fail to ask him to come in with her, to see where they would be put, and after that to have some tea, for which it was late already.

And then he stayed (as, perhaps, he should not have done) to look at photographs of the Earl's country home, which were certainly a pleasant contrast to the ornate dowdiness of the high and narrow house in Claverdon Place in which they then were, and which was Violet's home during the winter months, so that it is easy to understand her wish to show the family resources in a fairer light, without imputing any more personal motive to a young lady who was of a notoriously reserved disposition, and whose previous approaches to matrimonial alliance had consisted in an embarrassingly-expected proposal of marriage from a sporting stockbroker, and an embarrassingly unexpected one from an obese peer.

And so Bill, who had been acutely miserable since his last meeting with Violet, had a somewhat longer opportunity of comparing a first-rate article with one which was both second-rate and second-hand, and though the shy friendliness of his reception did not lift the cloud of his dejection, it changed its character, so that it might be said that while Violet was explaining the identity and character of her visitor to the Earl, who was now somewhat better, and had heard their voices as he sat by the fire in his overhead room, Bill was walking home in a condition of no less acute but much pleasanter misery than he had experienced previously. It is a debatable point whether Margaret's superior qualities in salesmanship might have overcome the disadvantage of the inferior article she had for disposal, had she been on the spot to sell it, but she was some hundreds of miles away, and could do nothing further to delude Bill as to the nature of the friendly sympathy which she had exploited so skilfully at the garden wall. So Bill realized quite clearly at which market he wished to deal, though in a tortured doubt as to whether he had placed his order already.

Yet the cloud of his misery was now pierced by a shaft of light. Violet had told him that she would be at the sale on Wednesday week—but what an age away!

And tonight—or perhaps tomorrow afternoon would do—he had to write to Margaret again about the infernal cat.

CHAPTER XXVII.

TO understand the somewhat crowded events of weekend preceding the execution of Thomas Mogson it is necessary, in the first place, to consider the document which he had indited, and which reached Mr. Whitaker's hands at about two o'clock on Friday afternoon. It read thus:

> I didn't think they'd believe that Constance had done it, because she wasn't the kind, and if she got off, I supposed I should too, 'specially as I'm not the one that's guilty at all. She said she wanted to try it on the cat, because the cat was a thief, and she wished it dead, and she didn't want to kill it in a way that Constance would know. I want to write all the truth, and we did have a talk about what a power it was if it was a poison that no one could guess, and how anyone who had it would feel that everyone round them was only living by their permission, but it was no more than talk, and should I have done anything that would have given all the money to Constance, things being as they were? I can't think why she did it now. Not at that time, anyway. But it wasn't ever more than talk, not to me, and that's the truth, so help me God.
>
> It was Margaret that did it, so I suppose. It must have been her, because she had it from me, and she couldn't have let Constance know, because she wouldn't let her know that she knew me at all.
>
> It began with Constance telling Margaret about the money I spent on her at the Yellow Cat, and I suppose she wanted a bit of fun too. So she came once to the Yellow Cat, and I don't suppose anyone there remembers that. It was a good many months

ago, and they wouldn't know who she was, but she got in by asking for me, and after that we used to meet at the Merrythought. That's easy to prove. Tommy Parrott there's served us about twenty times.

It was easy to keep them apart, because they couldn't ever come out at the same time, and I never went near the house, and Margaret was one who could keep her mouth shut better than most, and the other didn't know.

Constance was all right for a lark, and you could do what you liked with her taking her home in the taxi, or if you got her upstairs, when she'd gone a bit over the edge, but she wasn't the one to choose, if you knew both. She was a bit on the tough side, and she'd got a temper like a dog with the mange.

But Margaret was up another street, and she knew I'd have married her any day if she hadn't wanted to hold on till the old woman died, and get a grip of the cash.

So it isn't hard to see that she might want to hurry things up, though how she meant to get through, the will being as it was, or why she put any of it where she did without throwing it away is more than I've been able to guess, not having seen her since. Not to talk to, that is.

But it wasn't Constance at all. It couldn't have been, things being as they were, and I'll give evidence of this on oath anywhere that I'm wanted, and any time.

And I say that this is the real truth, so help me God, and I wish I had written it before now, but I didn't get much chance when they came to me and said it was no use denying anything, as it had all been found out, and it hidden in Constance's drawers. It didn't seem much good to deny that it came from me, or to say that I had given it to the other one. If they were in a mess it was not for me to help to get them out. I was in trouble enough that I didn't deserve, and I thought the innocent one was more likely to come through than the one that wasn't, and I saw I'd got to sink or swim in the same boat, because they showed they meant to fix it on me. But I'd have spoken before if I'd known how it would go, which I couldn't guess, and I don't see how anyone could. I only wanted to get myself out, as a man would, I not having meant any wrong at all.

As witness my usual signature this Twenty-Seventh day of March, Nineteen Hundred and Thirty-One.

THOS. MOGSON

Thomas Mogson had felt a glow of virtuous satisfaction as he had concluded this document. He felt that he had written it in a simple manly style which could not fail to impress any reader favourably. He had not whined. He had not concealed his "goings-on" with the two women. He had expressed his regret for the death of Constance Hillier in a generous way, though the responsibility was not really his. He had not arrested the woman. He was neither jury nor judge. He was no more than another innocent person in the same mess. And he had admitted (a certain amount of) responsibility. He had said that they had asked of poisoning people, though he hadn't taken it seriously. That admission would convince almost anyone of the simple truthfulness of the whole narrative. He had not made any profession that he was a saint. He had admitted that he was a "man of the world," and kindred spirits stretched out imaginary hands to shake his own. He felt himself to be the author of an admirable and convincing document, and that night he had slept well.

Mr. Whitaker read it with rather different feelings. In the first place, a long experience of such documents led him to anticipate mendacity.

In the second, he was much more concerned with the credit of his own department than with the vertebrae in the back of Thomas Mogson's neck.

He had been prepared, by the telephone conversation of the earlier day, for the allegation of Constance Hillier's innocence which it contained, and he examined it with a mind which was unsurprised, and somewhat sceptical. If it were true, it was not merely a most regrettable incident, it was a devilish nuisance, and the scoundrel should have spoken earlier, or held his tongue now.

Of the assertions of personal innocence which the document contained Mr. Whitaker took no notice at all. He knew that they would be there without looking, and his eye glided over them at a practised speed. The time for proofless assertion was over now. The jury had decided that, and, in the case of Thomas Mogson, they had shown their sense. Even had there been any doubt of that, the tone and substance of the document would have removed it easily.

The only question was whether it were true that Margaret was guilty, and, if so—it was less than a logical consequence—had Constance been innocent?

Should he admit these very doubtful premises, what action, if any, should follow?

He sat for more than half an hour examining the position from every angle in a cool, and fair, and very exact mind. At the end of that time he knew clearly what he would do. He would file the confession, after endorsing it briefly with his decision, which would be to do nothing at all. Looking at the matter in the broad way which he conceived to be his duty, he saw little possibility of good, and much of harm in disturbing it further.

But it had to be reported to Mr. Armfield, and his reaction, as Mr. Whitaker could foresee, would be very different. Had he simply picked up the receiver and been put through to the prison governor, he could have closed the incident at once and for ever, with an instruction that the execution should proceed, and that the confession must (of course) be treated as strictly confidential pending such action (if any) as his Department might decide to take.

Had he done that, it would have been millions to one against Mr. Armfield or anyone else ever hearing a word concerning it. But it is an illuminating fact that such a solution did not even enter his mind. As it was his first duty to decide what should be done, so it was his second to bring Mr. Armfield to a like opinion. This was hard on Mr. Armfield, who had been invited to Chequers for the weekend.

He was just ordering his car to be ready in ten minutes when a dispatch box was brought to him containing a brief memorandum of the substance of Thomas Mogson's literary effort. Even in the cold official words in which the information was given, the full horror of the possibility struck Mr. Armfield like a physical shock. And he had never wanted that woman to hang! It was Whitaker who had done that—who had overruled him, as he always did! The document quivered in a shaking hand as Mr. Armfield cancelled his car.

CHAPTER XXVIII.

MR. WHITAKER'S private office was a broad-windowed room, high and light, and having an interior which was coldly clear, after the order of his own mind. Even the bright cheerfulness of the fire-filled grate could not greatly reduce the effect of the bare austerity of distempered walls, the absence of anything beyond the needed minimum of furniture, the expanse of the unlittered desk. It was from this austerity that Mr. Whitaker issued his unhurried, unemotional orders, and the roar of the London that he ruled rose faintly from far below.

Into this atmosphere of quiet strength Mr. Armfield burst like a discordant note. He walked backwards and forwards in uncontrollable agitation, and the slow and well-constructed sentences of the Permanent Secretary had no power to subdue him. "I never wanted it, Whitaker! Never wanted it! You'll do me justice there. She ought never to have hanged while the scoundrel lived."

"It's an unfortunate affair, however you look at it," Mr. Whitaker conceded, without discussing the extent or nature of his responsibility. "But the real question seems to me to be whether we are to let the fellow save his life for the sake of attempting a conviction of the other sister, which it may not be easy to get."

In saying this he was making a calculated attack on Mr. Armfield's weakest side. Had he been talking to another official of his Department he would have put forward a very different argument, which must wait its turn. Mr. Armfield swallowed the hook.

"Let him live, Whitaker? Let him live? I think one of us must be mad. You can't credit that tale that he didn't know. A child wouldn't believe that. You've got a woman who'll let an innocent sister hang, and a wretch who'll connive at the same thing because he thinks there's a shade better chance of saving his own neck. We don't have lynching in this country, but I wouldn't trust that man's life for an hour if we let him loose, nor the woman's either when the truth's known. She'll find a gaol's the safest place for her own skin, till the hangman calls."

"Yes...if we make it public. And if it's proved. But it seems to me that if you are set on hanging the woman, you have got to let the man go. Of course, he is building on that."

"I don't see why you should. Suppose it turned out to be a pack of lies from end to end? You wouldn't let him off then?"

"I don't see how we can help it, even then. And we can test whether it's partly true in a few hours...But we have got to take his tale for truth if we arrest the woman. We can't go on blowing hot and cold. And we shall depend on his evidence. You could not depend on a man like that unless you have bought him, one way or other, and I am not saying that his evidence would be worth much at the best, but if he thought we meant to hang him when he had said what we required, you couldn't tell what he might do or say. He might refuse to open his mouth. The statement we have got wouldn't be any use at all. It's not even on oath."

Mr. Armfield saw the force of this argument, but, though his reason was convinced, his determination remained. The only possible conclusion to his mind was that the memory of Constance Hillier should be cleared, and the two murderers meet the fate they deserved. And, as a successful politician must, he had a very agile and flexible intellect. His experience had taught him that if he had made up his mind to reach a certain goal, he could usually arrive there at the end, though he might have to double and dodge on the way. His mind was of a more feminine quality than that of Mr. Whitaker, which was primarily concerned with the administration of justice, and abstract considerations of practical government, while his was disturbed by personal antipathies or regards.

"Look here, Whitaker," he said, "suppose we arrest the woman? It's ten to one she'll confess, or make some statement that'll twist the rope round her own neck. I don't know why, but they almost always do. I needn't tell you that. And she'll be taken by surprise, when she thinks she's got clear. You must allow something for that. If you act at once, we might see our way through, and let the fellow hang on Tuesday, just the same."

Mr. Whitaker hesitated. Not as to whether that might be a good plan—he knew that it would be an impossible risk to take on any evidence they yet had—but as to how best to postpone the decision till he could steer it more easily in the way he would.

He said: "I think there's one thing we ought to test first, and we can do that easily enough between now and Monday. We ought to know whether it's true that Mogson used to meet Margaret Hillier in the way he says. If that turns out to be false, we shall know that it's nothing more than a lie from end to end to save his own neck, and if it's true we shall have something more to go on than we have now."

Mr. Armfield agreed to this. Inspector Cleveland, who had conducted the previous investigations, would be the man for the job. He was fortunately an officer of proved discretion as well as ability. Mr. Whitaker would telephone the Assistant-Commissioner at once, and ask that he should be placed at the disposal of the Home Secretary. By 10:30 A.M. on Monday morning, Mr. Whitaker would have his report.

"Very well, Whitaker. We'll just do our best to forget it till then. It's quite likely it's no more than a rotten lie. We've got to hope that's what it is."

"Yes, sir. I'm sure that's the best way."

Mr. Whitaker said "sir" quite respectfully. Had he had occasion to write to Thomas Mogson, he would have assured him that he was his obedient servant. He was one of the rulers of England, and that is the traditional manner in which they behave and write. He did not really think they were taking the best way. It would have been better to leave a matter unproved which could not be pursued to any useful end. He had simply humoured a difficult child.

As to not thinking of it till Monday, that was absurd. It would receive just as much thought, or as little, as could be profitably spent upon it. Mr. Whitaker was used to deal with difficult or vexatious problems, and to resolve them in an atmosphere that was free from the agitations of Mr. Armfield's mind.

CHAPTER XXIX.

BUT Mr. Armfield could not forget.

He was not sure that it was wise to mention it (there might be nothing in it after all), and he had made up his mind not to do so, but after two or three successful repressions he let it out at last as he was sitting up with the Premier that night over a final pipe. He was surprised to find that Sir Robert Pengwyn's attitude, though not identical with that of Mr. Whitaker (as far as he had been allowed to understand the latter), was of a similar caution.

"It's hard to tell what to believe," he said reasonably, "when you're dealing with persons of that class." He paused and altered his phrase to "of that kind," as a democratic premier should. "You don't want to stir up such a dust unless you're quite sure you know what's underneath. And, if it's really true, the poor woman's past saving now. I used to have the same worry when I held your office twenty years ago. The judges say they never make any mistakes, and take good care the juries don't either. It's only we amateurs who worry about that. I suppose they're right, as a rule. Anyway, you can trust Whitaker. He's got a level head. We don't want anything to make you unpopular just now. You can never tell what the reaction will be."

Mr. Armfield was silent. He certainly didn't want anything to make him unpopular. He became more thoughtful than before. Sir Robert Pengwyn filled his pipe, and went on.

"I remember a tale I was told by Ashton Earle when he was a young man. I doubt whether there's anyone else alive who could tell it now. It wasn't known to more than five or six, and they were much older than he. I won't mention names, but it was a famous case, and a good deal like you're telling me now, except that they never knew who did the crime; but they found out that the man who'd been executed *couldn't* have done it, because he'd been twenty miles away at the time, as he'd always said. Well, Earle said they worried over it for months, and at last they decided to say nothing. They couldn't bring the poor man back to life, and it was trouble enough to get murderers convicted as it was. He said it was a question of public policy against private interests, and there could be no doubt which he ought to put first. I shouldn't wonder if you find Whitaker looks at it in much the same way."

"Ye-es. I daresay he does. I wish I knew what the truth is."

Mr. Armfield was a man of a restless energy, and of some originality of mind. He owed his popularity in part to some picturesquely unexpected episodes in his political life. He did not like Pengwyn's suggestion that his own reputation might suffer. He did not intend that it should.

Very early on Sunday morning he succeeded in getting Inspector Cleveland on the telephone, and learned that Thomas Mogson's tale was so far true that he had been known to visit the Merrythought regularly, and to meet a woman there who was of the description of Margaret Hillier. Did the Inspector know where Margaret Hillier now was? Yes, he did. She was at the hotel at Trethegar. She could be laid by the heels any time in less than an hour. She was, in fact, being already watched by the local police.

Mr. Armfield said he did not want her arrested. Nothing would be decided before tomorrow. He rang off. He wished that she were somewhere a bit nearer. Had he known that at first he might not have allowed the idea to take hold in his mind. On the other hand, the hotel was a stroke of luck. Anyone may go to a hotel. It had been a lifelong boast that he was a good judge of character. He had always engaged his staff without references, trusting to this instinct, and he had yet to make a mistake. He would go and see for himself.

Taking no one into his confidence, he left a message of apology to the Premier (who was a late riser) and by forming an energetic combination of car and train he was able to walk into the public room of the hotel toward the end of the afternoon, and order a substantial meal in the name of Mr. Percy Cross.

CHAPTER XXX.

MR. ARMFIELD did not know Cornwall. He came from the North. He took his holidays abroad. He did not expect Cornwall to know him. He travelled as inconspicuously as possible, finishing his journey with a third-class ticket. The reception clerk at the hotel accepted his assertion that he was Percy Cross without emotion. He had no cause to doubt that he had concealed his identity, until a man entered the room clothed in policeman's boots, and other articles of less certain origin. This man regarded him for an instant with a glance of amazement, which passed as quickly as it came. He sat down at the further end of the common table, of which Mr. Percy Cross was the only other occupant, and ordered his own meal. But Mr. Cross was annoyed. He had seen the glance. He had not come there to be recognized by stray members of the Metropolitan police, such as he supposed this man to be. He was sure that his eyes were on him again, though he would not return the look.

Then he considered that, if he were recognized, he would have a right to require secrecy from a member of the force of which he was the official head. If he were not recognized—well, it would be well to know. He looked at the iron-grey bullet head and brown intelligent eyes of Inspector Cleveland (whom he had not met previously) and opened conversation with him.

The Inspector accepted the offered gambit with a ready adroitness. He admitted, like Mr. Cross, that he had only just arrived. "It's wonderful," he added, "how quickly one can get about in these days, and talk all over the country to whom you please from wherever you are. I was in London myself this morning, and talking through to Chequers before I started coming down here."

Mr. Armfield understood the calculated indiscretion, which is one of the subtler devices of political warfare. He took the hint without difficulty. "Inspector Cleveland, I presume?" he inquired pleasantly.

"Yes, sir," the Inspector answered.

"Then come over here by the window, and we'll have a quiet talk."

They walked toward the open window, for the weather is warm in Trethegar, even at the end of March. They looked on to a narrow climbing street, some ten feet below.

"I should say that's the party, sir," the Inspector said, indicating a young woman somewhat gaily, but not tastelessly attired, who was coming up the street with a rather long and buoyant stride. The mourning garb had been discarded, perhaps not without reason. Who would wish to draw inquiries as to her recent loss under such circumstances?

Mr. Armfield looked at her, but his instinct failed. Perhaps the fact that he had made no previous study of the physical attributes of female poisoners put it to a test too hard.

"She hardly looks—" he said doubtfully.

"No, sir. They never do."

Mr. Armfield changed the subject, though his eyes were fixed upon the advancing figure as though fascinated by a monstrous snake. "Would you tell me, Inspector, just why you're down here today?"

"I came to find out the truth."

"I thought you were only required to ascertain if the tale were true so far as it related to the Merrythought meetings."

"I've done that, sir, and sent in my report. I thought if I could phone Mr. Whitaker in the morning, you'd be glad to know, with the execution fixed for the next day, and if you should want an arrest—well, here I should be."

"And how did you expect to find out?"

"Oh, when I've had a talk with the young woman I shall know right enough," the Inspector answered grimly.

Mr. Armfield thought quickly. He was not sure that the Inspector was not exceeding his instructions, and he had a side-doubt as to what those instructions were. (Had Mr. Whitaker let him down?) But the plan might be good, all the same. And he must be in London tomorrow morning, which meant the night train. There was no time like the present. Now the young woman was actually standing at the open door of the room. She was telling the waiter what she would like to be taken up to her apartment. With the quick audacity of decision which was characteristic of him in moments of action, however much he might worry or hesitate under the discipline of Mr. Whitaker's official mind, he stepped forward. "May we have a few words with you, Miss Hillier?"

Inspector Cleveland had not meant it to be quite like that. He would have preferred to manage the interview in his own way, but he saw that it was too late to prevent it now. There was an instant's silence, tense and antagonistic.

"Yes, if you want—if you've anything to say." The moment's hesitation may have been a sign of inward agitation, but, if so, it was the only one that they were destined to get. She added: "You can come upstairs, if you like."

They followed her into the private sitting-room that she had hired, and sat down at her invitation, one on a horsehair sofa, and one on an antimacassar chair.

"Perhaps," she said, in her pleasantest voice, "you won't mind telling me who you are?"

The question had the effect of giving the initiative to the Inspector, for Mr. Armfield (apart from the fact that he was somewhat breathless from the steepness of the stairs they had climbed, which had not troubled his more active companion) hesitated as to the advisability of disclosing his name. But it was the Inspector's wish to conduct the conversation in his own way. He said promptly: "I am Inspector Cleveland of Scotland Yard, and this is a—magistrate—Mr. Percy Cross. We want to ask you a few questions about the murder of your aunt, Lady Catherine Middleditch."

"Then I'm afraid, unless you can give me a very good reason for answering them, I must decline. I came here to escape all that. I hope never to hear the subject mentioned again as long as I live."

"I'm afraid I must ask you to hear us now, all the same. I may shorten matters somewhat if I tell you that Mogson has made a complete confession."

"Confession of what?"

"Of the full details of the crime."

"Well, what of that?"

"His confession implicates you, and exonerates your sister equally. I regret to say, Miss Hillier, that he charges you with the crime, and I ought to warn you that anything you say may be used in evidence against you."

"I have told you that I never wish to mention the subject again."

"At the same time, if you can give any explanation of the allegations he makes, they will be fairly considered, and this is your opportunity."

"Inspector Cleveland, you must think I'm a fool. You've hanged my sister on that man's evidence, and now you say he accuses me. I suppose, if he says my cousin did it tomorrow, you'll go off after her. How many more?"

"Miss Hillier, I must say that the attitude you are taking is hardly that of an innocent woman."

"And my reply is that unless you're in the habit of accusing innocent women, you're not competent to judge."

"I must tell you further that the evidence against you does not rest on Thomas Mogson's confession. Your visits to the Merrythought can be proved, and the fact that your acquaintance with Mogson was suppressed at your sister's trial—"

"Did you expect me to shout it out? If you'll look up the evidence, you'll find that I wasn't asked. I should have said so at once. Do you suppose I *wanted* people to know that?"

"It was a material fact, which—"

"Which the police could have discovered, if they had tried. I don't suppose you've come here to tell me that you don't know how to manage your own business, but what other reason you can have isn't very easy to guess. I don't want to be rude to the gentleman with you, but I'll be glad, Inspector Cleveland, if you'll leave my room." She rose with the words, her eyes hard and bright with anger or indignation.

Her visitors rose also. "Yes, Miss Hillier, we'll leave—now," the Inspector answered unperturbed by this outburst. They went out.

"What do you make of that?" Mr. Armfield asked, as they regained the public room, which was still vacant.

"Full of beans," was the reply. "It speaks well for the Cornish air. I Suppose you'll be getting back, sir, and I'd better stay on. You've learnt about all you can here."

Mr. Armfield was puzzled. He felt that the lady had had the best of the encounter, and yet the Inspector seemed to regard it with equanimity, if not satisfaction. And, beyond that, she had left him in greater doubt of her guilt or innocence than he had felt previously. He did not disclose this uncertainty, preferring to draw out the Inspector's opinion, while he reserved his own.

But Inspector Cleveland had no doubt. He answered at once. "Guilty? Yes, of course. She as good as admitted that, and put her tongue out at anything we could do. And she mayn't be far wrong either. I wonder how many times she's thought over what she would say, if anyone walked in on her like that. But I think I'll stay on a bit, all the same. You never know when you're near the end of a woman's nerve."

CHAPTER XXXI.

"THE point is," Mr. Armfield repeated, "that if she were inno-cent, we oughtn't to let the conviction stand. That's what I can't get over, Whitaker, and what's more, I'm not going to take the respon-sibility of letting this man hang without the truth being told. You don't know what it might mean, if it should come out after all."

"Well, sir, I've said what I think, and I've given you the best reasons I can." The words were harmless enough, but the tone was as nearly approaching the sarcastic as Mr. Whitaker had ever used to the various Home Secretaries who had paraded across his horizon and gone down, one by one, to their natural insignificance, or (more rarely) risen to greater heights. But it must be excused as being at the end of an hour of futile argument, and no man's patience is in-exhaustible.

The radical difference between them was one of conflicting standards of morality, of which neither was clearly conscious, though they caused each of them to regard the other as advocating that which was ethically contemptible.

Mr. Armfield's contention was one which may win an instant and instinctive sympathy. He wished to clear the memory of a dead woman from the stain of a false condemnation, and (perhaps quite as strongly since he had experienced the contemptuous rebuff of the previous evening) to bring the actual culprit to the place of trial. It seemed intolerable to him that one who (as he concluded) was guilty not only of her aunt's murder, but of having tricked an innocent sis-ter into the punishment which she herself deserved, should go free, and in actual enjoyment of the wealth which her crime had won. He had also the natural caution of the politician lest he should take a step which might ultimately reduce his popularity, should the truth become known in another way.

But Mr. Whitaker considered that these were no more than triv-ial issues when weighed against the public good, which it was their first duty to guard. If public policy should demand it, he would have sacrificed a dozen Miss Hilliers, whether guilty or innocent, without hesitation. He would have sacrificed any number of Home Secretaries. He would (in all probability) even have sacrificed himself.

But Mr. Armfield was too genuinely perturbed to resent, even if he noticed, the sarcastic tone of his subordinate. The trouble to him was that Whitaker would not give way, and he lacked the moral courage to defy him on such an issue.

"Well," he repeated, "I won't do it on my own responsibility. I'll have it over with the Premier, and I think you'd better come along. I'll fix up a conference before the day's over. It's too much for one man to decide."

So it happened, at four o'clock that afternoon, being the hour at which the wretched Mogson had calculated that his reprieve would be sure to come, and while Margaret Hillicr lay on the Cornish sands, trying to persuade herself that she was not really worried by the fact that Inspector Cleveland was on a garden-seat about eighty yards away, that there met, in the Premier's private room, a little group consisting of the Home Secretary, the Attorney-General, the Minister of Labour (who was a solicitor by profession, and a recognized authority on criminal law), Mr. Percival Whitaker and, of course, the Premier himself, to decide what, if anything, should be done in consequence of the document which Thomas Mogson had indited with such mistaken complacency.

"I think, gentlemen," the Premier began when they were all seated, "that as Mr. Whitaker has a ripe experience in these matters, and as he has given some attention to this case already, it will be a convenient course if I ask him to give us the benefit of any conclusions he may have formed. The facts, apart from the latest development, are sufficiently known to you already, and a copy of the confession of Thomas Mogson, whether true or false, will be found before each of you. Mr. Whitaker, if you please—"

Mr. Whitaker glanced at some very brief notes, and commenced to explain his views with the confidence of one who deals with a subject which he is conscious of understanding better than those to whom hc is spcaking.

After a brief but very lucid summary of facts with which we are familiar already, he continued to this effect:

"The sole question requiring immediate consideration is whether a reprieve shall be granted to Thomas Mogson, so that he will be available to give evidence in the event of Margaret Hillier being brought to trial.

"To resolve this, it appears to be necessary to consider, first, is this confession deserving of any credence? Second, assuming it to

135

be true in its material allegations as against Margaret Hillier, could a case be made out on a foundation which would justify placing her upon trial, with a reasonable prospect of a conviction being obtained? Third, if there appear to be such a probability, is it desirable, as a matter of public policy, to reopen the case? There are also two side issues arising, of subordinate importance, but not relatively so, if we regard the main question as being whether or not a guilty woman shall escape the gallows—first, what will be the ultimate fate of Thomas Mogson, if he be reprieved now, in the hope that a further conviction will be secured? Second, if we credit his confession sufficiently to conclude that Margaret Hillier was guilty, does the innocence of Constance Hillier logically follow from that conclusion?

"Approaching these queries in the order in which I have stated them, the document is one of a kind to which we have learnt to attach a very limited importance, so far as they deal with either the guilt or innocence of the convict himself, or accusations against his associates. Had Thomas Mogson's statement gone no further than that, I should have had no hesitation in advising that it should be ignored entirely. But it has an unusual feature in that it suggests the innocence of his fellow convict, who has, unfortunately, been already executed, and the suggestion that Constance Hillier may have been an innocent woman involves the supposition of her sister's guilt. I have given some consideration to the question of whether any credence should be attached to this allegation, or whether it may be dismissed as a last desperate effort to avoid the gallows. In its self-revelation it discloses the character of the writer in such a way as to discredit his unsupported evidence on any serious issue, quite apart from the implications of the crime of which he was, no doubt, rightly convicted. But I regret that I am unable to advise that it can be dismissed in this way. Investigation has already shown that the statement of his acquaintance with Margaret Hillier is substantially correct. If that be allowed, her guilt is, at least, a possibility. I have gone over the record of Constance Hillier's trial, and I am bound to advise you that the nature of her defence, futile as it appeared, and as it proved to be, supports this supposition. Inspector Cleveland, an officer of reliable judgement, interviewed Margaret Hillier yesterday, and his impression was that he had met a clever and unscrupulous woman. He goes so far as to say that he has little doubt of her guilt. This opinion is perhaps the more valuable, because Inspector Cleveland was in charge of the case against the two persons already convicted, and is fully conversant with the circumstances of Constance Hillier's arrest, and her demeanour under that ordeal. He might also be supposed to have a natural reluctance to accept a new theory which involves the conclusion that he had been instrumental in obtaining the conviction of an innocent woman. For these reasons I am unable to advise that Mogson's statement be disregarded on the ground of inherent improbability, or as being unsupported by independent evidence.

"The second question naturally follows—if we accept Mogson's allegation against Margaret Hillier, could we bring her to trial, with a reasonable prospect of a conviction resulting? This is not a question which can be answered confidently. Absolute proof would be almost impossible to obtain. Mogson's evidence would be regarded with a proper suspicion, and he would make a very bad witness if handled by a hostile counsel of average ability. Yet a conviction is possible. Absolute proof—I will revert to this point—is not usually required in a trial for capital crime. Much—very much—would depend upon the demeanour of the accused. A proportion—a large proportion—of murderers are convicted as the result of the preliminary inquisition which is held by the police immediately after, or technically before their arrest. In such a case as this the procedure would be to invite Miss Hillier to a police station where, probably after she had been kept waiting for several hours, and would be physically and mentally tired and perturbed, she would be questioned by the police for as long as there might appear to be any prospect of obtaining damaging admissions, or inaccurate statements which would discredit her subsequently. Such a procedure, without legal advice or protection, is often of great practical value, and in some instances may be the foundation from which a case is built. But I am sorry to say that Inspector Cleveland is not sanguine as to the result of such procedure in this instance. He regards the woman as one whom it might be very difficult either to cajole or threaten successfully. It would be a trial which would certainly attract public interest, which might result in popular championship of the accused woman, or an opposite feeling of equal strength if there should be a general belief that she had allowed, or even tricked, her sister into paying the penalty of her own crime. I cannot go further than to advise that the result of such a prosecution must be regarded as quite uncertain.

"The third consideration, that of public policy, is, of course, by far the most important; and here I have already put certain arguments before Mr. Armfield which appear to me to be of a conclusive character. It will be readily admitted that the crime of murder should be discouraged—and, in particular, the crime of the poisoner—by every available means, and, of such means, the arrest and conviction of suspected persons (with their subsequent execution) is of obvious importance. Yet such crimes are difficult to trace, and, from their nature, particularly difficult to prove. From these reasons, a custom has grown up in our courts of admitting a class of evidence in murder trials which would not be allowed in connection with any other criminal charge.

"For instance, if a man were put in the dock on a charge of burglary, and the court were then asked to consider evidence that he was known to be in financial difficulties, and therefore might be supposed to be inclined to steal, no judge would tolerate it. He would say at once that if there were evidence of the man's guilt it should be submitted, or, if there were none, he should be discharged. In either event, mere evidence that he might be supposed to be a man who would be prepared to burgle was a mere waste of the time of the court, if it were not open to more serious objection. Yet, in murder charges, evidence of motive is not only admitted, it is the common practice to present it to the jury as being a material and important part of the case against the accused; and the tendering of such evidence is, in itself, a tacit admission that the prosecution is unable, or is not expected to prove the crime. They invite the jury to guess, where the police (probably with better material than they can lay before the court, and being in other ways more competent to do so) have guessed already.

"The public is vaguely conscious of this difference, which is reflected in the debate as to the innocence or guilt of accused persons which frequently follows their conviction, and it may be largely responsible for the recurrent agitations for the abolition of the death penalty. I submit that, as a matter or public policy, it is not advisable that anything should transpire which might tend to produce a condition of public disquiet as to the way in which such convictions are obtained, or increase the difficulty of persuading juries to agree upon a verdict of guilty in such cases.

"The standards of public morality can never be identical with those of individual conduct, but, as a practical issue, I can assure you that very careful attention is given to every case, to avoid the risk of the execution of any innocent person. Even in cases which cannot be said to amount to more than a very strong suspicion, there may be a subsequent confession, of which the public are not informed, or the man or woman may be of such a character as to make it unreasonable to interfere with the legal result of the opinion which the jury have formed.

"As to the two subordinate considerations, it will be apparent that we cannot support a prosecution of Margaret Hillier with the evidence of Thomas Mogson unless we are prepared to put him in the witness-box, with some reasonable certainty of the evidence which he will give. It is not reasonable to suppose that a man of that character will be amenable to our requirements without receiving some assurance that his reprieve is not merely of a temporary character. Against the possibility of the conviction of Margaret Hillier, you have to put the fact that one of the worst criminals of our times will escape the gallows. I am aware that—for what it is worth—he still asserts his innocence of the murder of which he has been convicted, but, on his own statement, he gave false evidence against Constance Hillier which was material to her conviction, and with no better excuse than that it appeared to give him a slightly better prospect of escape himself. A decision of this kind should be independent of any personal feeling, but, if the issue were no more than that of supporting a further prosecution, I will own that I should reprieve that man with regret.

"The only question remaining is whether an assumption of the guilt of Margaret Hillier involves that of her sister's innocence. It seems to me that that is something less than a logical consequence. We do not know what may have passed between the two sisters, or what guilty knowledge they may have shared. I should agree that this probability is discounted by the amount of credence we give to the assertion that the acquaintance of Mogson and Margaret was kept secret from the elder sister, which I am disposed to believe. But, even then, these is no certainty that Mogson may not have worked upon both of them to the same end, offering them the opportunity of an undetectable poison, and a release from a condition of life which was equally intolerable.

"After carefully weighing the considerations which I have now put before you as briefly as possible, I have already submitted my advice that the execution of Thomas Mogson should proceed, and that no further action should be taken, unless or until there should be some further evidence against Margaret Hillier, from other sources (which is improbable), though the police will doubtless keep her under their observation, and continue their investigations."

It was a tribute to Mr. Whitaker's lucidity, and to the pauseless fluency with which he had spoken, that he concluded his remarks without interruption from his naturally talkative audience. As he ceased, the Premier turned to Mr. Armfield, and said: "I think that about clears the deck, doesn't it? It's a nasty affair, look at it any way that you will, but what Whitaker feels is that if we don't stop where we are we may go further and fare worse, and I should say he's about right." Then, as Mr. Armfield remained silent, he turned to the Minister of Labour, "What do you say, Ballinger? You know more than most of us about these matters."

"If you make this public," Mr. Ballinger said, in his slow deliberate way, "you won't get another murderer convicted for five or ten years to come. Not unless you've got two or three eyewitnesses to the actual deed. Whitaker's right about that."

There was a murmur of assent, from which Mr. Armfield saw that it would be useless, and only result to his own detriment, for him to make further objection.

"Very well," he said, "let him hang. It wasn't that I had any wish to keep him alive. But I thought it best for us to consult together, it being a rather—"

His words trailed off vaguely, seeing that it was regarded as settled, and that two of his colleagues were already talking between themselves on a quite different matter. Mr. Whitaker put his papers neatly together, and said good afternoon to the assembled ministers, with a faint and formal deference. "Shall I let the Governor know that you don't intend to interfere?" he asked Mr. Armfield in a toneless voice. He certainly did not mean to cause further difference, but the final word was not chosen with his usual precision, and Mr. Armfield was in a mood to resent it. "Interfere?" he said, rather sharply. "No, you can leave me to deal with it."

But he did not bring himself to the point of telephoning the prison Governor. There was no hurry about that; indeed, no necessity, though it would have been a courteous thing to do. He went on to the House in a dissatisfied mood, feeling that he had been rebuffed, and half-admitting to himself that Whitaker was right in a bloodless way. But why did the fellow put things so objectionably? Public morality must be inferior to that of the individual? He couldn't remember exactly, but it had been something like that. He became conscious of his surroundings as the Chancellor of the Exchequer was answering a question concerning some minor inequity in the levying of the Income Tax (Schedule B). The right honourable gentleman replied diplomatically. He admitted the injustice of the existing System, but its adjustment would cost the Treasury about £200,000. In the present state of national finance he could give no undertaking, though, under other circumstances, he would have been glad to do so. Nobody seemed surprised. Expediency, not honesty, was the national standard of financial conduct. If a taxpayer should.... Yes, Whitaker was right. But why put it so bluntly? There was a nakedness about his habits of thought which was almost indecent. As to the Hillier case, he hoped never to hear of it again.

BOOK THREE

MARGARET HILLIER

▲

CHAPTER XXXII.

MR. ARMFIELD, feeling that he had done what he could in a cause which had enlisted his emotional sympathy and indignation rather than the support of his cooler judgement, turned his mind to other things, in the belief that he had been overruled, and that his protest had made no difference to the course of the events with which it had dealt. But in this supposition he did something less than justice to the influence which he had exerted. It is true that Mogson was hanged, and his confession had been silently pigeonholed as Mr. Whitaker had resolved to have it. The innocence of Constance Hillier had not been published, and her sister remained free to enjoy the results of the crime of which he believed her guilty.

Yet he had succeeded, beyond his knowledge, in deflecting the course of events, however slightly; and that deflection, widening as it advanced, must lead at last to a most different end from that which would have been reached had Mr. Whitaker had his way at the first, and Inspector Cleveland made no inquiries at the Merrythought Club, nor followed Margaret to the Cornish coast.

Even Mr. Whitaker's mind had not been entirely uninfluenced, and it was with a distinct sense of relief that that gentleman, reading sedately next evening, after his quiet dinner, in Paley's *Moral Philosophy*, came upon the support of this very comforting passage:

> The other maxim which deserves a similar examination is this: "That it is better that ten guilty per-

sons escape, than that one innocent man should suffer." If by saying it is better, be meant that it is more for the public advantage, the proposition, I think, cannot be maintained. The misfortune of an individual, for such may the sufferings, or even the death of an innocent person be called...cannot be placed in competition with this object.

He felt that William Paley was a safe man. A very sound and discerning guide. Yet he could observe nothing in the discourse of *Crimes and Punishments* to suggest that Margaret Hillier should go free....

He did not anticipate that anything further should be done nor would he have been disposed to advocate the prosecution of Margaret Hillier, even on the clearest evidence, without full consideration of all the consequences involved, but he felt that there was no particular reason to withdraw Inspector Cleveland from observation of the suspected woman. Knowledge is power—a fact that is nowhere better appreciated than in those quiet rooms in Whitehall and Somerset House and Scotland Yard where the real rulers of England work, while its politicians chatter in Westminster, and its lawyers fatten in the Strand. When he got back to his office next morning he sent instructions to Inspector Cleveland to follow up any possible channel of inquiry into the connection of Margaret Hillier with Thomas Mogson, or the crime, and to report direct to himself. The case was still so much on his mind that he discussed it in discreet generalities with a colleague at lunch, who was disposed to support the practical wisdom of the Rev. Canon of Carlisle, though he remarked acutely that the recognition of those who suffered innocently as being martyrs for the welfare of the state rather increased than diminished the responsibility of utilizing them in that manner. That a state should follow a procedure which has such results for its own benefit might be compared to a marooned party sacrificing one of their members to feed the rest, but being morally less defensible as the occasion were less extreme.

"Still," he said, "as a practical issue, what can you do? Three men burgle a house, and murder an inmate. Which of the three did it? No one can tell. One may have protested. Yet you must hang them all. Otherwise, the three burglars would stand in a row defying you to say which had done the deed, and walk off together." He also remarked, with some truth, that persons who are wrongly convicted are rarely of good character, or otherwise of very attractive attributes. Constance Hillier illustrated this proposition.

* * * * * * *

The presence of Inspector Cleveland in Trethegar certainly did not improve Margaret's holiday, though at first she did not allow him to observe that it made any difference to her enjoyment. It had one practical consequence, in that she did not feel disposed to go back to the neighbourhood of Castlemaine Gardens while she was under such observation. Otherwise, she might have done this, for she had a very disquieting letter from Bill Langford, after several days' silence. Not that it said much. The trouble was in its brevity, and in what it didn't contain, in view of how she had written to him three days earlier. Also, she had had a letter from Violet. Quite a nice letter, written on a necessary occasion, and going beyond its necessity in friendly expression, and in the news it gave. The trouble here was that there was mention of Mr. Langford's help and kindness, and Bill had not mentioned her. An angry and jealous mind leapt at a conclusion that was nearer the truth than such conjectures usually are. Margaret Hillier, whether poisoner or not, had a fighting spirit. Her instinct was to return at once in a tigress mood, to do battle for her selected prey. She did not doubt that she would be a match for Violet Scovell. Once on the scene of action, it was a position which would be very quickly restored.

But warring with this impulse was another which urged her not to return, but to fly further from the sight and memory of that hated house. And how could *anything* be forgotten with this policeman at her heels? Her plans had been so clear, so carefully thought. Bill had told her that he could take his holidays almost at his own date, so long as it was before mid-summer, before the time when the heads of the firm took theirs, and there was competition among the senior members of the staff. Very well. He would come somewhere that she would be, or at which she would join him. Up to then, there would be no word, no suggestion of marriage, unless it should be his. But when he met her there, differently surrounded, differently dressed, in the vitality of recovered youth, and free from the gloomy associations of that chapter of her life that would be dosed for ever, would she not wake more ardent feelings than had first sprung from the sympathy of his inexperienced youth? And by then he would be in possession of the money, whether much or little, which he was inheriting. He was of age and free to make his own choice. How easy in the imagined idleness of summer days to draw him into the mood which would ask, "How long?" and "Need we wait?" And she, a lonely wanderer with no occupation, with no settled home, what excuse could she make? What could she do but yield?

So she had planned, in a mind that was subtle and clear and hard, and which kept a cold rule, though she had passions that were warm and fierce enough in their own place. She knew that his mother would be a strong foe. That had been plain, without words, from the time when they had exchanged courtesies in her own house. But she did not doubt her strength to overcome in that conflict. It was partly because of her that she planned to conceal the suddenness of her purpose, screening her field batteries till they should be ready to advance to the decisive action.

She could deal with her when the time should come. But the annoyance of this flank attack was unforeseen. She could neither be sure of its import, nor dismiss it, as she would have liked to do, from a contemptuous and angry mind.

She lay awake in the sombre hours of the night, watching the procession of stars in a clear sky (there was no moon at this time) through the small uncurtained window of the room in which she slept, and looked back at the past (at which she had thought never to glance again) with a stubborn courage which would not flinch. What was there really to fear from the damnable meddling law? What, for that matter, but for the same damnable meddling law, would there have been to regret? Not, as she was fair enough to observe, that the balance was all on the wrong side. Thomas Mogson was dead. On the other hand, she had lost a sister for whom she had never greatly cared. She had lost her in a publicly disgraceful way. She had also had some measure of anxiety as to whether she might herself have been attacked by the same interfering law. That had been an inevitable anxiety in view of her own association with Thomas Mogson, which had seemed, somehow, to be more sinister in its implications because it had been unmentioned and unguessed. Even Mogson had kept it secret—until the last. But did it matter now? Did it matter, whatever he might have said, either of truth or lies? *Thomas Mogson was dead.*

She thought of it for a long time, as the night hours passed, and she came always to the same conclusion. It did not matter at all. And then she recommenced to consider it. That was how she had often lain awake in the heavily-furnished, dark-curtained bedroom in Castlemaine Gardens, seeking some method of release which would not risk the loss of the fortune for which she served. So often, through the slow-passing years before her sister's talk had led her to make the acquaintance of Thomas Mogson at the Yellow Cat. So resolute she had been not to lose a chance—and not to make a mistake. *Had she made a mistake?* She could not see that she had.

It was true that her acquaintance with Mogson could be proved easily enough. But what of that? As she had told those policemen, it was not a thing that she was likely to shout in the street. And she had not been asked. Whose fault was that? If they did not know their own business, were they to blame it on her? Besides, they had found the poison in Constance's drawer, not hers. And they had "proved" that she was guilty. And now Constance was—dead. Her frightened, stupid, reiterated denials would be heard no more. No more on earth at least. And there is nothing beyond. It is a foolish dream. (Margaret knew this, because she had learnt it from the modern prophet, Mr. H. G. Wells, who is an exceptionally well-informed man regarding the purposes of the Creator, if any, and the destiny of the species to which he belongs.)

And Constance had left her the money. That was a point on which, till she had heard the will, she had always had to subdue a lurking fear. To try the effect of the substance, when Mogson had told her its reputed nature, had been an obvious thing to do. If her aunt did not die, who would be the worse? If she did, several people would be the better. It was the interfering doctors and lawyers who had made all the trouble, not she. It had been an obvious thing also to do it when her sister was on duty. So easy, by just waiting till she had heard her go along the landing, and the click of the bolt. So safe, while Ivy Parker was in the basement fetching some needed article for the landing-cleaning. So quietly done, while her aunt lay sleeping in the familiar position. *Of course*, she had put the packet in her sister's drawer. They would say, in their unreasonable illogical way (she did not anticipate sympathy, if the truth were known), that she had done it to throw suspicion upon her, and, of course, it was absurd. It was not to throw suspicion upon another, but to remove the risk of it from herself, which had been a very natural thing to do. She had not wished that suspicion should fall upon anyone. That had been no doing of hers. Aunt Catherine was dead, and quite time too. She had been no loss. It would have been a happier world for that death—if they had not interfered.

When she had put it in Constance's drawer, she had not expected that anything would really happen. She had not thought that anything would be discovered, or could be proved. She had not supposed that they would search the house. It had been a simple natural precaution, in case they did. Just as she always tried to think things out carefully in advance, and avoid mistakes. It was no different from stepping behind someone else when bullets begin to fly. If the one behind whom you shelter be shot, are you the assassin? It would be absurd to say that. The interfering, blundering, hateful law!

There had been the one fear, she acknowledged that, the little secret lurking fear that Constance might have heard her when she stole in to take the key in the night. Doing that had been the one small inevitable risk. Of course, when Constance had turned over, she had remained motionless for nearly half an hour, and then withdrawn. She had left it till the next night, and then she had been *sure* that Constance had slept throughout. Quite sure. No needless risks for her. But she had always had that little lurking doubt that Constance might have heard her move, and have suspected...till she had heard the will. But she was sure now. If Constance had had the faintest, smallest doubt! She knew Constance too well for that.

She had told Constance at their first interview at the gaol that she believed the policeman had put it there himself, to fix her with the crime, and Constance had believed it, more or less. She was sure of that now. And how could Constance have suspected her when she did not know that she had ever met Mogson at all?

And Mogson had held his tongue—long enough. She had never owed him any gratitude for that. He had only done it in a faint hope that he would save his own neck, and then betrayed her later with the same object. He would have denied everything, if he hadn't been such a craven fool!

No—there was no fear from the law. No fear that it would move to her destruction in its heavy, deliberate, unimaginative, relentless way.

But she saw clearly that there was one fear, one difficulty, that she might have to meet. If her association with Mogson became a public tale, inferences might be drawn, whispers might pass. How would it sound to Bill? There could be no two opinions about that. But she saw that to be a risk which she could not alter, whether small or great, and put it aside the more easily with a resolute will. It would be time enough to think of that if it came. And the night must be half-gone and she had not slept! That was not the way to improve her health, or her looks. Fortunately, Inspector Cleveland could not know that he had cost her these hours of sleep. Fortunately, she had no need to rise till the hour of her own choice now. Thinking of that, could she doubt that she had done well?

The next morning she had another impulse. She came on the advertisement of summer tours in Switzerland in the hotel lounge. Why should she not go where, she supposed, this policeman would not be able to follow? Probably, if the opportunity of annoying her should cease, he would get busy with other things, and she could come back in peace before the time for which she planned, or Bill might come out to her there.

But could she be accused of attempting to fly, if she should do this? Could he, would he, attempt to stop her? Even to arrest her? She did not think so, but she was puzzled that he should hang about as he did. Suppose it were his aim to worry her into a panic flight, which might be twisted into an admission of guilt? With the thought, there came determination to face the issue in a bolder way. She would write to Bill, and tell him that the police were annoying her, and ask him that his firm should take it up. They might send him down to represent her, and ask the Inspector what he meant by the molestation from which she suffered. That would suit her plans in more ways than one.

And yet—would it? Would he not be certain to mention the acquaintance with Mogson, to tell him of the "confession"—the accusation that Mogson had made against her? He might be driven off, but the harm would remain. So she gave up the idea, but she was shrewd enough to hold to her resolution that she would face the Inspector with a legal witness. At the worst, if they should prosecute her (which she did not think), it would look well that she had challenged them in that way.

Coming back from a morning on the sands, she noticed the neat brass plate of Timothy J. Trewennick, Solicitor, Commissioner for Oaths, at the side of a door that opened on to the cobbled street. She would not enter on a sudden impulse, but went on to her lunch at the hotel, and after that (not too soon, for she must give Mr. Trewennick time to have his lunch also; she did not wish to make an abortive call) she went down the street, and entered the legal office, in full view of the Inspector who was strolling up from the shore.

CHAPTER XXXIII.

"I AM being annoyed by a policeman," Miss Hillier stated coming to the point with her usual directness.

The solicitor to whom she spoke, and who had received her name without obvious recognition or interest, was politely attentive. He was probably the only man in Trethegar who was not aware that his visitor was the sister of Constance Hillier and that she was now being watched by a detective from Scotland Yard. The explanation of this ignorance is that he was not Timothy J. Trewennick, who, for nearly fifty years, had been concerned, on one side or other, in every dispute that had arisen within ten miles of his High Street office, who had drawn more than half the wills, and received costs in almost all the bankruptcies of that considerable district. He was Jonathan, the son of Timothy, who had come down from London, where he was a junior partner in the firm of Tult, Tult, and Bettesley, to protect his father's practice while the old gentleman convalesced from an attack of arthritis which had finally overcome his obstinate determination not to absent himself from an office over which he had presided for nearly fifty unbroken years. But Jonathan Trewennick, after ten years in London, following the intermittent absences of school and college, was a stranger in his native town. He may have been liked for his father's sake, and not disliked for his own, but in speech, and manner, and attire he was as one of the invading aliens on whom the people of Trethegar lived, but with whom they had no confidences. Absorbed in mastering the various matters of which he had taken charge, and in the effort to modernize, as far as his intrusion permitted, the traditional methods of an office which, though it tolerated a telephone, had not yet permitted the introduction of a typewriter or a filing system, he had heard nothing of the excited gossip around him.

Now he looked at his well-dressed and not unattractive visitor with a somewhat preoccupied mind, and wondered vaguely what might be the nature of the annoyance which she was experiencing.

He saw that she was not a native. It was unlikely that she was complaining of the amorous advances of an uncongenial suitor. How else should a policeman annoy her? As he thought, he asked.

"How does he annoy you?"

"He follows me about."

"You have no idea why?"

"Yes. He pretends to believe that I was concerned in some way in my aunt's death. But I don't think that's any excuse, even if he does. I can't go on like this. I don't want to stay here always, and I don't want to seem to be running away from him. I want you to do something to make him stop."

"You'd better tell me from the beginning."

"There's really no more to tell. I suppose you know who I am. Everybody seems to. I'm Lady Catherine Middleditch's niece."

Mr. Trewennick's eyes opened to a livelier interest. He looked again at the name which the office-boy had laid before him. His thought went back to a case which was too recent, in which the public excitement had been too great, for its details to have left his mind. Yes, of course. The other niece. Probably more or less of a nervous wreck after the ordeal through which she had passed. And trying to fly from a publicity which must be almost intolerable to a sensitive mind. Poor woman. Imagining now that the police were pursuing her! Suppose they *had* shown a little special interest? What could it be, but in a kindly protective way? He supposed hysteria, but observed that she showed no certain sign of that condition. She looked a remarkably healthy young woman. And self-possessed. But, to a keen eve. worried. Yes, certainly worried.

"You'd better tell me all about it," he said in as fatherly a manner as can be promptly assumed by an unmarried man of thirty-three. "We'll see what we can do."

The tone irritated Margaret rather than soothed her. There was a note of asperity in her voice as she replied.

"It's just what I've said. I came here to get some peace, and in walk these two men."

"Two?"

"Yes. Inspector Cleveland, who had charge of the investigation before. He came with a man named Cross. A magistrate, he called him, and said that Mogson had accused me, and said that Constance was innocent."

"This was before Mogson was executed?"

"Yes—just before."

"And I suppose they questioned you about what he had said? Were there any questions that were—difficult to answer?"

"I don't know. They didn't get that far."

"You refused to answer their questions?"

"Yes, I told them to clear out. I came here to get some peace."

"I think, Miss Hillier, if I may say so, you acted with unusual discretion. And after that Mogson was executed."

The last remark was rather to himself than to her. He had a moment of reflective silence.

"And since then they have been following you about?"

"Inspector Cleveland has."

Mr. Trewennick thought again. He was not as clear as to the limits of police power as he would have liked to be. The police force (he knew) is only a century old. Its powers and numbers have been extended rapidly as a hundred years of restrictive legislation have struck their ceaseless blows at the individualities and freedoms of the English race. The work of disciplining them to the required patterns has required a semi-military force of some hundred thousand men, and it is almost impossible for the present generation to imagine a community which managed its own affairs. But the legal authorities of the organization are not clearly defined, and have been notoriously exceeded in recent years, particularly by the police of the Metropolitan area. This he knew, but what remedy, if any, might be in the hands of a citizen annoyed by a detective's observations was a point on which he found himself to be in some doubt.

His father would have expressed his ignorance without hesitation. He had gained a reputation for wisdom which he knew to be impregnably fortified. His son, being younger, was less quick to confess to anything less than omniscience. Had he been in his London office he would have said that it was a point on which he would take counsel's opinion. But he knew that that was not the custom in Trethegar Timothy Trewennick dispensed his own law. He would have risen in his accustomed way, and run his hand along one of the rows of law books which adorned three sides of his private office. He would have read oracular, incomprehensible, and possibly irrelevant words. He would probably have got the local police-superintendent on the telephone and discussed the position in a friendly but authoritative way.

His son asked diplomatically: "What would you like me to do?"

"I want him to say what he means, or else to leave me alone."

"Where is he now?"

"He's lodging over the confectioner's, at the Porth Street corner. At least, he comes out from there."

"You mean at Mrs. Evard's? I'll ring him up now, if you like, and see what he's got to say."

"I don't think he'll be in now. He was coming up the street, as I came in here."

"Very well, I'll try later. Do you mind telling me just what Mogson said, as far as they told it to you?"

"He said it was all lies that he swore at the trial, and that Constance hadn't done it at all, and that I had. Of course, it was only a last try to get a reprieve."

"No doubt. And it evidently failed. I thought you hadn't known him at all—if I recollect the case accurately.

"I did know him, but it didn't come out at the trial. No one asked," she added, as she observed a shade of gravity on the solicitor's face at this statement. "I told them I wasn't likely to shout it out."

"No—I suppose not. Well, leave it to me. If you look in tomorrow, I shall probably have something to report."

CHAPTER XXXIV.

INSPECTOR CLEVELAND declined to discuss the matter on the telephone. He said he would call.

He came about an hour later, having utilized the interval to get through to Mr. Whitaker, and acquaint him with the invitation he had received. He had been thinking over the case in the leisure of the last days, and while he had never had one in which it was more difficult to see how to proceed, he had never had one either which he would have felt more reluctant to leave. The more he reviewed the events of the arrest and trial, the more disposed he was to admit that a very terrible miscarriage of justice had occurred, and to blame himself as the cause. Ought he not to have taken Constance Hillier's denials more seriously? Why should he have assumed that Mogson was only known to her? A dispassionate verdict may exonerate him from any suggestion of negligence. The fatal packet being found in her drawer might have been less than conclusive, standing alone, but when Mogson admitted that he had given it to her, and when the circumstances of their meetings were considered—well, it is difficult to contend that he should have started a blind inquiry on the assumption that Mogson might have had a separate acquaintance with the other sister It is always the weakness of circumstantial evidence that no circumstance, and no set of circumstances, constitute a complete whole; they are tangled inextricably with others in an endless chain—and each modifies the significance of the rest. There are those who can tell the truth, and fewer who can tell nothing but the truth, but the whole truth is something that no one will ever tell.

He saw that, if he were to bring the one whom he now believed to be the real culprit to justice, it would mean a public acknowledgement of his previous error, and it is to his honour that he did not shrink from this possibility. But he was shrewd enough to see also that it would be a very difficult if not impossible thing to do, and that there might be reluctance on the part of his superiors, as a matter of public policy, to authorize such a prosecution, even though he might place the necessary evidence before them.

When he spoke to Mr. Whitaker, he asked for a free hand to conduct the investigation in his own way, and received this permission, on the obvious condition that no overt action would be taken against the remaining sister without the authority of the Home Office, to whom he was now directly responsible. Mr. Whitaker asked whether he thought it wise to discuss the matter with Margaret Hillier's solicitor in its present stage. But about this he had no doubt. It may often be well to avoid alarming a suspected criminal. But that question did not arise. Margaret Hillier was alert already. If he could alarm her into some indiscretion, he would be pleased to do so. He walked up the High Street to Mr. Trewennick's office at a brisk pace and with the grim expression on his mouth which had been ominous of the doom of many.

Mr. Trewennick Jr. received him affably. He alluded lightly to the weakness of feminine nerves, and the ordeal through which his client had passed. He felt confident that there was no intention of causing her any annoyance, and a word of assurance from the Inspector to that effect.

Inspector Cleveland did not respond to this mood. "Feels annoyed, does she?" he inquired. "As you've asked me here, I suppose you won't object to a straight talk?"

"No. Tell me what's on your mind, and we shall know where we are."

The Inspector paused, choosing his words. He was not a man of fluent speech. Now he said, with a slow deliberation: "I don't want to make another mistake. But I'm hoping to see that woman hanged."

Mr. Trewennick took this with an expressionless face, but his tone was more serious as he replied "*Another* mistake? Then you admit to one already?"

Again the Inspector was slow to answer. "Yes," he said at last, "I'm afraid I do. About the worst mistake that a man in my line can ever make. And it's too late to put it right now. Yes, I'll own to that."

Mr. Trewennick recognized the strength and honesty of the feeling which underlay this admission. His respect for Inspector Cleveland increased. His confidence in his own client may have diminished, but he held to the advocacy which he had undertaken.

"But if I am correctly informed, the whole basis of your present suspicion is an accusation from the lips of a man who was making a last desperate wriggle to escape the rope, and who must, on his own statement, have perjured himself up to the neck previously."

"No. It's more than that."

"And the tale of a man who's been hanged, so that you can't have taken it seriously enough yourself to keep him alive to answer to it?"

"That wasn't for me to decide. But I don't say Mogson's word, standing alone, would be worth much, dead or alive."

"What else is there?"

"I can't say that." (It was far better to frighten her with the vague suggestion of other evidence than to say that it was no more nor less than that she could be identified as having been in Mogson's company.)

"Very well. I can't press that, of course. What I do ask is whether my client is supposed to be under any form of restraint. She doesn't mean to stay here all her life, and she doesn't mean to make herself liable to be accused of running away."

"She's not under arrest."

"Then she's free to go where she will? To France or Switzerland, for example?"

"I don't know that I should advise her to try that."

"That isn't quite what I asked."

"I'm afraid it's all the answer I can give."

"I see. Well, if she decides to go, you'll understand that you've been told in advance. She's not running away."

"No, she's no fool. I've never thought she was that."

Inspector Cleveland went.

The next morning Margaret called again at Mr. Trewennick's office, and heard the substance of this conversation.

"What do you advise me to do?" she asked with her usual directness, and without comment upon it.

"I can't recommend you to go abroad, if you are confident that you have nothing really to fear. It might lead to an unpleasant experience, at the least. Suppose you were refused permission to land at a French port? Such things may be arranged. I doubt whether you can do better than to remain here for a time, and then go back to London. You can let me know if the Inspector should be any real annoyance. You can't prevent him taking a holiday here. It would only make it more conspicuous if you move from place to place, and he's always in the next compartment."

Margaret thanked him, and went. She noticed that he made no motion to shake hands, and the omission stirred her to a sudden rage as she walked back to the hotel. She would never enter that office

154

again! But the next moment her anger changed to a mood that was almost terror. If she could not maintain her self-control better than that!

In the end she resolved that she would stay where she was, and tire the Inspector out. After all, what could he do, hanging about here? If he thought to frighten her, he would learn, sooner or later, what a fool he was.

So she stayed on until one morning she had a letter from Mr. Risdon which changed her plans. She wired that she would be at his office at 4:00 P.M. the next day, which was the appointment that he proposed.

CHAPTER XXXV.

MR. RISDON'S letter was short and noncommittal. It was not one to excite alarm under normal circumstances in a normal mind. It said:

DEAR MISS HILLIER,

Constance Hillier, deceased.

Would you kindly arrange to call at these offices at 4:00 P.M. on Thursday next to discuss a matter of importance which has arisen.

Yours faithfully,

RISDON AND CLARKE

But Margaret Hillier was already worried by the following shadow of a crime which she had thought to leave behind her for ever when the drop fell beneath Thomas Mogson's feet. She had never liked Mr. Risdon, from the first time when she had heard him take down without protest the terms of a will which would have left her sister and herself unprovided, and had coldly declined the opportunity for a subsequent conversation which she had contrived to offer. She had always felt that he did not like her.

Now she wondered what sinister "matter of importance" could have arisen in connection with her sister's will. It was true that the letter did not forecast anything of an unfortunate character. But what matter could arise of a satisfactory kind and sufficiently important to justify a request that she should return to London to hear it?

After dismissing less probable suppositions, she decided that Inspector Cleveland, or his superiors, were at work again. Believing her to be the murderess of her aunt, as they professed to do, might

156

they not have taken some action which would deprive her of the fruit of her crime? She was too ignorant of the legal issues involved to judge the probability of such procedure, or its results, but she reacted to this new fear with the fierce courage of a cornered wolf. The money was *hers, hers*. They could prove nothing, *nothing*, let them hint and whisper as they would. So she lay and thought through the night. The darkness hid the lift of a snarling lip, which distorted her face to an instant of some primeval ferocity, as she turned in imagination upon the pursuit of the tireless hounds. Was it for this she had sinned? To be poor again, and with the horror of that surrounding whisper that would not cease, that she was a murderess who was beyond the law?

No, she saw now, as she had seen from the first, that she must face this menace boldly, or it would bear her down. She must outface this new danger of her imagination, and overcome it, or it would have been better for her to be in the grave where her sister lay. She would tell Risdon to fight—to fight for that which was hers, to the last ditch.

But would he fight for her? Would he not ask for funds, if her own, which were still entirely in his control, were menaced, and from where could they be found? She had no confidence in Mr. Risdon's goodwill.... Perhaps it would be better for her to consult another solicitor. She might see Mr. Trewennick before she left. But she rejected this possibility. Deep in her inarticulated thought she knew that, since his interview with Inspector Cleveland, he had believed her to be—that which she was, that which it was intolerable that she should be thought to be. She felt that suspicion was round her like a thickening mist. Of course, there was Bill. She did not want him to know anything of this trouble, or of Mogson's dying accusation against her. But if it had got to be, it could not be told too frankly, nor too soon. She would go to his firm for help, for them to take up her case. If she could make Bill think she was wronged, if she could make a new call on the generous sympathy that had responded so well before, it might even be the means of strengthening a bond which she felt instinctively that her absence weakened. And Bill had come into money—much or little—and might be able to champion her cause in a way that Mr. Risdon would be unlikely to undertake.

On this resolution she slept, and the next day, being Wednesday, she looked up the trains and found that, if she left sufficiently early on Thursday, she would arrive at Paddington at 3:45 P.M. She wrote to Risdon and Clarke that she would keep the appointment, though she might be a few minutes late.

CHAPTER XXXVI.

TRETHEGAR, as we know, is at the terminus of a branch line, and travellers to London must change for the express at the junction, ten miles away. The single local train brings in those who have come down by the night express, and returns to the junction station with the morning passengers who are going up.

Margaret arrived at the station in good time, and in fairly good spirits. She had succeeded in persuading herself that she had probably misinterpreted the ambiguity of Mr. Risdon's letter. The morning was bright and pleasantly cool. She was of a disposition to be of improved spirits when the moment for action comes, and she felt some confidence that she would be able to deal successfully with whatever difficulty she might be going to meet. She was conscious of the increased vitality that had come to her from these weeks of rest and good feeding in the Cornish air. Her step, which had always been brisk, was buoyant now. Her appetite, which had always been good, had a keenness which she had never known during the narrow servitude, and occasional unhealthy pleasures, of the old hateful days. The very fact that she was about to take the journey to London, and was able to do so at her own will, was an exciting pleasure to one confined and limited as she had been through so many of her youthful years. Inspector Cleveland had thought to bluff her, and had brought his witness in vain. He had tried to frighten her by hanging about, and had given up a useless attempt (she had seen nothing of him during the past week). Now she would go back to London, and would get this matter of Risdon's off her mind (probably it was really nothing at all!) and would see Bill, and resume the ascendancy that she had found so easy when he had sympathized with her in her lonely trouble. If there were really anything serious with Risdon—well, she would have the better reason for appealing to Bill!

But there were two incidents at the station to disturb her serenity. She was on the single platform as the little fussy local train steamed into the station, and was standing not ten yards away when Tommy Parrott got out.

With commendable coolness, she turned quietly away, without pause or haste, and strolled through the throng of waiting or alighting passengers till she was at the further end of the train. There she got in, and took a quick glance along the platform, which by that time was comparatively vacant. As she expected, Tommy Parrott was no longer there. That, she thought, was a good escape. She had no wish to be recognized by him as Thomas Mogson's one-time companion. But what was he doing here? Had the Inspector sent for him to identify her? The idea was not of a comforting kind, though she could still smile at the annoyance it would be, if that were so, to find that she had left as he arrived. But then she had another shock, and must readjust her ideas again, as Inspector Cleveland came along the platform, and, without appearing to see her, got into the next compartment.

By this time, the engine had been reversed, and the train commenced its hard-puffing, laborious return to the junction-station. When it got there, the express was already in. Margaret had no more than time to transfer herself and her luggage, and she settled down into a corner of a rather crowded compartment without knowing whether the Inspector were still following her.

But, in fact, he had not seen her. His thoughts were on other things. The fact was that he would not have stayed so long in Trethegar had his mind not been diverted by another matter. After his interview with Mr. Trewennick he had decided that he was wasting his time where he was, and that he would have a better prospect of obtaining additional evidence against Miss Hillier (poor though it might be) if he were to resume his inquiries as to her relations with Thomas Mogson, commencing with their admitted visits to the Merrythought Club. He could easily arrange for the local police to keep her under observation, and to inform him of any move she might make. That was all he could do, if he remained himself. Even if she were about to leave the country, he had no authority to interfere.

But just as he had reached this resolve, he happened to come upon a local resident whose appearance reminded him forcibly of a man against whom he held a warrant that was nearly ten years old. He was one of the four men who had been concerned in the famous Glaston bank frauds of 1921. Three of them had been arrested and sentenced, but neither the fourth man, nor the money, had been traced. He had waited patiently, thinking that when, at the end of four or six years, the other men were released, they would get in touch with him, or he with them. Probably there would be the plunder to be shared. But the closest watch on these men had been fruit-less, nor did they show any sign of having money at their disposal. It had always been said that the missing man had escaped to the Continent, and so, it was concluded, he must have done. But Inspector Cleveland always kept him in mind, with a dozen others whom he would be pleased to meet. Now he thought he had seen him, and he resolved at once to stay in the district while the excuse that he was watching Margaret Hillier enabled him to follow another trail without the necessity of asking leave at the Yard, or communicating his suspicion to anyone. With a pardonable human weakness, he desired to avoid the risk of reporting an unfounded suspicion, or otherwise to have the credit of an unaided capture.

It was in this connection that he had boarded the local train that morning, which he had left at the Junction, and Margaret's fears and suspicions were doubly wrong as she sat in her crowded corner, for though he was not on the train, Tommy Parrott was.

Tommy had seen her as she turned away, though he had given no sign. He had passed on into the booking-office, and observed her from that convenient refuge. He had not come to see Inspector Cleveland. He desired few things less. The sight of him boarding the train was an unwelcome complication. But, at the last minute, he followed. At the Junction, he observed with satisfaction that the Inspector left the station, and that Margaret continued the journey to London. Nothing could have happened better for him. He had come solely to see her, and had not hoped that he would be able to use the return half of his ticket so promptly.

He spoke to one of the attendants in the dining-car. He gave an accurate enough description of Margaret Hillier, though it was not one that she would have cared to hear. He was exact as to where she sat. If she asked for a lunch ticket (as she probably would) he wanted to be next to her, at a single table. The attendant looked dubious. Tommy Parrott did not inspire confidence at a casual glance. A ten-shilling note passed. He became more hopeful. Another was promised. It could probably be arranged.

CHAPTER XXXVII.

TOMMY PARROTT had not always been the manager of a night-club of the baser sort, drawing his salary on the uncomfortable understanding that he must be the one to accept responsibility, and go to gaol, if bribery and luck and evasion failed, and fines should be considered inadequate penalties.

He had once claimed to belong to the honourable profession of journalism. His activities in that direction had been of a peculiar kind. He would study the life of one of his fellow citizens diligently, preferring one who had encountered adverse circumstance in his domestic or commercial experiences, or whose position or character was such as to render him particularly susceptible to any hostile publicity.

He would then write a biographical article in which he would exhibit a practised skill in the statement of half-truths in such a manner as to convey sinister inferences which a close and logical analysis might fail to reveal as being there at all, or in the isolation of a selected fact which might be in itself beyond denial, but which would contain implications absolutely contrary to those of the complete circumstances to which it belonged. He would then call upon the subject of these biographical details and explain that he had written an article for which the editor of *Jack Sprat* would pay him £30. He was a poor man. He could not afford to destroy an article of such a saleable nature. But he was indifferent as to who should purchase it from him....

There had been no deception in these statements. If the offer were declined, the article would appear in *Jack Sprat*, and Tommy Parrott would receive a cheque for £30 from the editor of that periodical. Tommy throve until he encountered an individual who lacked either the good sense to kick him out, or the complacency to purchase his composition. He made a second appointment, at which he promised that the money would be in readiness. But he was not a straightforward man. There was a cupboard in his room large enough to hold a detective, and on the second occasion a detective was there. Tommy got three years to think it over. When the Editor of *Jack Sprat* heard about it, he was extremely surprised. He said he had always regarded Tommy Parrott as being an exceptionally high-minded man.

Tommy came out of gaol a considerably healthier man than he had gone in, but his business was ruined. During six industrious years, he had built up a connection which could be relied upon to contribute more or less regularly to his income in return for his continued efforts not only in self-restraint, but to avert the activities of his journalistic acquaintances. A sound business instinct warned him that these springs of sustenance were dried up for ever. He looked round for other fields of activity where his peculiar talents would be appreciated, and became the manager of the Merrythought Club.

When Inspector Cleveland had strolled into the Club on the Saturday afternoon which was to be the last of Thomas Mogson's life, and said: "I want a word with you, Tommy," in that abrupt manner which was so bad for the nerves, and Tommy had led the way to his private room, he had not been surprised at all when the Inspector's hand had abstracted a fat black pocket-book from the breast of his coat, and it had been with a very pleasant reaction that, instead of the expected slip of white paper which would invite him to one of those expensive interviews with a stipendiary magistrate which are so difficult to refuse, he had drawn out a portrait of Thomas Mogson, with the laconic inquiry: "Seen him before?"

Tommy Parrott had a good memory for faces, as his occupation required. He knew all about Mogson's visits to his club, though he had concluded too readily that the Miss Hillier who had accompanied him had been the same one who had been known to do so at the Yellow Cat. He had debated whether he should endeavour to acquire merit by reporting these visits to Scotland Yard, but his natural aversion to any avoidable contact with the police, and a faint disinclination to betray a customer without being sure of any substantial benefit to himself, had combined to produce a state of hesitation which had never reached the point of decision which a voluntary action requires. So he had let the days pass. Now he had the adroitness to shape his recollection to the Inspector's satisfaction without the risk of incurring blame for his past silence. Recognize the portrait? Rather. Prepared to swear to him anywhere, or the young woman who used to come with him. He gave details of appearance, clothes, and manners. That was Thomas Mogson, who had been convicted in the Middleditch case? Not *really*? Who'd have thought it? He *was* surprised. Keep his mouth shut? Of course. Anything to oblige the

Inspector. He turned the conversation to the exceptionally innocent character of the establishment over which he presided. Had Inspector Cleveland noticed how well it had been conducted since that last little unfortunate episode, when he had admitted that his control had not been quite so strict as the law, and his own proprietors, desired? Did the Inspector know that some of the shares were now held by a second cousin of the Home Secretary? The Inspector had replied unsympathetically that second cousins are queer fish, now and then. He had repeated his warning, and gone. Tommy Parrott had considered this visit in an alert and curious but very cautious mind.

He considered the fact that Constance Hillier was hanged. The police could hardly want to know anything further about *her*. By the following Tuesday he was able to observe that Thomas Mogson was hanged also. They could hardly want to know anything more about him. And why was he to keep a closed mouth? He began to examine the problem with the patient thoroughness which he had developed in the days of his journalistic prosperity. He procured the back numbers of Sunday papers reporting the trial. As he looked at the crude representation of the younger sister, he almost heard the voice of Thomas Mogson. "*Come on, Maggie.*" That was what he had called her. Margaret, of course.

Tommy Parrott, possessed of this surprising information, had done nothing for several weeks. Except think. Even then, he did not guess all the truth, but he got near it in several particulars. He concluded that Thomas Mogson had confessed, and that, in some way, the confession had implicated Margaret in the crime. He watched for her arrest, which did not occur. He considered the significance of the fact that Mogson had not been kept alive. He concluded that, whatever the police might suspect or know, they lacked legal evidence on which to proceed. It did not occur to him that Constance might have been innocent, but he supposed that Margaret was under suspicion as being a party to the crime.

He reflected also that Margaret must now be a wealthy woman. When wealthy women are in trouble, it is often profitable to be hanging around. They may pay, even for the information that trouble is liable to come. They will pay for other things. He did not forget the Inspector's admonition that he should hold his tongue. It was a policy which it suited him to observe. But that was not inconsistent with a discreet inquiry as to where Margaret Hillier was now living. He did not control the resources of Scotland Yard, but he had others, which were not contemptible. The man who received a five-pound note to ascertain her address was puzzled as to why Tommy should require it, but failed to guess. You can't blackmail anyone whose troubles have been advertised in the Press already. At least, so he supposed.

Tommy gave it a few more days' thought, and decided that it was worth the risk.

In all this we may observe, if we will, the superiority of the judgement of Mr. Whitaker, whose first decision would have been to bury Thomas Mogson's confession in the usual silence, instead of starting inquiries which might lead in the end to who could say what of embarrassing publicity? He may have been somewhat deflected in his subsequent judgement, or he would have called off Inspector Cleveland more promptly, but that only shows the trouble that may result when amateurs interfere. Besides, the harm had been done by then.

CHAPTER XXXVIII.

THE attendant brought Tommy Parrott a ticket for the first lunch. "The lady's," he said in a discreet whisper, "is No. 23." The ticket which he handed over was No. 24. Tommy sat still for a time. He did not wish to be in his place before her. She might say that she did not like the seat when she observed his presence, and seek accommodation elsewhere. Let her be at least halfway through the soup....

She did not notice him when he sat down. Her eyes wandered from her plate to the Wiltshire fields. She declined to recognize him, even when she gave him a casual glance. He saw that he must open the conversation. The time was not unlimited. There was a second lunch to follow.

He said: "Excuse me, Miss Hillier, is it not?"

He spoke in a professionally friendly voice, which had been part of the regular equipment of his earlier business. Margaret looked at him for one bewildered, frightened moment before she answered. (Did everyone know her now? Would she always have this sudden quickening of the heart at the unexpected sound of her spoken name?) She looked at the small, rotund, gross-featured man with the curiously bulging forehead, and said coldly, "You were at the Merrythought Club, were you not?" She knew it to be a foolish thing, even as she said it. Why mention the club? Why admit that she had been there, or that she knew this man at all?

She was even more annoyed at a note of diffidence, if not of anxiety, of which she was aware in her own voice. Of what had she to be afraid? And she had never been lacking in courage when a crisis came. But this had been so unexpected. Her self-control had been warned to be in readiness for the interview at 4:00 P.M., or earlier if it should encounter Inspector Cleveland, but this attack had taken it off its guard.

"Yes," he said cheerfully, "I remember when you used to come with Mogson often enough. You must be glad to know that business is over. What a capable officer Inspector Cleveland seems to be."

Margaret answered in a monosyllable, as she gave the waiter an order. She gave Mr. Parrott no further glance. She had herself well in hand now, He saw that he must be more explicit in attack if he were to bring the conversation to the point he would.

"I'd like a talk with you some time, Miss Hillier. This isn't the best place, but I don't suppose we'd be overheard. Not with the noise of the train."

She had a thought that Mogson's sudden arrest might have left an unpaid bill for which he wished to make her responsible. "I don't see why you shouldn't say anything you want now."

"Of course," he began easily, "we never give our guests away. It's the first rule of a club like ours. But it hasn't been an easy thing, in a case like yours, as you may suppose. There are too many that know."

"Know what?" she asked with a curt directness that made him wonder for a moment whether he had misread the earlier symptoms. Perhaps she was not going to be so easy a victim as he had thought. But he felt that the end was sure.

"Of course, Miss Hillier," he answered indirectly, and with a ready mendacity, "you're not the kind of lady that's forgotten easily. There's too many at our place who remember you now. That's been the trouble all along. And with the Press willing to pay. Well, you can see what it's been to us. But I shouldn't have said anything about that. Only now, with the police coming round again.... "

"When?"

He met the curt monosyllable and the challenge of the hard inquiring eyes without losing the assurance of his manner, or changing the ingratiating intimacy of his tone.

"Inspector Cleveland came round himself a few weeks ago. Of course, it makes talk, and with the Press ready to pay.... I thought I'd better find out what you'd wish me to do."

Margaret thought rapidly. The last information relieved her mind of part of its earlier fear. There was no new move by the police. Inspector Cleveland must have called there before he intruded upon her at the hotel. The fact that the man admitted that it was some weeks ago was a relief. It also inclined her to give him more credence than she might otherwise have done.

Keeping to the train of thought in her own mind, and still holding him off, she asked again:

"Nothing since then?"

166

"No. I wouldn't say that there has. But I ought never to have mentioned that. If he was to get to know.... It's not a thing I would have done, if we didn't always put our own people first."

There was a fraction of truth in this also, which gave some sincerity to his voice. He would, indeed, be perturbed if Inspector Cleveland should know that he had given him away. But he had not anticipated such a possibility. Did not still, though he felt increasingly aware of having taken on an unusually difficult subject.

There was an interval of silence. Margaret went on with her lunch, as though there were nothing more to be said. Her parry had turned the point of his last sentence, and he saw that it must be repeated.

"I thought I'd better ask what you'd like us to do?"

"Do?" she asked vaguely. She may have understood more than she showed, but she was would give him no help. She was not of a kind to be deceived easily by such as he. She knew how much of real kindliness he had to offer, to her or to any.

"I mean, there are a good many employed at the club. We can't make them all keep their mouths shut, unless it's worth their while. The Press will always pay for a good tale."

"I don't see that there's much to tell."

"Oh, well, if you look at it like that...."

He almost contrived to hide the disappointment in his voice, the more easily that he only half-believed in the sincerity of her attitude. Had she said no more, she might have freed herself from that annoyance. But she thought: "If there's anything more published like there was before, and Bill sees it, as of course he will." She remembered that she had never told him of her association with Mogson. Implicitly, she had denied it a hundred times. If the tale had got to be told, as perhaps it might, she must do so from her angle with some excuse of loyalty to her sister to explain her silence. But if he learnt it first in the way that it would be handled in the *Sunday Press*. She said weakly: "I suppose they oughtn't to lose, if they don't talk. How much ought they to have?"

That was more like the expected tone. He concealed his exultation without difficulty, for that was a long-practised art. How much should he venture to ask? Not that it mattered much. It was the start that was the main thing. After that....

"Well, a hundred might do for now."

"A hundred pounds! I haven't got twenty."

She had not thought of such sums. She had no idea of what the Press paid. Her idea had been of distributing nothing more than some good tips to servants at the club who had remembered her, and

167

had been sufficiently loyal to hold their tongues. She might have gone to five pounds, and thought it well spent, though she would have grudged even that, for she was not of a generous kind. There are some who spend shillings with care, but who will give pounds with an open hand: there are others who spend carelessly on themselves, but to whom a small gift will seem a large sum. Margaret was of the second kind.

"But you could get it?"

"I don't know that I could." ("And I shouldn't either," she thought venomously, "Does he think I'm a fool?")

It wasn't true that her resources were less than £20. She had reserves. But it was true that the sums which Mr. Risdon had sent had been of quite moderate amount. The estate was not yet realized. Heavy death duties must be provided. So he had explained, before she had left London. But any money she might need from week to week.... She had "needed" a good deal, and now had a full note-case and about £27 in the bank. She had written for another fifty nearly a week ago. No doubt, he would give it to her this afternoon. Or—she put the doubt from her mind.

"I don't think I could get much," she answered, after a pause, of the length of which she was hardly conscious. "There are death duties and things; that comes first. I don't know why I should either. I don't mind giving them five pounds."

Mr. Parrott explained. He saw that he had hooked his prey, and could haul in the line with a leisurely skill, limited only by the fact that they were at the cheese-and-biscuits stage. He ordered coffee for two, while he explained the huge sums which the Press would pay for such a tale as that she had consorted with Mogson without her sister's knowledge, and that it had not come out at the trial. It would be difficult, but if he had twenty pounds he would do his best.

"It's no good giving it, if I'm not sure," she said, with some return to her first asperity, and he found he had gone too far, and had to give her explicit assurances of the authority he would exercise, and the conditions on which he would hand over the money to these imaginary clamourers, before she drew the pocket cheque-book from her bag, and commenced to write.

He viewed the cheque with the disfavour of an experienced blackmailer. "You'd better make it to self and endorse it," he exclaimed hastily.

"Why?"

"You don't want the bank to see that you're paying money to me. You don't want anyone to be able to prove that."

That was true. Neither did he. They were at one on that point. With another hasty exclamation he prevented her crossing the cheque. He examined it with a practised swiftness, as he folded it, and put it away. Thank Heaven, it was on a London bank. He thought that there would be many of such cheques in the years to come, and for better amounts than that. But he didn't flatter himself that they would be over easy to get. No, he wouldn't call her a good milker. You had to watch all the time, or she'd kick the pail.

CHAPTER XXXIX.

THE interview left Margaret without cause for any immediate anxiety from that quarter, but it had been a strain on nerves and temper which rendered her less fit than she might otherwise have been for the further ordeal that was before her.

It had concluded with a little incident which Tommy Parrott considered had been very neatly executed. When the head waiter had come round to make out the bills, he had said "Both in one," with a careless wave of the cigar which he had now lighted to celebrate his success. But the next minute, before the return procession on which the money would be collected, he had risen, and left the car. Margaret, her mind too occupied at the moment to notice the unpaid bill, had been thankful to see him go.

When she did, she had an impulse to send the waiter to find him. But she did not know where he might be on the train. She must avoid, above all things, any dispute which would bring them into a common prominence. The sense that she had been duped over this petty amount swept her with a sudden tempest of anger, so sudden and fierce that her hand trembled as she drew out her note-case to discharge the bill.

The sudden ungovernable anger frightened her, as it had done once before. Self-control, she told herself, above all, self-control was that which her welfare, even her safety, needed. But she had wanted to get away! To separate herself for ever from a dead, most hateful past! Had she been able to do this, might she have become a good wife, perhaps a good mother, under fairer, more favourable conditions of life? How many must there be who have looked over the very edge of the pit of guilt, and been deterred by fear, or prevented by circumstance, and have gone on, unconscious of abnormality, and honoured by those among whom their afterlives have passed? How many have sinned, even to the taking of life, by a crime which has remained unguessed, and may afterwards have expiated it in a long repentance, or put its memory away with a firm will? A mistake. A wrong. An unrepeatable thing. But irrevocable, also. And what use is regret for that which we cannot change?

A man may hesitate on the impulse of violent crime, and a trifle, a mood, a meal, may decide it. "Well," he will say to himself the next day, "I'm thankful I didn't do that. But, of course, I didn't mean to. Not really. Though I was mad enough to do almost anything at the time. But I shouldn't really have done that." And he goes on as before. He will be just a normal, ordinary man till his life's end.

Or else—the scale tilts so slightly further on the other side, the event is so slightly different, the provocation, the mood, the temptation, or the opportunity, so slightly varied. And in one moment there is the unalterable thing. And nothing will ever be the same again.

Margaret Hillier had not sinned on impulse, but with a steady will. Yet her instinct had been sound when the end had come, to cut herself loose from sight or memory of a closed and hated thing. Her moral nature had acted as would the body struggling for air beneath a suffocating weight. It must get free—get free! Had she been able to do this— She was not of those who find it hard to forget. She did not find self-explanation and self-forgiveness hard. Her aunt was better dead. Anyone could see that. And if the law *would* interfere! It was no use blaming her. If it had left them, Constance and she might both have been enjoying life now, and nothing have happened to stain their names, or to trouble their peace. She had done it for the good of both, but if one of two has *got* to be hanged—well, you wouldn't let it be you, if it could be helped? Now would you?

No, she was not of a temperament that would get thin with worry over an ended thing. She would have made full use of her gains, and, as to the rest of her life, it might have been well enough, or even better than that. Who can say?

But she was not destined to know. The past had her in a relentless grip. It was like a steel trap on her leg. She had felt the bite of its teeth for the first time when she had snarled in the night. And she could feel them still, though she might summon courage enough to pretend that they were not there.

CHAPTER XL.

THERE was a quiet happiness in the eyes of Violet Scovell, as she entered Mr. Risdon's room, and shook hands, wishing him good afternoon in the voice which was usual to her with those she liked, and with whom she felt fully at ease. It had a note of sincerity, of being personally meant, which rendered it something more than the empty form that conventionality required.

She, surely, was not troubled by any anticipations as to what Mr. Risdon might have to say at this interview to which he had invited the two beneficiaries under Constance Hillier's will.

"Grandfather asked me to say that he would like to see you as soon as you can arrange to come. Any morning after ten-thirty. He wants to make some change in his will...oh, no, he's not worse. He's seemed much better the last few days."

Mr. Risdon had a moment of hesitation. Had he known this earlier.... It was partly the form of the Earl of Weyford's will, and the critical nature of his illness, that had influenced him to the decision that had caused him to propose this meeting. Even now, it would not be too late. He could make some plausible excuse as to some matter on which he had wished to consult. But no, he would not change his purpose again. He was not one to take a decision lightly, or to alter it when it had been made. He would go on as he had resolved.

"Miss Hillier has written that she will be here, but I think she may be a little late. Her train was due at 3:45."

They talked on indifferent topics for a few minutes. He knew just what had to be said. Even the words had been rehearsed in his mind. And he was not going to say it twice.

At 4:15 Margaret came. Yes, she said, her train had been late. She looked worried. Now that the moment had come, she had a nervous dread of what she might be about to hear. It was with a conscious effort of will that she controlled her fear, and answered Violet's friendly trivial questions as to the weather, and her enjoyment of the Cornish coast.

Mr. Risdon commenced at once, when they were seated, to explain the reason for which he had asked them to meet him together. He spoke with the unemotional exactness which had become the habit not only of his business, but of his private life, and it would have been difficult to believe, even by one who had the knowledge that his hearers lacked, that he was about to make a confession which might involve the loss of his own reputation and liberty, or any consequences of magnitude to those who heard it.

"I am sure," he began, "that you will understand that I should not have troubled you to meet me in this way, if there had not been a matter of importance which it has become my duty to lay before you, and which will involve some explanation to which I must ask, in justice to myself, as well as for other reasons, that you will give very careful attention. I am sorry that I cannot explain the position that has now arisen without going back to the events of fifteen years ago, more or less, when I was left, by the decease of my senior partners, as the sole proprietor of the business. You may, or may not know, that the death of Mr. Clarke occurred about a year after that of my father. While they both lived, my father had dealt with what I may describe to you as the estate department, chancery and conveyancing work, and Mr. Clarke had handled the common law business, and had been, as far as I then knew, and as subsequent evidences indicated, in entire charge of the books and the financial side of the firm. For the year following my father's death, Mr. Clarke was entirely in charge. I was legally a junior partner. Actually, I was no more than a clerk. It is due to myself that I should make that clear.

"When Mr. Clarke suddenly and unexpectedly died, I found myself in sole charge. I had to take up and unravel all the financial responsibilities of the firm, of which I had known nothing previously, while carrying on the practice. At that time the affairs of your grandfather, Miss Scovell, the Earl of Weyford, had been unreservedly in our hands for many years, and his securities were, or should have been, deposited with our own bankers.

"A position had, however, arisen through which it was necessary to marshal the resources of the estate for the purpose of paying off certain mortgages that had been called in, and making a general charge upon it. The alternative was to sell a portion of the estate, which the Earl was unwilling to consider.

"But when I went into the matter I found that some of the securities were not there, and others had had charges created upon them the cause for which, or the use to which the money had been put, were not easy to understand.

"Finally, I found a little book in a secret drawer in Mr. Clarke's desk which left no doubt of what had occurred. The confidence of the Earl had been abused, and his securities had been used to supply funds for the use of the firm. Even now I do not know for what purpose this money had been used, or how the deficiency had arisen.

"But the fact was plain, and the deficiency was a very substantial sum. I saw, at first, no alternative but to disclose a deficiency which would, of course, have been ruinous to the reputation of this firm, though I might have had no moral responsibility, and which would also have placed the Earl in a position of great and unexpected embarrassment. While I hesitated, Lady Catherine Middleditch, having quarrelled with her previous solicitors, placed her affairs in my hands. Her physical condition, and the unreserved confidence which your family had always placed in our firm, gave me an opportunity of which, rightly or wrongly, I took advantage. I pledged or realized sufficient of Lady Catherine's securities to adjust the deficiency in those of the Earl of Weyford, resolving that the major portion of the future income of the firm should be devoted, from year to year, to the adjustment of this new deficiency which I had created. I resolved that I would not marry, nor draw more than £400 per annum (actually I have drawn less than that), until the deficiency should be made good, if I should be so fortunate as to have the necessary time allowed me to do so. It is due to myself, in view of the statement of the present position to which I am leading, that I should make these facts clear."

He paused for a second, and Margaret's voice interrupted, sharp with the anxiety of a rising fear. "Are you going to tell us that the money's gone?"

She had heard the first sentences with some relief, as it became clear that she had not been asked there to hear that the law was moving against her, to deprive her of the benefit of her sister's will. But this slow explanation was a torture to hear. She had a dreadful growing suspicion that it was to end with a cold-blooded statement that the money for which she had risked so much was a vanished thing, and it was not to be his fault at all! Of course not! He would give his slow, precise explanation, and tell them they were penniless, and show them to the door, and that would be the end of *that*. Of course, *he* would have done no wrong. You wouldn't be able to touch *him*. And you could starve for all he'd care. Probably he'd rather like it than not. She didn't believe a word he said. He was just a clever rogue. That was what she had always thought. But why didn't he come to the point? When his voice paused, she could wait no longer. She must know I But she was not to know yet.

"I think, Miss Hillier, that I must ask your patience while I explain this in my own way. I shall not be long." (But why not tell them at once in a straightforward way? She would have broken in again, but remembered the resolution she had formed. She must be calm. It is when you lose control that you let slip the foolish word, that you cannot recall. To keep cool. What was he saying now?) "And during that time the amount was reduced each year. Sometimes by a few hundred, sometimes by over a thousand pounds. Had Lady Catherine lived, there is little doubt that a time would have come when it would have been adjusted entirely. Had I died, there is insurance, which would have been sufficient for that purpose.

"But the fact is that the death of Lady Catherine, coming when it did, under the circumstances that we all know, found me with a deficiency of nearly £5,000. It was an amount which I could not hope to adjust within the period which is allowed to an executor for realization—"

"You mean the money's about that much short?" Margaret interrupted.

"I am coming to the present position. You will understand that, during all these years, I have had to consider what my position would become, if circumstances should arise such as would require me to find the whole of the missing amount. I was unwilling—perhaps you can understand that—after so long a struggle, to contemplate the possibility that I might be defeated at last. I often considered the possibilities of speculation to relieve me promptly and finally from the shadow under which I lived. But I rejected a course so hazardous, feeling that I had no right to attempt it, even when I saw those around me enriching themselves in periods of boom. I determined that I would only resort to such an expedient as a last resort. But I made a diligent and regular study of stock exchange fluctuations, so that I might fit myself to engage in such operations with a reasonable prospect of success, should it appear that there was no alternative, apart from such an explanation as I am making now.

"When Lady Catherine died, and I considered the deficiency that still remained, I felt that that emergency was upon me. Had her life continued for a few years, all would have been well. But it is useless to regret that. But the course which I took was to draw upon the money which was in the bank, as soon as probate had been obtained, and to utilize other sums which were already under my control, and to apply them as cover for certain speculative operations by which I hoped to make a sufficient profit to relieve me of any further anxiety.

"You will anticipate that I did not succeed, or I should not be explaining the position, as I now am." Margaret looked at her cousin. Violet's face was anxious and pale. Beyond that, it gave no sign of her thoughts. But the tumult of wrath and anger and indignation in Margaret's mind was beyond further repression. She could no longer doubt that these measured deliberate sentences were leading by a slow torture to the confession which must sooner or later come, that the money was lost. And when there came that maddening hint—with an implication to her own mind which he could not guess—that all would have been well had her aunt lived for a few further years, it was beyond the limit of the self-control that she was so hardly exercising.

Looking at Violet, she said, with a bitter anger in her voice: "I don't think we need listen to any more. It seems to be a case for the police."

Violet did not answer for a moment. Her mind had been following Mr. Risdon's explanation with its own anxiety, and she looked vaguely at Margaret for a moment before she answered. She had supposed, even sooner than her cousin, that there was adverse financial news to be faced, because she had had no alternative fear as to what might have occurred. She saw, as the explanation proceeded, that she might have to go back and tell her grandfather that all the hopes which had been built upon this extra money being available must be cast away. If it were anyway possible, of course he must not be told. It was to this lifting of his financial worries that she attributed his improved health. It was owing to the prospect of this money that he wanted Mr. Risdon to revise his will. Probably he would have to be told. But if so, she wished to be able to give a lucid and accurate explanation. One that would not worry him more than would be inevitable. And she knew that she was very ignorant of financial matters. She wanted to listen and understand. Of course, she was sorry for Mr. Risdon's troubles, as far as she understood them, but it was of her grandfather's disappointment that her mind was primarily concerned.

"The police?" she said vaguely. "But they couldn't do anything in a case like this."

She spoke without conscious ambiguity. It seemed a silly suggestion. The police wouldn't offer to make good the deficiency. They wouldn't arrest the missing money, and bring it back.

Margaret stared at her. It seemed such a silly remark to make I She said: "But, of course they could. It's what they're for."

"Perhaps, Miss Hillier, it might be worth while to listen to the conclusion of what I have to say, and to learn just what the position is."

"But you've told us that plainly enough. You've speculated with what was left of our money, and lost the lot."

"I didn't say exactly that. In the first place, there is the lease of the house."

Margaret felt some part of the fear to be lifted from her heart at these words. After all, there would be something left! But, as the worst fear went, her anger against a man that she had always disliked rather increased than lessened. And how could you tell whether even that were true? And who would leave anything in his hands, after what he had said? If it hadn't gone today, it might tomorrow. And where would she be with only £27 in the bank—no, not £27. *She had given £20 to that man on the train.* Suddenly, the thought of that £20 assumed a new and portentous magnitude. She had only £7 in the bank. And for—how long?—if ever—there would be no more to come. It was what she had thought before. She would be shown to the door by this smooth-talking lawyer, penniless, ruined, and he would go on as before, unhurt, uncaring. Did he think her a fool? He would soon learn something different from that! Perhaps he hadn't lost it at all. It might be all a trick, and the money just hidden away. But she had resolved that she would not lose self-control. What was he saying now?

"...And there is a good deal besides the lease. I am sorry that the way in which I was putting the matter before you—which was really necessary for a correct perspective—and, if you will pardon me saying so, the perhaps natural interruptions which have occurred, may have occasioned an impression which goes somewhat beyond the fact.

"I said that the transactions in which I have recently employed the more liquid assets have not been successful in so far as that they have not produced a sufficient profit to make good the existing deficiency. I neither said nor suggested that they had resulted in any serious loss. The operations in which I engaged them dealt with certain leading securities of the United States of America, upon the assumption that the adversities of that market are not yet over. In the result, I have both lost and gained considerable sums. At one time, I could only have withdrawn with a loss of at least £2,000. Last week, I found that by closing my account very promptly I could avoid loss entirely. Indeed, after some rather heavy expenses have been deducted, I have a net profit of £157 8s. 10d.

"It was when I realized that I could get clear without any deficiency in the accounts which can be said to have originated in my own misfeasance, that I resolved to do what I should have done at first, and explain the position frankly to you, rather than expose your fortune to any further hazard.

"It only remains to lay before you certain proposals for the appropriation of the major portion of my business income until such time as the balance of this old-standing deficiency shall have been completely discharged. With such rate of interest as you may think it right to require. The amount of this net deficiency as on the 31st of March last, and before crediting the balance of £157 8s. 10d. already mentioned, was £4,830 4s."

Mr. Risdon paused for a moment. He had made his statement, as he had rehearsed it beforehand, as clearly, coldly, and fairly, as though he had addressed a business meeting of creditors on behalf of a defaulting debtor, whose affairs it had been his duty to elucidate. Now he was about to add a few words of a more human kind. Words of regret and explanation, and assurance of the continued efforts that would be made to adjust the deficiency. With the completion of that humiliating statement he felt more human, more at one with his kind, than he had done for the last fifteen years. He had had something of this feeling from the moment when he had abandoned the perilous attempt to retrieve by speculation that which had been lost by (as he supposed) the fraud of his predecessors.

As he paused, his glance met the friendly troubled eyes of Violet Scovell. "I'm not sure," she said, "that we ought to let you do that."

The words seemed dear to her—would have been understood easily enough by one of her own kind—but they had a different meaning to Margaret's ears.

She was in a mood of sudden relief from the worst fear that had shadowed her but three minutes ago. Free also from the dread with which she had approached this interview. The law did not threaten the property which was hers, nor, it seemed, had its bulk disappeared as she had too hastily concluded. As these fears went, in the reaction of recovered confidence, she felt equal, and more than equal, to the overcoming of any difficulty with which she had still to deal. But she had had frights enough. She would not leave her property in this man's hands for a day longer. It should come into her own. And if he could not find it all, well, so much the worse for him. But she did not believe that. When he recognized that she meant to have it, you could trust a lawyer to find a way. At the worst, would not his business sell? Was not that what was meant by goodwill?

Even the furniture in that sober, substantial, soft-carpeted office would fetch a useful sum.

"No," she said, following Violet's remark, with a quite opposite meaning, "I don't think we should."

CHAPTER XLI.

THE two ladies might misunderstand each other, but Mr. Risdon understood them both without difficulty. He answered Miss Scovell: "It's very kind of you to hesitate on such a point, but in my view there is no alternative to consider." He still spoke with something of his habitual formality, but with a note of gratitude in his voice. Violet had a sense, which she did not define, that he was as a man who rejoins his kind after a prolonged isolation.

He turned to Margaret, and his voice had recovered its accustomed monotony, "Will you tell me, Miss Hillier, what I am to understand by your last remark—exactly what you intend to do?"

Margaret Hillier did not lack courage, though it was most easily roused by the baser impulses. Mr. Risdon had no cause to remark any lack of precision in the reply he received. "I mean to have my money out of your hands the first moment I can, and if I find it's short, I'll see what the law can do."

"And how soon do you consider that you are entitled to it?"

"I think after what you've said—"

"Yes," he said, as though considering an impersonal problem. "There might be ways. It might not be as easy as you think. Nor as quick. And it might cost more than you'd care to pay. But there would be methods you might adopt. They would all be alike in this, that they would cause you a loss which you might avoid. Probably a much larger loss than I have indicated as the present deficiency."

"Well, we'll see what Tult & Co. say about that."

"Do I understand that you mean to place your interests in their hands?"

"I shall ask them to get my money—what's left of it—out of your hands, and if there's anything much short I suppose the police'll know what to do next."

Miss Hillier had risen as she said this. She turned to make for the door.

Violet interposed. "Margaret, if you would leave it for a day or two...I think Grandfather ought to know."

"Of course, he'll have to know. But I don't see any good in letting things go on. I shall tell Mr. Tult to get the money the best way he can."

She went out, without further formality. She had no intention of being talked over by Violet.

If we seek the impulses of her action we find that complication of motives, logical or instinctive, which makes justice so impossible in human hands, and might be thought to trouble the accuracy of an Archangel's scales.

There was the angry fear that the money for which she had risked so much was diminished by a substantial sum, which might be lost unless she exhausted the arguments of coercion and threat. There was the pleasant change from being dogged by the law and blackmailed by Tommy Parrott to being in the position of one whose trust had been betrayed, and who could cast the shadow of the gaol which had fallen across her own on to the path of another.

There was the quick realization that she could now go to Bill with a request for legal help of a different kind from that which she had feared that she would have to do. This offered her the gain at which she aimed, that she could resume their intimacy by meeting him away from his mother's home, without the price which she had feared that she would have to pay in the telling of that awkward tale, which she had been trying in vain to shape into a credible and sympathetic form. It was not a chance which she was likely to throw away at a pleading word from a foolish, inexperienced girl.

Beyond that, there may be many to agree that her attitude was not unreasonable in desiring that her interests should be in the hands of others more experienced than herself, more competent to judge whether the full truth had been told, to do whatever might be necessary to protect the remaining assets, and to take such steps as should seem expedient to recover those which had been alienated.

She had a feeling (which was not quite accurate) that Violet would say, "Oh, well, never mind. Does it matter so much? Anyway, it can't be helped now." No, thank you. Not for her. What was the money to Violet? She hadn't expected—ought not to have had it at all. She hadn't—shall we say, exerted herself to get it in exceptional ways? Perhaps Violet would ask him to take a bit more, to reimburse him for what (he said) he had put back in the earlier years! Margaret congratulated herself on having more sense. She would go to those who would deal with it in a business way.

Violet hesitated when Margaret had gone. She felt awkward, and very troubled, and uncertain what she should say.

"I am very sorry, Miss Scovell," Mr. Risdon was saying, "that I should have had to trouble you in this way. I hope that the matter may be ultimately adjusted without loss, or any real difference to yourself. I do not think that that will be a difficult, nor, perhaps, a very lengthy business, if I can prevent your cousin from making any serious trouble about it, as I am hopeful to do."

Violet said: "I must talk it over with Grandfather."

Mr. Risdon looked his unwillingness. "I had hoped," he said, "though I recognize that I have no right to ask it, that that might have been avoided."

She answered with regret and apology in her voice, but without hesitation, "No, I don't think it could. No, I must tell him."

He did not protest further. He may have recognized that it would be useless to do so. He was a good judge of character, as a lawyer often is, and understood the tenacity with which she would hold to the course which she thought it right to take, her courage screened behind a front of timidity, as when she had challenged an interview with the Editor of the *Sunday Pail*.

He merely asked: "Then shall I make the appointment for which your grandfather asks, or shall I wait till I hear again?"

"I think—you'd better wait. I'll write to you tomorrow." She held out her hand. He saw that she did not wish to be questioned further, and let her go.

Then he rang for a stenographer. The clerk who answered the bell asked: "Can you take an affidavit now, sir?"

"Who's it for?"

"It's Tult, Tult & Co."

"Well, they must wait a moment. I must dictate a letter first. Tell Miss Thomas to come in."

The letter which he dictated was brief, and he instructed that it should be typed at once. It seemed to him to be a curious coincidence that one of Tult & Co.'s clerks should be in his waiting-room now. He would ask him to take the letter back with him. It read:

Dear Sirs,

Constance Hillier, deceased.

Miss Margaret Hillier, one of the beneficiaries under the will of the above, has seen us this afternoon.

182

We gather that she is not satisfied with our conduct of the estate, and she intimated on leaving that she would be placing her interests in your hands.

Should she do so, we shall be pleased to make an early appointment to discuss the position which has arisen.

Pending such an interview, we are sure you will appreciate the possibility that Miss Hillier may not be entirely accurate in her facts, nor correct in her deductions.

Yours faithfully,

RISDON & CLARKE

Messrs. Tult, Tult, and Co.
12, Pettifer's Court, W.C.2

He felt that that disposed of any possibility of immediate trouble from Margaret Hillier. If he knew Alfred Tult, he would be very, very slow to do anything except to restrain Margaret Hillier, when he got that letter. In any case, such matters do not move quickly. He had no urgent fear of any hostile legal step, either criminal or civil, being commenced against him. It was the more distant ultimate issue that he had to consider, and, meanwhile, that the prestige of the old name of his firm should not be damaged. He was surprised when Margaret Hillier walked into his office again, about half an hour afterward.

CHAPTER XLII.

WHEN Violet left Mr. Risdon's office, she was undecided on two points, both of which contributed to her decision that she must inform the Earl of Weyford of the deficiency in Lady Catherine's estate.

In the first place, she had understood that this deficiency was part of a much larger amount which had originally been missing from the Earl's own money, and which had been made good from Lady Catherine's in a way which was legally and morally indefensible. In view of this circumstance, she was unsure whether the Earl would not feel it a duty to restore the money to Constance Hillier's estate. The practical effect of this would be that Margaret Hillier's portion would be made up, and that the whole loss of nearly £5,000 would fall upon the Earl or herself. In view of the use to which the money was to have been put, it did not seem very important who, of her own family, should be debited with the loss. The point was that the funds which would be available in the event of her grandfather's early death would be nearly £5,000 less than he had supposed, and she could only vaguely guess how serious a difference this might be, or how far it might affect the alterations in his will which he was proposing to make.

Had she alone been concerned, she would have said at once that Margaret's portion should be made up from her own, and the trouble would have been at an end. But she had already offered the use of this money to her grandfather, and it must be for him to decide.

Her other doubt had been whether, the loss having occurred before Mr. Risdon succeeded to the business, she ought to accept his offer to continue to devote his life, as she recognized that he had been doing, to making it good. That, for the same reasons, was another impulse that she had left half-spoken. She saw that the Earl of Weyford must know, however reluctant she might be to worry him, and that he would be worried was a very certain thing. Another thing of which she was sure was that he would not want any legal action or publicity. He would want to restrain Margaret, at any cost. She felt that she did not like Margaret. She had always had a suspicion of that, but she was sure now.

As she went out through the clerk's office, she was surprised to see that Margaret was still there, and that she was talking to Bill. She was talking in a low voice, but with passionate inflections that caused some of her words to sound clearly in the silent room. The three clerks in the background were listening keenly.

A tall man, heavily made, in the attire of a prosperous farmer of the older type, was standing near to Bill in an unconcealed impatience.

"Coom, lad—" she heard him address the office-boy, as she passed. She supposed that she had kept him waiting and he was impatient to be announced. But what was Bill doing there? Had he met Margaret by appointment? If he were going to do that, why hadn't he said so last night, when she had told him that she—that they both—would be there? She was not of a distrustful nature, but Bill looked ill at ease. She saw that he would have withdrawn from Margaret to speak to her, but she had a hand on his arm, and did not stop speaking as Violet came out. The farmer also seemed to be expecting Bill's attention. She said, "Good afternoon," as she passed, but did not pause as she did it. She did not want to talk to Margaret again.

Bill Langford cast a miserable look after her (which Margaret did not fail to observe), but what could he do? He had Mr. Moorhouse on his hands, and the affidavit to get sworn. He went into Mr. Risdon's office, after a few minutes of further delay. Margaret said she would wait.

CHAPTER XLIII.

IT was not by appointment that Bill Langford met Margaret at the offices of Risdon & Clarke, nor was it by one of those coincidences by which destiny weaves the pattern of life, nor (he would have said with emphasis) was it by the interposition of a friendly Providence. It was the unwelcome fruit of his own deliberate misdoing.

Ever since last night, when Violet had told him that she would be at Risdon & Clarke's at 4:00 P.M. tomorrow, he had been wondering how best he could contrive that she should not get home without meeting him in that casual way which had become so bewilderingly frequent of late, and which usually ended either in Bill leading her to the nearest tea-shop of a suitable character, or on her invitation that, as he had so clearly nothing to do, he should come home with her to see her grandfather, whose loneliness it would be a charity to console. But when he learnt that Mr. Moorhouse was up in town from the West Riding, and would be calling at 4:15 to swear his affidavit in *Moorhouse v. Charlesworth and Another*, he saw (as he then thought) the interposition of an indulgent Heaven.

"We can't swear you ourselves," he explained, when Mr. Moorhouse had put his signature to the document, "I shall have to ask you to come with me to a Commissioner." Mr. Moorhouse expressed no surprise. He already knew that, being an experienced litigant, though this was the first time that his neighbourly skirmishes had risen to the dignity of a Chancery action. He went out with Mr. Langford, followed by the puzzled and regretful eyes of the junior clerk, who was usually delegated for such expeditions, and who found them to be a pleasant interlude to his interior labours.

Bill found his trouble to be that Mr. Moorhouse knew too much, and demurred from the simple processes of his own mind. A Commissioner for Oaths was required. Mr. Risdon was a Commissioner for Oaths. Violet was, in all probability, still in Mr. Risdon's office. It is to Mr. Risdon we must go. Few things can be clearer than that.

Yet Mr. Moorhouse thought differently. When they had walked about a quarter of a mile at a pace which would have been impossible in a turnip-held, and was objectionable anywhere else to a fourteen-stone man who had had a very comfortable lunch, he distinctly jibbed. He began to examine brass-plates for himself. He had a natural difficulty in believing that Commissioners were so thinly distributed in the legal quarters of London.

"It's no good going there," Bill assured him, as he pointed to one appropriate legend, "we should only be losing time." There was sincerity in his tone as he said that, but he was soon driven to more elaborate and complete mendacities. He gave Mr. Moorhouse the impression that the solicitors in their own immediate neighbourhood would be unlikely to swear the affidavit without perusal, and that the risk that its contents might be prematurely conveyed to Charlesworth and Another was too great to be ignored. Mr. Moorhouse missed his train without further protest.

But in his concentration on the One Important Thing in Life, Bill had failed to give due consideration to the fact that Margaret was also to be there, or to make any plans against the possibility that she might be the first to encounter him. Not that he had any quarrel with her. He was still very fond of her, poor girl. He told himself this quite frequently, and he was in a good position to know. But he didn't feel any overwhelming impulse to be fond of her that afternoon. He was quite content to be fond of her by correspondence, about once a week. This may show more than the advantage of propinquity. It may demonstrate that Bill was of changeable and unstable character. Perhaps it does. If so, it was very lucky for him.

But the penalty of his betrayal of Mr. Moorhouse was that he had to take Margaret to tea, and although he remembered that it had become urgently necessary for him to get back to his office (he really had got a letter in his pocket which Mr. Risdon had asked him to pass to Mr. Alfred Tult's own hand) which enabled him to hurry that meal, yet he could not avoid a promise that he would meet Margaret during the evening at the Billington Hotel, where she would be staying, after he had mentioned her case to his firm. In the meantime, she accepted his suggestion that she should go back to Mr. Risdon, and ask for the money which she had told him she was needing. Perhaps he would not have suggested this, if she had not given him a somewhat exaggerated idea of her financial stringency, and been somewhat less than just in regard to the amounts which had been advanced already. But she wished to excite his sympathy, and there were some payments (particularly £20 that afternoon) which it would have been foolish to mention.

But she accepted the suggestion very willingly. It was her programme to look to him for advice, and to be meekly and gratefully obedient to it, and she had a restless desire to be doing something. She was quite willing to quarrel with Mr. Risdon a second time.

CHAPTER XLIV.

BILL returned to his office to hand Mr. Risdon's letter to Mr. Alfred Tult, and to tell him of the new client which he had obtained for the firm in the person of Miss Margaret Hillier, and of the nature of her charges against Mr. Risdon. He was somewhat embarrassed by the information that the letter he had been carrying from Mr. Risdon dealt with the same subject, though from a different angle It is evidence of the preoccupations of his mind that the probable contents of that letter had not occurred to it already. Mr. Tult, a shrewd and cautious man, thought that there was something that he had not been told, and was not relieved of that doubt on asking why Bill had been in Mr. Risdon's office, and receiving the explanation that he had taken Moorhouse there to swear an affidavit.

Still, Margaret's charges, as she had given them to Bill during their somewhat hurried tea, were too detailed and explicit for it to seem a possible explanation that they had been entirely invented. Mr. Tult felt great difficulty in believing that Mr. Risdon had been guilty of any financial irregularities. He knew him as an exact and very scrupulous man. There had been, at times, substantial transactions between the two offices. Mr. Risdon's settlements had always been of a punctilious promptness. There had been none of those delays which are too common in the profession, and are so hard to resent. Still, it was a detailed accusation. Strange things do happen. Very unexpected things. He would certainly take up the case, but he would proceed as cautiously as Mr. Risdon himself had suggested.

He wrote at once, asking for an appointment at Mr. Risdon's office for the following afternoon. He would telephone for confirmation in the morning. He told Bill to let Margaret know that he would see her at 11:00 A.M.

Bill rang up his mother to say that he would be late, but not very, and went to the Billington Hotel.

Margaret received him in a private sitting-room which she had taken. She was dressed with care, not having reverted to the mourning which she had worn when in London previously. She guided the conversation to explain that it made her too conspicuous. She was longing to forget the past! And who could wonder at that?

Then she turned to the subject of Mr. Risdon, and became a very angry woman. He had asked her at once whether she still meant to go to Tult & Co., and when she told him that she had made the clerk who had been in his office at the time the messenger of her instructions to them—without mentioning that she had known him previously—he had declined to do anything, except through them.

"I don't mind telling you, Miss Hillier, that I had a cheque made out, which I should have handed to you this afternoon, had you not left rather abruptly, but now—well, I think it would be better to do nothing except through the solicitors who will be acting for you. They will advise you of the time at which you will be entitled to require a settlement of the estate."

Then he had touched his bell, and said to the promptly-appearing boy, "Show this lady out."

She had restrained herself with difficulty from a display of undignified passion, fortified by the thought that his triumph would be short, and that Tult & Co. would know how to deal with *him*. Her hurried exit was not destitute of effect on the minds of the clerks who had partly overheard her conversation with Bill, with an eager if somewhat incredulous curiosity, and now half-regretfully concluded that she was no more than an hysterical female, with whom the gov'nor had dealt as she no doubt deserved.

To leave her with only £7 in the bank, while he had thousands of her money at his disposal!—if it were not all lost already. Bill said she need not worry about the immediate future. He could lend anything she needed. He had just come into a legacy of £250. But she said, no, she would not take his money. (So it was no more than that! She had thought, from the way he had spoken, that he had expected a large sum. It was a natural expectation that it would be large, his mother being a wealthy woman.)

No, she would manage as best she could, relying upon his firm to protect her rights, and secure an early settlement of at least part of the money which was her due.

Bill knew enough of law to have his doubts of a speedy settlement—doubts which were not decreased by the measure of credence which he gave to her representation of Mr. Risdon as an unconscienced villain—and enough of finance to know that £7 would not carry her far while occupying a private sitting-room at the Billington Hotel.

He did not know that she had created various reserves totalling more than £100, which she had determined to leave untouched, unless at a last extremity.

She did not wish him to know that. She wished to appear dependent on his advice and help, while refusing his money, so that he should exert himself to the utmost, and so that she could be properly grateful in due course. She could pay off her first week's bill from the £7. And for the rest—well, it could wait a bit, at the worst.

She managed the interview with adroitness, establishing a footing of intimacy without the embarrassment of demonstrative feeling. Bill stayed rather longer than he had meant to do, and left with a somewhat warmer regard for her than he had felt while she had been away. She had certainly had enough hard luck previously, and this money trouble coming on the top of everything—well, it was too bad.

CHAPTER XLV.

WHEN Bill got home, his mother met him with the news that Miss Scovell had rung up, and had asked that he should speak to her as soon as he got in. There was nothing very unusual in that, Mrs. Langford's only surprise being that Bill was late and that Violet was not with him; and she would have been unlikely to inquire as to the subject of the consequent conversation, but Bill took up the instrument in the room in which she was writing, and his own contribution was audible to her.

Bill got through quickly, and the instant sound of a rather troubled voice suggested that Violet had been waiting for his call to come. "Bill, I want to know whether Margaret's really doing anything foolish about Mr. Risdon."

"I don't know about anything foolish. She's instructed my firm to act for her. They're seeing Risdon tomorrow. It sounds rather a mess to me, but I hope they'll make him cough up, for your sake as well as hers."

"Bill, I wish you could stop it, at any rate till I've spoken to Grandfather. I couldn't say anything tonight. He's not been so well today, and he was asleep when I got in."

Bill was conscious of some masculine exasperation. Why trouble the Earl at all, especially if he weren't well? Why, if she didn't care enough about her money to do anything herself, try to obstruct those who have more sense? Did she want to lose the lot?

"I'm sorry to hear that," he answered, "but I don't know that there's any hurry about telling him. As far as I can see, if my firm are looking after Margaret's interests, they'll be doing all they can for yours too. You're both in the same boat."

"I'm not sure that we are, but, if so, oughtn't we to act together? I don't think it's nearly as bad as you suppose, and interfering may do more harm than good. I'm afraid of Margaret doing something that'll bring it all out in public, and I know Grandfather would hate that."

"Isn't that a reason for letting Margaret act on her own? He can't mind the publicity if you only sit back and watch. You needn't be in it at all."

"But why not wait a day or two, till we can talk it over together? I don't think Margaret's quite fair to Mr. Risdon. I thought we might all see him together again, and fix it up among ourselves."

"I don't know about that. Margaret says he owns that he's blue'd about £5,000 already. You don't know what may be happening any day with a man like that. He's probably over his ears in debt."

"Well, I wish I could get her to wait. I thought you'd have done that for me, when you know how I feel."

"I'll...I'll do what I can. It isn't easy to stop a thing that's just started, without any good reason to give. But I don't suppose anything'll be done tomorrow. Not to matter, that is."

But Violet held to her point. "You could stop Margaret if you really wanted to. You don't know what she'll do or say when once she begins."

Bill was not sure that he could, and still less sure that he ought to attempt it. He had heard her tale, and his sympathies were on her side. He could not see why Violet should be concerning herself about this lawyer crook, against the protection of her cousin's interests. So he said.

Violet would not explain further. She said, "I've only asked you to stop it till I've talked it over with Grandfather, and we can all meet. I thought you'd have done that for me."

Bill said he'd do anything for her, and as for this—well, he'd do what he could.

His voice was not very convincing, but Violet recognized that it was the most she was likely to get from him that night. She rang off.

She left Bill in a very miserable state of mind, as she may have been also. It was the nearest thing to a quarrel that they had yet had. She was surprised to find that she had so little influence over him. No girl would have liked that. And he thought her request to be unreasonable. He thought also—perhaps too modestly—that it was beyond his power to grant. He felt that Margaret would not be easily turned from her purpose—and he was not sure, in her interest, that he ought to try.

He was about to ring up again, and reopen the conversation, thinking of several points which he could make, and that he might yet persuade her to concur in Margaret's more enterprising methods, but his mother's voice interrupted his purpose.

"Bill, what was that you were saying about Mr. Risdon?"

Explanations followed. He found another advocate for the policy of waiting the Earl of Weyford's opinion.

"I didn't think Mr. Risdon was the least likely to be involved in a difficulty of that kind. I should need him to tell it to me himself, before I believed it. Anyway, I shouldn't take it from that woman."

Bill understood the remark well enough. By gradual stages his mother had allowed it to become clear that she did not like Margaret Hillier. The question was assuming the aspect of a personal issue. His mother was taking Violet's side, and he Margaret's. He was conscious of an acute dissatisfaction with this position. And yet he felt that Margaret was right, and, be that as it might, that he had taken up the advocacy of her cause, and was unable to throw it up. In their exasperatingly feminine way, they did not give any reasons why Margaret should delay her efforts to protect her property. He had an instinctive feeling that, if he were to see Margaret before Mr. Tult interviewed her in the morning, and propose that she should alter her plans, it would not help him materially to say that his mother and Violet wished her to do so. He would need a better argument than that.

Then a new puzzle occurred to him.

"I didn't know you knew Risdon at all."

"I knew him before you were born."

"He may have altered since then."

"Yes, he has. I saw him at Wimbledon last week."

"Well, you can't tell what a man is in business, because you meet him like that."

Mrs. Langford admitted the general truth of this statement. She said no more, seeing Bill's difficulty clearly enough, and that he could not go beyond the vague assurance that it wasn't likely that much would be done tomorrow. But she found it hard to believe the tale.

She had known Mr. Risdon rather well in her early days. He had proposed to her before she was married, and again after her husband died. That was before he had succeeded to the complete control of the business. They had met a good deal after that, and she had half-expected to have to refuse him again, but the occasion had not recurred. He appeared to have accepted her refusal as final, as she had meant it to be, and had continued the friendship as far as she had allowed him to do so. She knew that, if she were engaged in a tournament of any importance, he would be there to watch her play, and it had been a powerful reason why she had striven to retain her form as the years passed, and they were kept apart by reasons only known to their own minds.

Meanwhile, Mr. Risdon was occupied in some very dirty work. His staff had left. His offices were ostensibly closed. But he was in one of the attic rooms, among the dust of forgotten deeds, burrowing for papers which might be required to prove the truth of the shadow under which his life had been passed.

The truth was bad enough. But even the truth might not be accepted on his own word. The affairs of the Scovell family had been so entirely in the hands of his firm for generations that there could be no corroboration of much that he might assert, apart from the evidence of deed or letter. Indeed, had it occurred to him to bury the deficiency in his own books, it is possible that, large as it was, he might have obliterated it in the course of years. Who, but himself, knew the details of Lady Catherine's estate? Who could have contradicted him, had he said that it was smaller than was, or should have been, the case? But it had not occurred to him to adopt this method of cancellation.

Now he would have everything in readiness for the preparing of a statement which would go even further back than the date when he had inherited the business, and the materials were here. The accumulation of documents and correspondence in such an office is of enormous bulk, nor is it usually safe to destroy them till they have acquired an almost antiquarian interest. He worked late, and was in a state of unusual nervous excitement when he returned to the office next morning, showing evidences of a sleepless night.

Among the morning correspondence, which he opened himself, he found Mr. Alfred Tult's request for an interview in the afternoon, and a letter marked *Personal*, at which he paused for some time, before unlocking his private drawer, and putting it away, though it was not one which should have taken long to read, or which was difficult to understand.

My dear Wilfred,

I know you will have the good sense to pardon this letter, should it be an impertinence (you will remember us arguing over the correct use of that word—how many years was it ago? Please don't count!) as I expect it may.

But I have £4,000 lying at 4 percent, practically at call in the East Middlemore Building Soc., and I heard (indirectly through Miss Scovell) this evening that a position has arisen in which you might be able to utilize such a sum to advantage.

If so, and if it would be worth your while to pay the same rate of interest, it is entirely at your disposal, and it will be a pleasure to leave its investment with you.

Always sincerely yours,

EDITH LANGFORD

He sat for a few minutes in thought, and then submitted himself to the tyranny of routine, and became immersed in the morning's work. He went out to lunch as usual, and returned in good time for Mr. Tult's expected call. Then the claims of the physical body became assertive. He dozed in his chair, and was actually asleep when Mr. Tult was announced.

Mr. Alfred Tult was a shrewd, genial, elderly man, enjoying a good constitution, and showing some signs of taking more food than exercise. He had the brightness of eye and dryness of skin and manner which is typical of the London lawyer.

He shook hands with Mr. Risdon with his usual affability, noticing as he did so that he showed some signs of being tired or worried which were unusual in one who was looked upon in the profession as a model of competent unemotional conduct. Risdon always seemed too impersonal to be either well or ill, or have any individual feelings. Was this really the opening scene of one of those tragedies of financial failure of which the legal profession provides several for every year? He wished he knew with greater certainty, but his duty was clear. It was really nothing to do with the matter that he had disliked the woman when she had called upon him this morning. He seldom remembered meeting anyone whom he had disliked more.

The feeling might have no logical connection with the inquiry which he had undertaken, but it was reflected in his opening words.

"Of course, Risdon, I'm not going to take anything that woman says for granted. It didn't need your note to put me on my guard against that. Thanks for sending it, all the same.

"I can understand anyone showing her the door, and if I hadn't had your own note, I don't know but that I should have done the same. But if I had, she'd have gone somewhere else, I suppose, and perhaps made more trouble. She's got the devil's own tongue when she gets roused. If the sister'd poisoned her instead of the old woman, she'd have shown more sense than she did, or dosed them both off and been able to feel she'd done some real good in the

196

world when she came to hang. But the point's this. I've told her that it's too early to begin worrying an executor for accounts, or expecting a settlement, and if she makes herself a nuisance about that you can just throw her out, or me either if I take up the same song. But she sticks to it that you told her with your own lips that you've made away with a good part of the estate, and she's prepared to make an affidavit to that effect. She says, in a detailed way, that you told her that you'd used her aunt's money to fill up a hole in the Weyford funds, and now there's no means of putting it right. And on the top of that she says that Miss Scovell won't be a willing witness, but if we ring her up we shall find that she can't deny having heard the same thing from your own lips. Of course, if all that were true.... Well, you'll see where we should be."

"Yes," Mr. Risdon replied. "It's the kind of tale that you're bound to investigate, whether you believe it or not. Suppose I gave you my word of honour that the Weyford funds have never been a penny short at any time, would you accept it?"

Mr. Tult became thoughtful. "No," he said at last, "it's my client's responsibility, and it may be all lies, but if she's prepared to swear to it, and Miss Scovell supports her account, I don't think I could."

Mr. Risdon seemed unperturbed. "Then it's no use offering that," he said, with a slight smile. "How should you propose to proceed?"

Mr. Tult had a moment's doubt of whether he were being laughed at, or were in the presence of a man who had given up hope of escape, and become cynically interested in the processes of his own destruction.

"There are several ways we might. There's no need to tell you that. I might decide to proceed for an account."

Mr. Risdon became thoughtful in his turn. "Yes," he said, "that would be the least you could do—and, perhaps, the least troublesome for your own client, in the end. Mr. Tult," he went on, with a change of manner to that of an unusual frankness, "I should like to speak to you without reserve, and I am convinced, whether you can believe me or not, that you would go away satisfied that your client's interests are unjeopardized. But my difficulty is that the interests and confidences of other clients are involved in such a way, as, without their permission, to forbid me to do so. For the moment, I neither admit nor deny all or anything that Miss Hillier has thought fit to allege. I will not forecast what Miss Scovell may say should you think fit to approach her, but I may point out that she has declined to associate herself with Miss Hillier in this matter.

"I will offer you this. Within seven days, I will have an account prepared of all the transactions of the two estates during the whole period when I have been in control of this office, which you can appoint any accountant of reputation to audit, together with evidences, satisfactory to you, that the assets of the one in which Miss Hillier is interested are in order, and, subject to realization, and the usual precautions, can be promptly distributed. You will appreciate that such accounts cannot be prepared in a moment, and if the business of this office were not carefully and systematically controlled, I should be offering you an impossible thing."

Mr. Tult answered at once. "I have, as you know, a rather difficult client to deal with, but I think she will have to take my advice to accept your offer." He rose to go.

Mr. Risdon rose also. He thought that he knew what was on Mr. Tult's mind, but he was not as certain as he would have liked to be. He added, with a smile, "Of course, Miss Hillier can commence criminal proceedings, if she likes, but I think she would be sorry afterwards. Still, she is an unusual young woman. You can never tell."

They shook hands and parted.

Mr. Risdon locked his door, and drew Mrs. Langford's letter from his desk. He read it again. It might be thought that it was in the confidence of the offer which it contained that he had met Mr. Tult in the way he did. He had, it is true, changed his plan of action since yesterday, when he had intended to repeat the tale he had already told, and trust to Mr. Tult's business sense, as well as to any friendly feeling he might have, to see that it would pay his client best to accept the money as it could be found. If he could show him that all the other transactions of the office were in order, and that he was free from any financial embarrassment. He had altered his plan of action, but from a quite different cause. He now wrote to Mrs. Langford a grateful letter of thanks, but ended by saying that he did not anticipate that he should require the money. He asked for her permission to call.

Mr. Tult walked away in some uncertainty of mind. Was Risdon putting up a clever bluff, to gain time? Perhaps just hoping that something would turn up, as a desperate man will? He had only accepted the offer subject to his client's consent. That meant he could still do as he would. He might apply at Bow Street for an immediate summons—or even a warrant. But would he get it? The position was unusual. An executor in default does not usually expedite proceedings by accusing himself. It would be an hysterical woman against a solicitor of repute. He felt that if he made such an application on her affidavit he would have to back it, in effect, with his personal reputation. If Risdon denied it in the box, and there were no corroboration, it would be dismissed, and he would look a fool, or worse. It might be a very serious matter for Miss Hillier. And yet Risdon's attitude had been—odd. He might so easily have denied it, and he had declined to do so. What had the words been, "I neither admit nor deny all or anything." They had been explicit, deliberate words. No doubt carefully chosen. And yet he had offered his word of honour for an absolutely inconsistent statement. But, had he? No, to be exact, he had only suggested that it would not be accepted. A queer business, altogether.

He concluded that there was only one thing to do. He would ring up Miss Scovell. If she denied Miss Hillier's tale, there was an end of the matter. If she confirmed it—well, he would see what she said.

He did this as soon as he got into his office. He got through to Violet. When he had explained his business, she asked him to wait a moment. She went away, and came back to the instrument after a short delay. Then she said, "My grandfather, the Earl of Weyford, says it would be best not to discuss it over the phone, but he wants you to know that he has absolute confidence in Mr. Risdon. He is writing to you tonight."

"And have you the same confidence, Miss Scovell?"

"Yes, of course."

After that there was nothing to be done, but to wait for the letter. In the morning it came.

Dear Sirs,

In reply to your telephone inquiry of yesterday, Messrs. Risdon & Clarke have managed the affairs of my family for generations, and have always had and deserved our confidence. Should you hear any contrary report, from whatever source, you have my authority to contradict it.

Yours faithfully,

WEYFORD

Messrs: Tult, Tult & Co., 12, Pettifer's Court, W.C.2

Mr. Risdon had a letter from the Earl by the same post.

My dear Risdon,

Please see me at once. I am terribly sorry about this, and would have come to you had I been able. Why did you not tell me before?

Yours most sincerely,

WEYFORD

Mr. Risdon was somewhat puzzled by this letter. Did the Earl know the truth—or, more probably, did he guess? Anyway, it was over now. The only real question was how Edith would reply.

If the quality of human actions is to be gauged by their consequences, then we must put it to the credit of Margaret Hillier that when she shook that little pinch of colourless dissolving powder into the glass of her sleeping aunt, she set light to the train of circumstance which was to unite Wilfred Risdon and Edith Langford, after they had both supposed—from different reasons—that that was no more than a dead hope. Youth may think it to have been no great thing, they being of the age they were. But youth is wrong about that.

CHAPTER XLVI.

THE Earl of Weyford was a sick man, but his mind was clear. If his hand was unsteady, it yet reached out to give that of Mr. Risdon a warm grip as he came to his bedside.

"I might have guessed, Risdon," he said, in a self-reproach which he could not still, "I might have guessed. I should have guessed, but I didn't want to see. And you've borne the burden for me for all these years?"

Mr. Risdon was precise. "It has been unfortunate for me, but I cannot say that I have done anything for which I should be properly thanked. I have paid the penalties both of a lack of courage, and of confidence in my predecessors. What I did was actuated by self-interest, or almost entirely self-interest, throughout."

The Earl looked puzzled. "You mean that you haven't known?"

"I hadn't the least idea until within the last forty-eight hours, when I came on a packet of Lord Broughton's letters. I shouldn't have looked at them then, if the rubber band that held them, being rotten with age, hadn't burst apart as I moved them, and, as I collected them again, I saw something that made me read more."

But it would rather add to confusion than reduce it to follow their conversation further. They talked of the dead, and of things which were familiar to them, but are strange to us. And the explanation itself is a short and simple thing.

The title of Lord Broughton, which was held by the eldest son of the Earl, and was now that of Violet's father, had first been held by his elder brother, who had died without heirs. He had been an exception to the rather timid probity and propriety of the males of the Scovell family, and had died at an early age of the effects of vicious living. But before his death his father had suffered from a long illness, from which he had not been expected to recover. Saying, perhaps, to himself that he was doing no worse than to forestall that which would soon be his by his father's death, he had obtained certain securities from the lawyers' office by a letter forged in his father's name, and, by a further forgery, he had realized upon them.

The deception having been discovered by Wilfred Risdon's father, he had cynically admitted it, and challenged him to report it to the Earl, and break the heart of a dying man. For a time, the two partners had decided to maintain silence, knowing that the Earl was not of a disposition to take any action against his son, and sharing the belief that he had not long to live. In the end, what difference would it make? But in the irony of events, the Earl lived, and it was his son who died. So did Mr. Risdon senior, being an old man. It is probable that Mr. Clarke was on the point of acquainting the Earl with the circumstances of his son's dishonesty at the time of his sudden death, for, two days earlier, the Earl had received a letter asking for an appointment for the purpose of a communication which he feared would be of a painful kind. As it was, he died, leaving Wilfred Risdon to the blind inheritance of a deficiency for which he could not account.

Yet, in fact, had he had the courage to acquaint the Earl, all would have been well, for he had already a suspicion of the truth from papers which had been found, from the words of his dying son, and from the amount of money in his possession at his decease. When he had had Mr. Clarke's letter, he had guessed the nature of the communication which was to be made.

When Mr. Wilfred Risdon had succeeded to the business, he had waited in anticipation of hearing that some of his securities were missing, or his funds deficient. As the time passed, and he found that a full account had been rendered, he was relieved but puzzled. Yet it was not a doubt he could voice. Could he go to his lawyer and say, "I cannot understand my estate not being short. Can you not produce some evidence that my dead son was a thief and forger?"

So the years had passed between solicitor and client in an equal silence, until Violet had brought home a tale which found an instant interpretation in its hearer's mind.

"You must let me know what I owe, Risdon; you must let me know what I owe," the Earl said, with an anxious reiteration. He felt that he could have no peace till he had done that much to remove the consequences of his son's disgrace.

But Mr. Risdon was not quick to accept the offer. He felt that it was sufficient relief, after fifteen years of straitened living, to know that he would have the enjoyment of the full income that he made. He knew that such a sum could not easily be found at short notice from the Earl's resources. Also, he had a more urgent matter on his mind. How should they deal with Margaret Hillier's hostility?

But that was in the Earl's mind also. "We've got to pay that woman off, Risdon, we've got to pay her, if it's the last penny we can raise. Let her have the money, and go. I hope never to hear of her again."

Mr. Risdon felt much the same, but a sense of equity caused him to add that, after all, he had caused the trouble himself by the statement which he had felt it to be his duty to make, and that there had been some reason for the way in which she had acted subsequently.

As to paying her off, it was a question of legal method, and of the amount to be offered.

Two days later Mr. Tult received a letter from Risdon & Clarke, saying that their clients, the Earl of Weyford and Miss Violet Scovell, were prepared to purchase the interest of Miss Margaret Hillier under the will of Constance Hillier, deceased, for the sum of fourteen thousand pounds, of which six thousand pounds would be paid forthwith, and the balance in six months' time, to be secured meanwhile by the deposit of certain securities of which a list was enclosed.

Mr. Tult had a long consultation with Mr. Risdon, and subsequently accepted the offer on his client's behalf.

Margaret was exultant with the success of her business methods, and grateful to Bill for the help he had rendered.

Violet looked on that help differently. When they met, she would not take Bill into her full confidence, not wishing to talk of the dishonour of an uncle whom she remembered with a child's affection. They parted, conscious of mutual misunderstanding. When the Earl asked her petulantly why Bill hadn't been lately, she turned the subject aside.

It was in the recovered confidence of her financial victory, and the hope that Bill was once more coming under her influence, that Margaret received an urgent call on the telephone from Tommy Parrott, and showed her contempt for his threats by hanging up the receiver.

She said to herself that if she hadn't been as worried as she was at the time, he would never have laid his hands on that £20.

CHAPTER XLVII.

INSPECTOR CLEVELAND wired to Scotland Yard:

Arrested Yardley the wanted man in Glaston case
1921 has confessed identity bring him night train.

It did something to restore his self-confidence and his self-respect after his ghastly mismanagement of the Middleditch murder—for such he now admitted to himself that it had been—to have captured this half-forgotten criminal. And it suited him well to return to London, where he could follow up the trail of Mogson and Margaret Hillier, as he had resolved to do.

Having delivered his capture, he reported to Mr. Whitaker, and inquired whether he required him to continue his investigation of the Middleditch case, or should he return to his routine duties at the Yard?

Mr. Whitaker showed a hesitation unusual to him in the pause which preceded his reply, but when it came, it did not lack clarity.

"I don't mind you going on with the investigation, Inspector, knowing you for the man you are, if you think you can make any useful discovery, and if you'll bear in mind the view we take of the case as it now stands. We have to look facts in the face, and there is at least a probability—a most regrettable probability—that an error of justice has occurred, which it is too late to put right.

"But that is, after all, no more than a probability. Even if it could be proved, it would not be in the public interest to make it known, and, apart from a confession by Margaret Hillier in a form which would exonerate her sister, it is almost impossible that such proof should now be obtainable.

"But if it be a fact that Margaret Hillier was guilty, it may still be possible to obtain evidence against her, either as principal or accessory, and if you could do that in such a form that the question of the innocence of the elder sister would not arise, and the confession of Thomas Mogson need not be put in—I am not sure that we could do that, even if we wished—it would be a service to the State in securing the conviction of a particularly despicable criminal. Have you any hope of obtaining such evidence at this date?"

"No, sir. I can't say that I have, though I'd give half the life I've got left to see that woman stand where her sister stood when the judge put the black cap on his head."

"Then you think there's no doubt?"

"No, sir. I wish I did. I've gone over the case a hundred times, thinking out just what was said, and how the poor woman behaved, and I don't think, I *know*.

"I think of the way that Margaret Hillier cheeked us at the hotel, and I'm more sure than I was before. I think if—"

Inspector Cleveland checked himself, and stood silent. He was not a demonstrative man, and Mr. Whitaker was faintly surprised at the evidences of emotion which he betrayed.

"You'd better tell me," he said.

"Well, sir, I understand what you mean about public policy and all that, and I've no doubt you're right, and it wouldn't be my place to criticize, if I thought differently. And you can't bring back the dead, I can see that too. But, all the same, I feel I can't go on as it is. I've got to clear it up, or resign. There's all the papers praising me now for this man I've caught in Cornwall, and more than half of them call me the officer who did so well in the Middleditch murder case, or something of that kind. They can't guess how it reads to me. I read one not an hour ago that said that but for me 'the Middleditch poisoner might never have faced the gallows.' If there'd been another officer on the case, he might have gone to work in a different way, and who knows what he'd have found?"

"Yes. I see how you feel. If it's any consolation, I can tell you that no one blames you at all. The way things went, I don't see how you could have come to any other conclusion. You can go ahead, if you'll bear in mind the lines I've laid down. There must be no mistake about that. How do you intend to proceed?"

"There's only one chance that I can see, and that's the Merrythought Club. If they only met there, it's there that the plot must have been hatched, and the packet changed hands. If I can find those who saw or heard anything of the right kind.... Well, I might invite her to Scotland Yard, and frighten her into making a statement that would do the trick. You know, sir, if we get them there, and leave them to sit and think till about midnight before we begin—well, you can mostly trust them to hang themselves with their own lies."

"And if you once get her there, you'll have a good try?" The Inspector made no answer, but the grim look on his face foretold an uncomfortable time for Margaret Hillier if she were ever to be the centre of one of those cross-examining groups who conduct preliminary trials of suspected persons in the privacy of police-headquarters during the midnight hours.

Mr. Whitaker saw the look on his face, and said, "I sometimes think it's a pity we've abandoned the sentence of outlawry. You might get enough proof to put a woman like that outside the law, and, if anyone knew that she deserved something worse—well, it was between themselves. I don't know that you'd let that woman live overlong, if that were the case today."

He spoke half-jestingly, with a freedom which he rarely allowed himself with his subordinates, and was a little startled at the tone of the Inspector's reply.

"No, sir. I don't say that she would."

There was so much menace in the words that Mr. Whitaker added quite seriously: "You won't do anything foolish, Inspector?"

"No, sir. You can trust me for that."

The Inspector went out with a resolution that had hardened as the conversation proceeded. He would have a double duty in making his inquiries at the Merrythought Club, for when he called at the Yard, Sir Edward had told him that it was under suspicion in connection with two crimes of violence which had occurred during his absence in Cornwall. It was believed that it had passed into the control of certain international crooks who had brought the methods of Chicago gunmen into a world that was too old to appreciate them. The Assistant-Commissioner would be glad of evidence which would enable him to close its door.

CHAPTER XLVIII.

TOMMY PARROTT was frightened. He had had one rather long term in gaol, and while he did not mind risking another three months, or even six, while his bank account went on mounting at its present rate, he had no wish to qualify for a much longer term. He was not only frightened of that. He was frightened of the man who had bought the controlling interest in the Merrythought Club. A man who was rarely seen in the street, or in the lower rooms of the Club. He was best known to the few who gambled high, and were admitted to the upper floor, the stairs to which had had solid doors fitted at top and bottom. If a police raid came, it might get through the lower door on the landing, either by force or trick, but it would only be to meet the door at the top, which would be secured long before a rush could get to the stair-head. And he was a man whose hands went too easily to those slight bulges in his jacket pockets, right and left. Too easily for Tommy's comfort, he being a man of peace. He had protested at something once, and would never while he lived forget the flood of Western profanity with which Mr. William Lorrimer—for so he called himself—had advanced upon him. It was such an instant, startling change from his suave habitual manner. And the things that were done now on these upper floors...the man wouldn't understand that he was not in New York or Chicago now...that he might run up against police that he couldn't square, even with all those rolls of notes in the safe in his private room. And now Inspector Cleveland was coming round again, inquiring about Mogson in his persistent way...much use it would be trying to square *him*. And Tommy would have liked to give him all the information he could...even to provide a little evidence of whatever might be the required kind...especially after Margaret Hillier had cut him off in the way she had...and Mr. Lorrimer had overheard, and must have it handled his own way, and the prophetic instinct of Tommy Parrott did not like it at all.

Mr. Lorrimer chewed his cigar, considering the tale that Tommy had told him, in an astute and very criminal mind. It offered business possibilities which he considered himself peculiarly competent to handle.

"Bumped the old girl off herself," he concluded, "more likely than not. Tommy, you'll get that dame here for a little talk. How? That's up to you. It's a hundred bucks to you if she's here on—no, I've got never-mind-what on then—not Sunday, on Monday night. So look slippy. There's no place for a guy here who can't do a little thing like that."

Tommy didn't like it at all. He was not quite clear as to how much—or how little—a hundred bucks might be, but he understood that the matter was being taken out of his hands, and that he was to receive a mere trifle of the expected blackmail. It was very different from when the Merry-thought had belonged to the Hebrew-looking gentleman with the highly respectable Scottish name, who had only inter viewed Tommy once a week to receive the accounts, and then usually at his own house. Tommy had done what he liked in those days.

Now he felt that he'd had about enough of the Merrythought Club. His bank account was in a very comforting condition. He wished he could have cleared out to the United States, where there must be many openings for such as he, but that unfortunate conviction. No, it would be Ellis Island, and a return ticket for him. A day's excursion to Boulogne—no passports needed—would be the best method. He felt that his health needed a change.

Still, if he could add a little of Margaret Hillier's money to that which he had already accumulated, there would be no harm in that. In the end, he planned with more elaborate subtlety than the occasion required.

He decided to visit Margaret openly at her hotel, and tell her that Inspector Cleveland was inquiring again among his staff, and unless she were prepared to square them with a substantial sum they would certainly give her away. If necessary, he would hint that a conversation had been overheard. He would decline to take money himself—let her come and see the man for herself, and she would understand how difficult it had been for him to keep them all quiet with the mere twenty pounds that she had provided. That ought to bring her along, and after that—well, he supposed it would depend mainly upon whether she had had her money or not. If she were already in funds, he thought Mr. Lorrimer would know how to arrange a satisfactory allocation.

But he did not forget that Inspector Cleveland's observation might be upon him. He decided to insure himself in this direction by asking the Inspector if it would be a good plan to get Miss Hillier to visit the Club, so that she could be identified by some of the waiters who had seen her with Thomas Mogson, but whose memories were now excusably vague.

To complete the simple truthfulness of his methods, he told Mr. Lorrimer of his plan of informing the Inspector of the proposed visit, and that gentleman, after a preliminary oath of impolite astonishment, thought it over again, and saw the advantage that it would provide.

If anything should go wrong, and the woman accuse them of attempted blackmail, they would be justified in advance. Of course, they would have had to make some excuse to get her there! The Inspector would understand that.

Tommy felt more comfortable in mind after that was arranged. He had been in some degree of panic as to the nature of the methods which Mr. Lorrimer might employ if Margaret proved difficult, as she was likely to do. There had been things done in the upper rooms of which it was not good to think. But with the Inspector informed of her coming, it was certain, at least, that she would be allowed to return in safety, let her attitude be what it might. It seemed to him that the only difficult problem would be that of persuading her to visit the Club, and about that he had no difficulty at all.

CHAPTER XLIX.

MARGARET HILLIER was in a condition of good health, and good spirits. She was at peace with a conquered world.

Yesterday morning she had had the pleasure of receiving the major portion of a preliminary deposit of £500. (Messrs. Tult & Co. had deducted their charges, but even she couldn't complain if they were a little high, in view of the settlement which they had obtained.) And she knew that there was a further sum of £5,500 to be paid to her on Monday next. She saw that courage had won, as it almost always does—as it had disposed of that slimy rat, Tommy Parrott, even after she had been weak enough to give him £20. But she *had* been rather upset that day.

Even if Bill Langford were proving more trouble than he was worth, she was not disposed to worry enough to lose any weight over him. For a young woman with five or six thousand pounds in the bank, and a lot more to come, "there were lots of good fish in the sea." She hummed the line quite gaily, as she made out a shopping-list which would take her two or three days to work through. And after that it would be a new country for her. A new country—and a new name. When she came back, married or single, Margaret Hillier would be forgotten. In the new world she would enter, who would she be likely to meet who had ever seen her before?

She had only waited to get the cash, and now.... "There's a gentleman named Parrott to see you, Miss."

Margaret looked at the page-boy with a frown. "Tell him I can't see him today. He can call again in a week's time."

But the boy had half-a-crown in his pocket which had not been there three minutes ago. And Margaret's tips had been few and small. He stood his ground, and while he hesitated, Mr. Parrott walked in.

She rose angrily. "Will you be good enough to leave my room?"

"I have a rather particular reason for wishing to see you, Miss Hillier. I shan't detain you more than a very few minutes."

The boy had gone now, closing the door.

Margaret stood for a moment of angry silence, and then her manner suddenly changed. She had looked ahead. She saw that if she did not end this menace now, it might trouble her as long as her life should last. She might defy him now, but how would it be if he should trace her when she had taken another name? She had shown before that she did not lack courage. She had already proved the benefit of its use. She had formed a confident opinion that she had nothing to fear from the police. They might still be smelling round the Merrythought, though she had only Tommy's word for that, but what could they find there? Nothing. Her bankers had sent her passport that morning. There had been no difficulty about issuing it. She may have overrated the significance of that, but it helped to make up the sum of the confidence with which she faced this annoyance.

She asked, coldly enough, but in a more placable voice than before, "Well, what is it now?"

"I wish you'd come round to the Club to see one of our waiters. Inspector Cleveland's been asking him to think back, and now he says he can remember Mogson saying something to you, and handing something over when you were downstairs in the hall. I've told him it wasn't you or Mogson at all. He's mixed you up with someone else. He'll know it isn't you when he sees you again, I daresay. If he won't see reason, we could get him to fix the date, and then prove from the books that you weren't there."

"When would you like me to come?"

"Monday night's the best time. He's on duty then...say, about one o'clock."

"Isn't that rather late?"

"He doesn't come on till 12:30. You can make it that if you like. Say between that and one."

"Very well. Then that will be all now." She had already touched the bell. The boy entered as she spoke. "Show this gentleman out."

He went satisfied that he could report success, about which he had been unsure. But he was vaguely uncomfortable. It had been almost too easy. A sound instinct, born of long experience, warned him of that. He was glad that he had insured himself with the police. For the rest, it was Mr. Lorrimer's racket, rather than his.

Margaret went to her desk. She did not believe that she had listened to anything more than a lying tale. She had the best possible reason for knowing that Mogson had not been seen to give her a packet in the Merrythought Club. Such an incident had never occurred. But she was determined that that chapter of her life should be put behind her for ever. She wrote:

Dear Sir,

I am being blackmailed by Mr. T. Parrott of the Merrythought Club in connection with my visits there with Thomas Mogson, of which you are already aware.

I am going there on Monday night to find out exactly what they are planning against me, after which I shall inform you of the result of my visit, and rely upon you to assist me to end the nuisance.

Yours faithfully,

MARGARET HILLIER

She addressed this letter to "The Superintendent of Police"—(Was that right? Well, never mind, it would do)—"Scotland Yard," and went downstairs to the enjoyment of a good dinner.

CHAPTER L.

MR. WILLIAM LORRIMER sat at the head of the table. The diet of good herrings and bad champagne, which was being dispensed at fantastic prices to the gulls in the lower rooms, was not for him. They were nearing the end of a six-course dinner, very delicately chosen, and choicely served.

Margaret Hillier, watchful, very sure of herself, but somewhat bewildered by the surrounding atmosphere, sat on his left, with Tommy Parrott on her other side.

This was not what she had expected to find. She had always regarded Tommy Parrott as being in control of the club, and she had made up her mind how to deal with him. But she had never suspected the luxury of these upper rooms. She had never met this suave-voiced, hard-jawed man, who talked openly of the beguiling of fools, as though she herself had been native to a life of crime, and who was watching her all the time with merciless appraising eyes. But she had no fear for herself. She had resolved to promise anything which might be demanded. If necessary, even to seem afraid, or willing to meet whatever exaction they might demand. Only, she would stipulate that she must pay the money in cash. There would be another appointment for that. At her hotel. That would be where the police would come in. They would be hidden in a cupboard, or behind a screen. That was the regular way. She knew all about that. What are the papers for?

But she was not being asked to pay anything. She was just being accepted as one of themselves. Rather more, indeed, than she quite liked, or could quite understand.

There was a woman opposite to her, of an obvious profession, floridly rouged and jewelled, whom Mr. Lorrimer called Muriel as a rule, but Sadie once. Margaret felt that this woman disliked her actively, even regarding her with a suspicious jealousy, for which there could surely be no occasion. She did not look any more pleased when Mr. Lorrimer remarked that they'd all know Miss

Hillier better in a few days. It was a silly remark. It almost sounded as though he thought she'd come there to stay.

There were four others of the party, two men and two women. They all seemed to Margaret to be intimates, rather than guests. They were coarsely familiar with one another in speech and act as the wine passed, though they were not allowed to drink to excess. There was a curt order from Lorrimer to the huge Negro who waited upon them, when another bottle was called for from the lower end of the table. Margaret noticed that, free as their manners were, they all showed a kind of respect for this man. When he said, "Now, ladies and gentlemen, please, I have a little business to discuss with Miss Hillier," they rose without protest or delay, and left the room. There was no one left but himself, and Tommy Parrott on her other side, and the Negro who had served them. A white boy who had helped him had gone, but the Negro remained.

Margaret did not feel as comfortable as she tried to look. There was too general an obedience to this man. She saw him get up and lock the door by which they had entered. "We shan't want to be disturbed for a bit now," he said in that suave snake-like voice that she was beginning to dread. For the first time she wished definitely that she had not come.

He came back to the table. "Now, Miss Hillier," he said, "I've an offer to make to you, and it's up to you to choose. Some men would talk all round for an hour before they'd come to the point, but that's not my way.

"If all I hear of you's true, and there's not much doubt, you'd be a very useful woman to us. The trouble with most is that they've more scruples than nerve, but you won't die of that. Not if it's true, as I hear, that you saved yourself, and let your sister swing. But that's your trouble, not ours.

"We've got the cops nosing round this joint now, and I don't say you wouldn't come in handy to buy them off, but I'm going to give you a square deal, all the same.

"There's three or four here who'll swear anything that they're told, and might find a bit of paper, too, with a few words written on it of the right sort. We've got one man who's very good with the pen.

"A straight talk saves time in the end. You can come in with us, and we'll see you clear, or it's the rope for you. It's what you've earned, if the cops haven't guessed wrong, and I'd say that you look the sort. Pete, fill the lady's glass."

The big Negro was behind her chair. He reached over her shoulder to pour the wine. The two men were on either side of her. She had a sense of being physically trapped in this deserted room, with the locked door. But there was another door to the room, that through which the others had gone. He had not troubled to lock that, probably because there was no exit by that way. It stood partly open, showing an empty carpeted passage, softly lighted, and a flight of stairs, going upward.

It was absurd to take this talk seriously, or to be as afraid as she was. It would be a case of price in the end. She would promise anything so that she could get out.

She looked at Tommy Parrott, seeking reassurance in the fact that there was nothing formidable about him. But he was not looking at her. She thought that he was almost as ill at ease as herself. She saw the truth with a shrewd mind. He had been a mere fool. A decoy. It was not with him that she would have to deal, as she had thought. He had done his part.

She gathered what courage she had, remembering the letter that she had written to Scotland Yard. It must be guile against guile. She looked at Lorrimer in a puzzled way. "You couldn't make up a tale like that. Not that anyone would believe. What do you want me to do?"

"Couldn't we?" he replied, with a slight sneer. "You'll know us better before long. What do we want you to do? You can stay here for the next few days, and...entertain some of the guests. After that, we'll see how you go on. Tommy, have you got a wife?"

Tommy said no to that.

"Then there's one for you here. That makes it all regular, and the cops won't have much to say. You'd better get busy, and frame it up. It takes a damned time in this country. And meanwhile Sadie'll fix her up here. You can write a note to the hotel, and we'll send someone to pack your things. I'll take care of the cash, Tommy. You know the rule here. But there'll be a thousand bucks to spend on the day you're hitched. No one goes short, if they toe the line, in this gang."

Margaret said, in a voice that was less steady than she would have had it to be, "And suppose I don't agree?"

"Then it's a hanging for you. But you'll agree slick enough. You've got sense."

He did not really mean her to choose. If he had ever done so, he did not now. This was better than getting part of the money from her by a process of gradual blackmail. Less trouble, and really less risk in the end. And you got all, instead of part. And he saw that she might be very useful indeed. Quite an attractive young woman. Probably an expert liar. And quite unscrupulous. She might begin trying her lies on him, but she would not gain much by that. Here she was, and here she stayed. She was really taking it more quietly than he had expected. There might have to be a few threats, even a little violence at first, but she would see sense in the end.

But he had made one mistake. He had his own methods, by which he had succeeded many times, but, in this instance, the brutality of his frankness had gone too far.

He meant to take her money! To take it out of her possession. She would be penniless, in his power. She would be—what was it called?—a white slave.

She might have kept her self-control at all else, at the idea of being confined there till she could find means of escape, of "entertaining" the guests, even of marrying Tommy, but that her money should pass into this man's hands, the money for which she had schemed and risked so much, and that was hers at last through her own courage! Courage. It was that that was wanted here.

She doubted that they would dare any physical violence, and she saw that, even so, if she seemed to acquiesce, she would be safe for the moment. She remembered again that she had written to the police. There *should* be violence unless she should go free, but it should be when she was ready to begin. They would not want a row in the club. She would get free in the end, and what weight would their accusation have after that? She was shrewd enough to see that they would have nothing to gain by elaborating false witness against her, if she were once free of their doors, and defied them to do their worst.

There was a knife, long and sharp, among the table cutlery facing her. It was within her reach, but she would have to stretch out. With that in her hand.... If they touched her, she could defend herself. She would be defending her honour! She saw herself in imagination as a popular heroine, boldly escaping from a very infamous trap. Virtuous innocence, not to be blackmailed or subdued.

She spoke softly to Mr. Lorrimer, as her hand reached for the knife. But she had underrated that gentleman's watchfulness. He had seen her first glance at the weapon, and his hand went to his jacket pocket. Not that he had any intention of shooting her. That was a merely instinctive movement. His eyebrow lifted to the Negro behind her chair. It was with him that the fault lay. His attention had wandered a moment from his master's face. Had he been alert, he would have caught her arm before the hand closed on the knife. Then he would have, in all probability, been carrying her out of the room in the next minute, with a huge black hand over her mouth, and it would not have been long before she would have learnt who was master there.

Or had he done nothing, seeing himself too late, there might have been no harm. Margaret had no thought of assaulting anyone. She merely wished to have the advantage of a weapon in her hand, while she argued this matter out.

But the Negro, seeing his fault, made a quick movement about half a second later than it should have been.

His left arm came round over her shoulder, the great hand fastening upon her throat. His right hand closed on her upper arm, just as she got a grip of the knife.

Margaret loathed the touch of a Negro worse than a black cat, as some white people do. Physical repulsion was reinforced by a panic fear, as she strove to bring the knife back to stab at the huge black arm that was beneath her eyes, and the hand that compressed her throat. Her strength was nothing to that which had her in its grip, but the Negro's hand having closed on her upper arm gave her more freedom than if he had held her wrist, as he should have done. She jabbed with the knife, but in too wide a sweep. It did her assailant no harm, but the point caught in something, and stuck. It was the side of Tommy Parrott's neck.

The next moment, the Negro had loosed her throat. He wrenched the knife with both hands from a twisted arm. Margaret stood bewildered. Her left shoulder and arm were soaked with blood. Tommy had slipped down from the further side of his chair, and was making spasmodic efforts to rise. Her own chair was thrown backward upon the floor.

Mr. Lorrimer kept his seat, surveying the tableau with cool, considering eyes.

Margaret was the only one who saw that Inspector Cleveland was standing at the open door.

CHAPTER LI.

INSPECTOR CLEVELAND thought quickly, as he had learnt to do. He had come down from the roof, where he had half a dozen of his best men. He was already in possession of the floors below. There could be no escape for any who were in that room—and no concealment of that which it contained.

It meant an inevitable inquest, from which Margaret might come off well enough. She could plead blackmail—self-defence—fear for life and honour in that den. They'd never hang her for that. Had he let things go on to that end, she might have found herself the popular heroine of her own imagination.

But the Inspector thought of other things. What might the inquest not reveal? It was beyond his guessing. It was just such a development as his superiors would avoid. He had promised Mr. Whitaker that there should be no publicity of the wrong kind. No, it was better to end it here.

He fired twice from the hip. Margaret Hillier sank a huddled heap on the floor.

"Put up your hands," he said sharply. The Negro stood in an abject terror. His teeth chattered. His arms were already lifted toward the ceiling.

But Mr. Lorrimer's hands did not rise. They were in his jacket-pockets. The table obstructed his left, but he had the Inspector covered with the revolver in his right hand.

"Officer," he said, "if we go quietly, you're not going to frame us with this?"

"We don't do those things here. You're not in Chicago now.... Do you know who she is?"

Mr. Lorrimer looked speculatively at the Inspector. What did the question mean? What trap might be opening beneath his feet? It was still in doubt whether the next moment might not hear an argument of a deadlier kind. "No," he said slowly, watching his opponent's eyes, "I'm not so sure that I do."

"If she knifed Tommy Parrott," the Inspector said, with a slow deliberation, "and he shot her in self-defence, it would be a likely thing for him to do. We can't take you for that. But I want to know who she is."

Lorrimer looked at the Negro. "Know her, Pete?" he said curtly.

The ugly pallor of the Negro's face changed to a broad grin as he looked down upon the body of the dying woman, that twitched a little upon the floor.

"Know that dame, boss? I should say! Sure, cop, she's the Pittsburg Kid."

CHAPTER LII.

THE next afternoon Inspector Cleveland called upon Mr. Risdon. He had been up all the previous night, and had had a very busy morning, but he seemed to be in better spirits than had been noticeable since the date on which Thomas Mogson was executed.

Perhaps it was natural that he should feel some elation in the success of the sensational raid upon the Merrythought Club, on which the morning papers were congratulating him in monotonous chorus. It was no fault of his that he had arrived too late to prevent a fatal quarrel between two of the gang, concerning which the police had taken statements from those who had been present when it occurred, but had been unable to intervene. They were both American citizens—one was a Negro—and they would doubtless be deported when the inquest was over. It was understood that the police accepted the truth of the evidence they were prepared to give.

It all showed the importance of suppressing places of such a character. Inspector Cleveland was a very jealous and capable officer. About eighty people who had been captured on the lower floors, and spent the night in the cells, had sadly endorsed this opinion, as they crowded the Magistrates' Court at Marlborough Street that morning.

The Inspector remained with Mr. Risdon for more than half an hour. The confidential information which he had supplied was of the kind to hold the attention of anyone to whom it might be addressed, but Mr. Risdon, when once its purport had been understood, was in an unmistakable hurry for him to be gone.

The door had scarcely closed before he put a call through to the London and Northern Bank, and when he got their reply to his query he said "Thank God!" with a most unusual fervour. Then he wrote a letter with his own hand which he sent round by taxi, and while that was on the way, he wrote one to Mr. Alfred Tult, also by his own hand—which he was not accustomed to do—and sent it round in the same way. Then, at greater leisure, he wrote a third to the Earl of Weyford.

The letter to the bank was no more than a formal authority to stop payment of a cheque for £5,500.

The one to Mr. Tult had required some adroitness of wording, hurriedly though it had been composed. It said:

Dear Sir,

Constance Hillier, deceased.

In view of certain information which we have received, we are advising our clients, the Earl of Weyford and Miss Scovell, not to complete the purchase of the interest of Miss Margaret Hillier under the above will.

We have therefore stopped payment of the cheque for £5,500 which we sent you yesterday.

We accept the forfeiture of the deposit already made, and, in the absence of any further instructions from your own client, we shall be obliged if you will close the transaction on this basis.

Yours faithfully,

RISDON & CLARKE

The letter to the Earl of Weyford may also be of some interest.

My lord,

Constance Hillier, deceased.

We have received confidential information this afternoon, from which it appears that Miss Margaret Hillier is not in a position to substantiate any claim to benefit under the will of the above.

In view of this circumstance, we have, of course, repudiated your agreement to purchase her interest therein.

The practical position is that Miss Violet Scovell is the sole beneficiary under the said will.

We are therefore holding the sum of £5,500 awaiting your instructions.

Yours faithfully,

RISDON & CLARKE

Violet, who had undertaken the opening of her grandfather's correspondence during the illness from which he had not yet completely recovered, read this letter a first time, and was puzzled as to what it might imply. She read it a second, and was afraid to think that it meant what it seemed to say. She read it a third, and had no doubt at all. She made a straight streak for the telephone. "Bill," she said, "if you're really keen on that house at Denham, you'd better make sure of it today. No, that's all right. I find I've got rather more money than I thought I had when we were talking last night."

ABOUT THE AUTHOR

SYDNEY FOWLER WRIGHT (1874-1965) penned over seventy volumes of science fiction, fantasy, classic mysteries, historical novels, poetry, and non-fiction, many of them being published by the Borgo Press Imprint of Wildside Press.

www.ingramcontent.com/pod-product-compliance
Lightning Source LLC
Chambersburg PA
CBHW031959240626
47153CB00003B/1037